David Strutt was born in London and, after graduating, trained as a specialist teacher for environmental projects. The onset of serious arthritis brought about early retirement and the beginning of a writing career. *Please Wipe Your Crutch on the Towel Before you Leave*, which evolved as a result of his hospital experiences, was published by The Book Guild in 2001. He and his wife have six children and live in Hampshire. His writings on educational and parenting issues have been published widely both in the UK and abroad.

ALL RIGHT, DAD?

Home Alone with Six Teenagers

David Strutt

The Book Guild Ltd
Sussex, England

First published in Great Britain in 2003 by
The Book Guild Ltd,
25 High Street,
Lewes, East Sussex
BN7 2LU

Typesetting in Times by
IML Typographers, Birkenhead, Merseyside

Printed in Great Britain by
Athenæum Press Ltd, Gateshead

A catalogue record for this book is
available from The British Library

ISBN 1 85776 763 2

For parents the world over.
Despite what you may feel, it is all worth it

1

At the risk of incurring the wrath of the child protection agencies, or, perish the thought, being secretly filmed by Esther Rantzen, I must tell you I have been contemplating purchasing a larger deep freeze: the extremely capacious sort used by family butchers. I am now convinced that the notion of placing children in cryogenic suspension the moment they hit puberty is the right approach. Freeze them at age eleven and when nine years has elapsed, pop them into the microwave on a heavy-duty defrost setting, give them a new set of clothes, and then send them off into the world to do their worst. It really is that simple. In one masterful stroke, adolescence could be banished from the face of the earth. Unfortunately, I fear I have missed the boat. I should have made the 'investment' years ago. My children are now too old. The horses, as they say, have bolted ... strolled more like. Our 'horses' don't bolt anywhere. Oh, that they did.

I have three *bêtes noires*, you see: unsolicited mail, bureaucracy and *adolescence*. If I count each of the six children as the glorious individuals they undoubtedly are, I suppose I have eight *bêtes noires*; nine if you include airports, which I feel strongly inclined to do following a recent marathon at Heathrow. More of that later. I am not certain what the collective term for *neuf bêtes noires* is. A herd, most likely. But I exaggerate of course and, as I relate this tale, I must avoid the juvenile obsession with constant hyperbole and the use of totally inappropriate language currently endemic in our household. Quite why a piece of Sunblest spread thickly with Marmite might be described as *awesome*, and an arrangement to

1

meet a *mate* at the pub be referred to as *wicked*, is a mystery to me. Such is life with an adolescent family. I am advised that I should not expect to understand more than a small proportion of what happens around me each day.

It was just before two o'clock that I returned from the airport and parked the car beside the cottage. There had been a shower of rain and the variegated ivy around the porch dripped tauntingly as I flicked one or two particularly long tendrils out of my face and opened the door. I made a mental note to do something about it; trim it back, thin it, anything to prevent its ceaseless wandering through windows and doors. It is the most extraordinarily vigorous plant which, given half a chance, will squeeze through tiny gaps in the children's bedroom windows and then propagate itself inside, even in the depths of winter, as it basks in the semi-tropical fug which is a permanent feature of adolescents' rooms. Quite why the children are so obstinately opposed to opening a window to allow some fresh air in, I will never know.

In the kitchen, a lone figure sat hunched over a bowl of cornflakes and the newspaper. I think it was a young man; he had slightly more stubble around his chin than most of the girls who are brought home by our offspring. I greeted him in the sort of 'cool' way that my children would wish me to greet all-comers in our house.

'Hello there. I'm Duncan; Greg's father.'

The figure gazed at me.

'Uh.'

He looked up from the finance section of my Sunday paper which, I noticed, was now liberally spattered with milk. I held out my hand in a gesture which would have suggested, at least to most inhabitants of this cultured isle, that I wished to shake him by the hand. He didn't move, or more accurately, he didn't move towards my hand, but instead again launched his over-laden spoon towards his mouth and, having done so, he spoke:

'Oroight then?'

2

I think this was a question which concerned my well being, so I told him that I was in good form, despite the traffic which had been chaotic, and that Mrs Dudgeon had arrived in plenty of time for her flight. He stared at me.

'Uh?' He shovelled another brimming ladle full of flakes and milk into his mouth, the surplus spilling over the share prices.

'Have you seen any of the others?' I enquired, filling the kettle, although I realised before the words were even out that such a complex question was likely to dumbfound this particular individual. It did. He stared at me, cereal dripping from the corner of his mouth. He shrugged. I left him and called up the stairs where the faint, bass beat of music could be heard above running water. There was no audible reply. Only the dog came down the stairs. He wagged his tail, and stretched in that inimitable way that large dogs do when they turn their nether regions towards one and then twitch, as they expose themselves in an unsociable manner which, really, I would rather he learned not to do.

My friend rose from the table as I returned to the kitchen. He stood looking pained, holding his breakfast bowl, as though searching for somewhere to leave it and, having decided that the dishwasher and the sink were somehow inappropriate resting places, left it on the *Sunday Times* and moved towards the door.

'Goddago. Cheers,' he muttered, and left.

Now I consider myself to be a tolerant sort of chap who takes a keen but realistic interest in his children. Mrs D wouldn't disagree with me, although she has been known to refer to me fondly as 'an irascible old stick' at times, and when she says it, she rolls the 'r' of irascible as though she might be thinking of me as a *wrinkly* old piece of stubborn laundry which refuses to submit to her steam iron. Generally speaking, I do not react to the youngsters' ways which are, at best, puzzling and at times irritating beyond all measure. I am fundamentally reasonable but when, for example, I discover, after a two-day absence, that one of them has decided on some spur of the moment whim to 'paint' her bedroom, and I return to find that not only are the bedroom walls now a deep shade of navy blue, complete with numerous pink stencilled impressions of the plant *Cannabis indica,* but also a considerable portion of the beige stair carpet is also now daubed in blue, then yes, I have been known to react less than favourably.

'Why on earth didn't you clean it before it dried?' I asked, staring at the Axminster, which by then bore a certain resemblance to a Jackson Pollock painting. 'It would have washed away if you had used enough water.'

'Spike did it for me. He said it would brush off when it was dry.' I had absolutely no idea who *Spike* might be and, clearly, he in turn had even less idea about decorating materials. I made a mental note to ask Spike, assuming he had the nerve to turn up at *Cromwell's Retreat* again, how many paints he was familiar with that 'brushed off when they were dry'.

On that occasion Mrs D and I viewed Angelica's bedroom with mixed reactions. She managed to beam benevolently at 'Glic', as our daughter's friends insist on calling her, ignoring the patchy walls and the overwhelming sense of gloom which pervaded the space as a result of painting a north-facing room, with a tiny dormer window, in a colour which reflected no light at all. Mrs Dudgeon might not have noticed that the white paintwork around the window, door frame, skirting board, ceiling and fireplace were now splurged in carelessly applied blue emulsion; but I did, not unreasonably, because I could remember only too well the hours I had spent sanding layers of old paint to achieve a perfectly even gloss finish.

'Did you use a brush, Angelica?' was my first comment, after Mrs D had remarked on 'what fun' it was, and 'what a transformation' she had achieved in such a short space of time.

Transformation! She had wrecked the room and half the house as well, and, when I went to the outhouse to see if anyone had, in our absence, remembered to fling some food at the dog, I had discovered my best lambswool paint roller and a priceless old sign-writing brush cast in the sink, completely gunged in solidified paint.

Mrs D, whose name should have been 'Patience', had chided me softly.

'They're only young, Duncan, they're not to know. Don't get stroppy with her,' she remonstrated with me as I held up my faithful old brush, which by then looked more like a navy-blue porcupine.

'But my brush ... the roller ...'

'I'll get you new ones, dear. It's not the end of the world.'

I seem to remember deciding to take the dog for a long walk at that point. How could that sort of thing be replaced? The brush had been like an old friend to me, like an old fountain pen; it knew how my hand worked ... it took years to ...

Having resuscitated the *Sunday Times* as best I could, separating the pages and laying them out to dry before they became glued together with milk, I set about preparing a simple lunch. I took my well-earned cup of coffee and my cheese and pickle sandwiches, and sat in the sun outside the kitchen door. At about two forty-five, Greg appeared in the kitchen.

'Wassfalunch?'

'I had sandwiches. Afternoon, Greg. Good night last night?'

'Crap,' he said, clanging the breadbin lid down and loading the toaster with four slices of bread. I should explain that 'Crap' is not a reference to the game played with two dice, but rather some sort of indication of the unsatisfactory nature of the boy's Saturday evening. My children do not play dice games on nights out – oh that they did.

'Who was Matey at the breakfast table just now?'

'Matey? Matey who?' he grimaced, as though he were being taxed by a *Mastermind* tiebreaker.

'The boy, I think, who was at the breakfast table when I came back from the airport. He was about six feet tall, he had dark hair and was pouring cornflakes all over the Sunday paper.'

'Oh, has the paper come?' Greg asked, as though the paperboy regularly delivered after two o'clock on Sunday afternoon. 'Can I have the Travel Section? What were you at the airport for?'

5

'Your mother, Greg, has gone to America, remember?'

He screwed up his face again as though dredging for some connection with reality. 'Course. Forgot. Yeah. Cool.'

'Greg, do you have any idea who the cornflake-slurping young man was?'

He raised his eyes from where he had been studiously comparing the costs of various flights to Thailand, and looked at me as though I was quite insane.

'Dad, please don't keep going on about him. You're hurting my head. I haven't got a clue what you're talking about.' He went to spread liberal quantities of Marmite, mayonnaise and cream cheese onto his toast which he then devoured in that inimitable way that kids seem to do, which involves managing to arrange their mouths around a toasted sandwich, sideways on.

Angelica was the next to arrive and a certain sort of sibling grunting went on as she tried to take part of Greg's Travel Section.

'Don't.'

'Wannit.'

'Get off.'

'Wait.'

'Ahcumorn! You donneed allorvit. Wassfalunch, Dad?'

'Afternoon, Angelica, my darling. How are you this lovely day?'

'Give over, Dad. Why do you always have to have a go at me the minute I get up? I've got a bad head. Where's the paracetamol?'

'On the shelf where they always are . . .'

Then the front door banged and Stevie arrived wearing what appeared to be a rubber wet suit. His brother, sister and father must have stared at him somewhat incredulously.

'Is that the latest gear for a night at the pub, Stevie?' I asked. 'Surely you didn't sleep in it?'

He looked at me, looked down at his garb, surprised, as though it might have clothed him by some sort of accident which he hadn't noticed, and said, 'Windsurfing with Leechie.'

I remembered then that he had actually announced his intention

6

to rise early and join some friends on the beach, to make the most of the spring tide and the brisk north-easterly wind which had been forecast.

'Of course. Sorry. I forgot. You did tell me you were going. Was it good?'

'Yeah. Wicked. I'm starving. Wassfalunch?'

'I've had mine. It is three o'clock and no one was up at the time.'

'I was up,' said an indignant Stevie. 'Can I make a cheese toastie? Just to keep me going 'til lunch?'

'Supper. Lunchtime has passed.'

'Whatever. I'm starving ... wassfasupper?' he enquired, as he stood at the pine table hewing great slabs of cheese from a block with the sharpest knife, which left a series of great digs across Mrs D's tabletop.

'Um, board, Stevie?'

'Yeah, right. Borrowed Leechie's spare one. Goes like shit in a storm.'

I gazed at him for a moment and then looked down the garden path to where a blackbird was being pursued by its fledgling offspring, its mouth gaping as the mother repeatedly dug worms from the rose bed and dropped them into its mouth. In six weeks time, I mused, that young bird will have flown the nest and its mother won't even recognise it should they ever meet up. What have I done wrong to be struggling still, twenty years later?

I tried once more to discover who our mysterious guest was, this time from Stevie.

'Stevie, any idea who the chap was eating breakfast in the kitchen earlier on? Caucasian, dark hair, unshaven, limited vocabulary, about five-eleven and a hundred and fifty-five pounds. I say this to distinguish him from all the other local young men who might well have felt a bit peckish and drifted in off the streets for a bite during the weekend.'

'Our kitchen?' he replied, slamming down the lid of the

sandwich toaster and leaning heavily upon it to compress one and a half pounds of cheese and a generous helping of baked beans. The machine hissed, and explosive glurps of melted cheese erupted from the side and dribbled down the cupboard door.

'Yes. *Our* kitchen,' I emphasised. 'Do you know who this chap was?'

'No idea,' he muttered.

'Well, *one* of you *must* know! We can't just have any old Tom, Dick or Harry dropping in, eating cornflakes, reading my paper and disappearing!'

Greg and Stevie looked at me, presumably stirred into response by the slight tone of annoyance in my voice.

'Chill, Dad.'

'Yeah, chill, Dad. Has he robbed us?'

'Robbed us? What do you mean, robbed us?'

'You know,' said Greg. 'Like, nicked any of our stuff?'

'Not that I know of. Why? Do you think he might have done?'

I thought for a moment of Mrs Dudgeon's immense and valuable collection of country and western records, but then, after a moment's reflection, decided that Jim Reeves wouldn't have been of great interest to our mysterious visitor.

'You ought to go to university, Dad. You'd chill about it then. People come and go the whole time. If you haven't been shopping and you get hungry, you just walk into some other hall of residence, have a look in a few fridges, make a sandwich and bugger off. Everybody does it all the time.'

'Well, thanks Greg. I really appreciate that savoury little insight into the domestic workings of one of our more prestigious educational establishments. The fact is, *Cromwell's Retreat* is not a hall of residence, and I'm not prepared to have a constant stream of unknown people wandering in here and raiding my fridge on a Sunday morning just because they happen to feel a bit peckish and they're too damned lazy to shift themselves to a shop as most people do.'

'Just one bloke, Dad. Just one. Not streams.'

Angelica, who had been very quiet until this point, broke away from her absorption with an account of a gap year spent lounging on the beaches of Bali, and looked at me.

'Dad, it was Bones, okay? Chill out. He slept on my floor last night because he couldn't find his door key. He had to go first thing this morning, and I told him to help himself to breakfast if he was hungry.'

The two boys stared at their sister.

'Bones!' echoed Greg, after a few moments. 'D'ja mean that psycho who was going out with Susie?'

'He's not a psycho!'

'Woh!' said Greg provocatively. 'In your room? Last night? Bones?'

Greg looked at me, clearly awaiting some sort of response. Stevie paused, his mouth stretched unnaturally wide around a double toastie, as baked bean juice dribbled down his unshaven chin.

'Glic!' he muttered, through his bubbling sandwich as he stifled an incredulous smirk.

'Angelica. Are you telling me you brought someone home last night and, unbeknown to your mother and me, you had him in your room?'

'Yes.' She looked at me indignantly.

'Well, who is he? How long have you known him?' I asked.

'Some time. Like, ages.'

'Ages?' repeated Stevie, with a hint of disbelief in his voice.

'Well, Friday. Look, Dad, nothing happened; he just slept on my floor, that's all. It's no big deal. Go up and look. The sofa cushions are still there. What do you expect me to do? Tell him to go and sleep on his front doorstep?'

At this point, Angelica jumped down from the work surface where she had been reading the paper, glared at me as though I might be the most unreasonable father in the whole universe, and stomped out of the kitchen in floods of tears, slamming the door behind her as she did so.

'Dad!' said Stevie. 'You didn't really need to do that to her, did you? You were a bit rough on her!'

'Rough on her? Do that to her? What are you talking about? I simply stated what she had told me, and asked her if it was true! *I* didn't upset her.'

'Well, shomebodgee didge and it shertainly washn't me,' he said, through a mouth stuffed full of baked beans and cheese.

I looked at the boys and began to reflect on what a long time three weeks might prove to be before Mrs D came home again.

2

Airports are not my favourite places. I think it's fair to say that this is something of an understatement. Whilst I appreciate that few folk are willing to undertake voluntary visits to such places, and presumably fewer still actually derive pleasure from them, you should understand that what I am referring to in my case could be called a pathological *loathing* for them.

I detest airports. Nothing will persuade me that there is anything remotely enjoyable about the experience; I would much prefer to be incarcerated in a fifth-rate Spanish hotel with my malodorous tax inspector and a jug of tannin-laden sangria. Even enduring a root filling without anaesthetic would be infinitely more agreeable than having to make another visit to Heathrow. Perhaps as a child I was once traumatised when, on a visit to the viewing gallery to see the aeroplanes taking off, I became separated from my parents. Quite how they managed to lose me, in the quaint old days of BOAC, when there was just a terminal for overseas flights and another for domestic flights; in the days when car parks actually had parking spaces, and *The Stack* was a youth club in Basildon, rather than an intricately poised conglomeration of mankind, metal and aviation fuel suspended hazardously above the streets of London, I shall never know. But lose me they did. All I am aware of is that now I am filled with an inexplicable dread, an overwhelming terror, as the first signs to '*London Heathrow*' appear on the gantries above the stationary traffic on the M25 west of London. It feels as though I have been doomed; as though nearly every mishap that might befall me in my entire life will conspire to act against me, and will do so, in a concentrated hour or two of purgatory. If it *can* go wrong it will, within three or four hundred yards of Terminal Three.

On that Sunday, the day when *Bones* came to breakfast, I set off early for the airport with Mrs Dudgeon so that she might arrive for a ten o'clock check-in and a midday flight to the USA. For the purposes of this story, not to mention my wariness of the Official Secrets Act, let us agree that she was travelling to meet her sister in Arizona, which is more or less true because she was due to stay at Winifred's for a few days on arrival. I may tell you that she carried a robust hand-case filled with papers which had arrived over a period of weeks, conveyed by a series of mysterious couriers from a certain government office near Bletchley. When we finally checked in at the airline desk, her first-class tickets awaited her in a sealed brown envelope. If you had lived with Mrs D for as long as I have, you would know not to ask too many questions. 'Just one of my old contacts, dear,' she will reply to any query following a transatlantic phone call at three in the morning.

The traffic sped along faster than ever as we approached the airport centre and, despite the speed restrictions, the mêlée of swerving cars all seemed to be changing lanes at break-neck speeds as the drivers sought to read the signs and make choices about their destinations. Not only does one have to negotiate unusually narrow traffic lanes amidst hurtling airline coaches and taxis but, simultaneously, one must choose between the various terminals available and also select the appropriate place to leave the car. Terminal One short stay; Terminal One long stay; Terminal Three intermediate stay; Terminal Three intermediate short stay; short stay domestic departures, and so on. You name it, they have a car park to suit, and if you waver for just one second as the chromed radiator grill of a bus looms large in your rearview mirror, you are lost, consigned for ever to the bowels of a distant exit-less car park, miles from your departure terminal, where you will spend your days wearily driving up and down those squealy ramps until, finally, the car runs out of petrol or you expire. Or both. There is a funeral parlour at Heathrow which, I am reliably informed, every year handles several cases of multi-storey car park fatigue. Death by NCP.

I found the correct car park slip road and pulled up behind a short queue of traffic at the right-hand ticket machine where the barrier rhythmically rose and fell, admitting a vehicle each time it did so. We shuffled forward as each driver took a ticket, the barrier lifted and the car disappeared into the depths of subterranean Heathrow ... until my turn came. The machine sulked, the barrier stubbornly refused to lift and a red light glowed ominously on the console. No ticket emerged from the slot. I pressed the green button. Still no ticket. A car hooted behind me. Mrs D scrabbled in the glove compartment for my reading specs and, so equipped, I discovered there was a 'Press for Assistance' button which I stabbed and was met by an overwhelming silence. After a few seconds, I applied my finger again and a voice, which sounded as though it was emerging from a high-speed food blender, could be faintly heard giving an instruction. Unfortunately, with stunning synchronicity, it coincided with the skull-rattling roar of four large jet engines attached to the ten o'clock 747 flight to Kuala Lumpur and Sidney, which passed overhead and drowned out everything emerging from the minute loudspeaker.

By then there were quite a few agitated drivers waiting behind me tooting on their horns. Quite why anyone should consider that is an appropriate thing to do under those particular circumstances, I cannot imagine. Did they think I was, out of choice, sitting at the barrier of a noisy car park? Did they think I was parked there having a brief respite after a long journey? A cup of coffee and ten minutes snooze with *Desert Island Discs* before I continued on my way? I have always admired the wherewithal of a driver of a broken down car at the Hammersmith Flyover who, on hearing the car behind hooting, calmly walked to the offending driver, and politely offered to sit with his hand on the car's horn on the condition that the impatient commuter would alight and fix the stubbornly inert car at the head of the congestion. He had style.

I sensed a certain quickening of Mrs D's breathing and perceived that she was about to do one of them a considerable mischief. Laying a restraining hand on her arm, I waved out of the window indicating that the cars behind should reverse and seek to switch lanes to the adjacent ticket machine, where the barrier was rising and falling with sickening efficiency as it admitted countless dozens of cars. It is quite a complex procedure to reverse half a dozen cars down such a busy road, and I watched in my mirror as my signal was repeated down the impatient line. Eventually, the car at the end of the queue reversed, changed lanes, and sped away to the next machine. No sooner had it done so, another car rounded the bend and took its place. Semaphore signals were repeated and the car duly moved away only to be replaced by another ... and so it continued until a gentleman in a turban emerged from an office, bearing a large packet. He opened the machine and, having installed a new roll of tickets, the barrier rose and we were free to drive into the car park. For ten minutes or so we then toured every level several times over and eventually found one of those exceptionally narrow spaces which is adjacent to an enormous concrete column and allows one to drive in, but not get out of, the car.

I hesitate to say this, but Mrs D is not the slim young thing she once was when she was in training with 'The Unit'. I imagine that her work with them these days is probably based more on cerebral involvement, as opposed to the physical. I reversed the car out, allowed Mrs Dudgeon to disembark, and then parked. Squeezing myself out of the door which was no more than eight and a half inches from the wall, was not beneficial for a back-sufferer who, on occasion, has trouble even bending down to pick up the dog's bowl. You will understand that I was not in the best of humour as we sought to control an uncontrollable luggage trolley and decipher the signing which eventually led to a long moving pavement heading towards Departures.

I need not have worried myself about being late. Airports seem to have contrived to persuade their customers that it is essential to

14

arrive three and a half days before a flight, and it is transparently clear why they do so; it is a multi-million pound persuasion aimed at separating innocent travellers from their money in the shopping malls which now surround every departure terminal. Buoyed up by holiday spirits, travellers with wallets full of nervous money are persuaded to acquire not just the essential accoutrements of flying, such as a good book and a packet of barley sugars, but expensive perfumes, electrical goods, leather handbags, briefcases, nine hundred and seventy-five piece jig-saws, new wardrobes of clothes, new wardrobes, soft furnishings and, most mysterious of all, suitcases. I have never managed to understand how one could possibly wish to buy a suitcase in a *departure* lounge. In Arrivals, yes. In Arrivals, it should be obligatory that vouchers be dispensed on the aircraft to allow one to claim recompense for the handles, trolley wheels and studs which are inexplicably knocked off during baggage handling. Our own luggage lasted for about twenty years when we holidayed in the car, but after one fifty-minute flight to Glasgow it emerged on the carousel looking for all the world as though it had been used as an obstacle in a steamroller race. But in Departures? Who has need of a suitcase prior to boarding a plane? How many passengers have you seen climbing out of a taxi clutching armfuls of shirts, dresses, trousers and underwear, only to smack their foreheads and say, 'Darling! You know what we forgot to bring?'

'No, sweet. What?'

'The suitcases!'

'Oh my goodness! So we did. How fortunate that there is a luggage shop just over there. Let's get two. They will make it so much easier at Mallorca airport.'

Mrs D checked in and was opening her brown envelope when a smart young man in customs uniform saluted her.

'Good morning, Mrs Dudgeon. Welcome to London Heathrow. I have instructions to escort you through the formalities. May I?' he asked, offering to carry her large black briefcase.

'Um, no. Thank you for offering, but I will keep hold of that one, if it's all the same,' she said, and with that she kissed me on the cheek, wished me luck with the children and the fitting of the new bathroom, and disappeared into that land behind the partition where only *bona fide* travellers may venture.

I turned to go, struggling to remember which of the many entrances we had used to join the thronging masses on the concourse. I found there was a considerable number of exits as I sauntered past the shops looking for a familiar landmark. Yes, we had come this way. No doubt about it. Here was the electrical store selling, amongst other things, a dishwasher which, when you come to think about it, is a jolly useful buy as you leave for a fortnight in the Canary Islands. I thought we had parked in Terminal Three short stay, but I confess that, when I reached that particular sea of cars, I was not so sure. All the car parks looked the same. I wandered through levels A, B, B1, C and D searching for my faithful mustard-coloured Lada which should have been sandwiched between a concrete pillar and an outside wall. There were plenty of concrete pillars, and even an outside wall or two, but no car. Perhaps I had left it somewhere else.

'Excuse me,' I asked quietly of the attendant sitting in a booth, not particularly wishing to broadcast my predicament to the flotsam and jetsam who all appeared to be retrieving their cars with remarkable ease. 'I seem to have lost my car. I can tell you what the parking space looked like . . .'

'Let's see your ticket, mate.'

'Ticket?'

'Parking ticket. You took it out of the machine at the entrance.'

'Ah that one. It's propped in the windscreen of the car . . .'

He gazed at me and simultaneously pointed upwards to a *massive* blue and white sign above the kiosk.

'*Do not forget to take your parking ticket with you as the fees are payable at the east end of the Departure Concourse where machines are located for the purpose.*'

'Ah.'

The car park attendant smiled patiently, if not a little patronisingly, and said, 'Don't worry, mate. It happens all the time. But you've lost your car you say?'

'I rather think I have,' I said, remembering the time I had lost the same car in our local town as a result of opiate-induced memory loss caused by taking morphine for pain relief before my back surgery.

'Tell me what you remember about the parking space.'
I described it as best I could. He wrinkled his brow as though trying to conjure up an image of where it might be.

'And where were the stairs?'

'Nearby. We came out on a long ramp that doubled back on itself and . . .'

'Level B, Terminal Two short stay. Right-hand side. Back corner. You need to go and get your ticket, chum. Then you pay in Departures.'

'In Departures? But that's . . . You mean I have to go *back*?'
He nodded and smiled.

Needless to say, the car was *exactly* where he had forecast it would be, the ticket was still in the windscreen, and it was a long walk back to the concourse where an eager machine gobbled two fivers and refused to spit out any change. That time I did not forget how to find the car. I sank gratefully into the seat and gazed around at the profusion of empty parking bays which, by then, surrounded me. I lit my pipe, listened to five minutes of *Desert Island Discs* and then realised to my dismay that if I did not leave quickly my stay would exceed the fee I had paid and, somehow, I would then have to re-enter the car park, collect another ticket . . .

3

I arrived home that Sunday afternoon at about the same time that Mrs Dudgeon would have been eighteen thousand feet above the Atlantic Ocean. How our arterial traffic systems can contrive to make a journey from Heathrow to the south of Suffolk so complicated and drawn out, I really cannot imagine. A proliferation of cones near Junction 21 lasted for about three miles, apparently re-routing the traffic via *Canterbury, Dover* and *Portsmouth.* Quite why we all stood at a standstill for an hour, as the three lanes of traffic sought to condense itself into one, I do not know. The only notable activity I could determine in that vast array of cones and signs was a lone man balanced on a platform, changing a light-bulb high above the central reservation. Can you imagine any other country in the world that would allow thousands of travellers to be delayed on the most significant road we have, so that a *light-bulb* could be changed? As Mrs Dudgeon said, later, when she enquired about my journey home, 'Back in Sierra Leone, one of the natives would have tucked a replacement bulb between his teeth and cheerfully shinned up the lamp standard and nobody would have batted an eyelid.' What is wrong with these people?

Personally, I blame the health and safety movement, around which an enormous, self-perpetuating industry has grown up. Much of this energy is totally misplaced and unproductive, apart from which it is at least partly responsible for the disfigurement of some of our most beautiful buildings. I happened to visit one of our great London churches a few months ago and, as I sat quietly

18

at the side, contemplating the sheer splendour of Wren's master-piece, I noticed on the wall beside me a fire extinguisher. Now, I would wish you to understand that I have no reservations whatsoever about the provision of such things – after all, we have lost York Minster and a sizeable portion of Windsor Castle, not to mention our local mock-Gothic post office, all savaged by fire in the relatively recent past. No, my question is why we need to have the fluorescent signs that are now situated above every fire extinguisher, each bearing a picture of licking flames and a jet of water squirting from the said appliance. Do the authorities really believe that it is not clear that a fire extinguisher is . . . well, a fire extinguisher, and that it constitutes the most useful and appropriate means for putting out a fire? What, in our confusion, do the authorities think we might try to do with it . . . turn it upside down and use it for a hymn-book rest? Everywhere one looks these days there is a plethora of signs, most of them unnecessary, all of them causing visual carnage to our most beautiful surroundings.

Not very long ago, I browsed a catalogue depicting the full range of signage which is now available as a result of this opportunist industry which grows on the back of the current nanny-state mentality. Imagine this: there are signs to put above hot taps reading *"Beware! Hot water!"* Can you believe that? What does any half-intelligent person expect to come out of a hot tap? Hot taps are usually marked in red with the letter *"H"* emblazoned across the top. Why do we need to spell it out further? I'll tell you why. It's because some nincompoop once held his hand determinedly under a hotel hot tap until he burnt his fingers. Deciding that there was substantial financial benefit to be generated from taking action against the hotel, he then sued the management and instead of the judge telling the complainant to bugger off and stop wasting the judiciary's time, the bewigged fool awarded damages. That's why. It's deplorable. You wait. As soon as someone sticks their fingers in a teapot, little notices will begin to appear on hotel tea trays: *"Take care. Hot liquid within"*. I'm surprised that we don't have a legal requirement for notices to be fixed above lavatories – *"Danger of Drowning"* – with a lifeline coiled nearby for good measure. The shower-head is damned dangerous. That should also have a notice affixed: *"Do not place this appliance in your mouth or any other orifice"*. The mind staggers at what one might get up to in the Jacuzzi . . .

The whole system of fire signing is misplaced and inappropriate anyway. Anyone who has had the misfortune to have been in a burning building will tell you that smoke rises to the ceiling, then thickens and gradually moves downwards towards the floor. Even a small fire will create enough smoke to obliterate the light from a sixty watt ceiling light, and the panicky escapee will find himself on the floor choking and spluttering as he crawls along the hotel's best Axminster, under the smoke, in near darkness. Tell me now; where do they put the faintly glowing *Fire Exit* signs? I'll tell you where: *above* the doors, just below the ceiling where they will be completely invisible and useless in an emergency. They should move all the signs and fix them at floor level where they would not only be more effective, but considerably less offensive to the eye too.

The catalogue I mentioned, the safety one, actually had a sign that read, *"Beware! Steps going down!"* Now, I could understand this if the sign was worded in Braille for the visually impaired, but it wasn't. It beggars belief that one might approach a staircase and somehow, even for a moment, consider that the stairs, which very apparently go downwards, do, in the depths of one's tortured imagination, mysteriously go upwards. Even my own children were, at the tender age of seven months, well able to determine whether the stairs in our house went up or down, long before they could read. Frankly, if you need a sign to tell you whether a staircase rises or falls, I really do believe that, and I write this with all respect, you are something of a monumental risk. You should actually reconsider whether or not you are safe to be at large.

I am not looking forward to the next rash of signs that will appear before common sense prevails and the pendulum swings the other way. They will all be aimed at saving someone's backside from possible litigation. The opportunities are limitless: *"Beware! Door!"* will appear everywhere (accompanied by a cameo of a person being smacked in the face by an opening door); *"Caution! Glass is dangerous!"* could appear above every piece of public fenestration in the British Isles; *"Danger! Floor!"* does, I suppose, have potential. It could be accompanied by an illustration of an androgynous-looking figure turning a somersault and head-butting the floor. The warning notices could then be displayed, screwed to the marble-floored interiors of hotel receptions, all at carefully prescribed EC regulation distances apart. There is no end to the nonsense, as one could then develop a series of signs warning of the dangers of tripping over signs. Take my word for it; if you have a few quid to spare, invest heavily in *Fluoro-Safety Signs Inc.* You'll be onto a winner.

The prize for the most absurd piece of signing, created in the first whiffs of metrication nonsense from Brussels, must go to British Waterways. For years, canal craft have plied their trade up and down the country's quiet canals. The rule was that you did not travel at more than four miles per hour; not that it was always possible to achieve such a remarkable turn of speed owing to the lack of dredging and the consequent build-up of glutinous silt. Four miles per hour is, give or take a bit, a rapid walking pace, and that is how people judged their speed quite satisfactorily for about two hundred years. As Brussels legislation loomed, some bright spark in the head office at Watford, not in the least deterred by the fact that road signs were to remain unmetricated, decided to waste licence payers' money by ordering hundreds of canal-side signs reading *"Speed limit 6.43 kph"*. The notion that boaters could possibly determine their speed to two decimal places is, as my eloquent children would say, 'total bollocks'.

The bottom line is that people do not read signs. Had I done so at the airport, I would have avoided a long and tiresome walk. In most cases, we are satiated with unnecessary written instructions. They no longer impinge on our consciousness, if they ever did. We have had enough of it. If you don't believe me, consider this. A notice on our station reads as follows: *"Ball games and skateboarding are prohibited on this platform"*. Now, who is this written for, I wonder? Children? Assuming they are old enough to read the sign but not old enough to realise that skateboarding under the six-seventeen fast train to Liverpool Street will do little for their complexions, why one wonders are they there? What are these youngsters doing on the platform accompanied by nothing more than their knee and elbow pads? The sign can only possibly be there for a parent to read who, one assumes, will, sign or no sign, instinctively deter young Johnny from doing triple somersaults across the branch line to Clacton. If they are genuinely old enough to be there in the first place, they might know that practising penalty shootouts under the overhead wires is foolish. So who is the sign written for? The answer is, solicitors. The notice is a piece of backside saving but, more than that, it is a justification from the safety officer that he is doing his job thoughtfully and diligently – except that just down the line there is a broken-down fence beside a footpath where toddlers and dogs can wander at will on the tracks where ninety-mile-an-hour expresses streak past. The point is that by placing smart blue and white signs on the station, the job is seen to be done (even if it isn't).

In every major concern there is undoubtedly a person appointed to turn out this appalling drivel, and most of it at considerable cost to the public. The long-term answer is simple. It is all avoidable. When a child is registered shortly after birth, the government should provide each with a bracelet akin to those bearing a medical alert. It should read: *"Life is dangerous; don't say we didn't warn you!"* Thereafter, as soon as anyone files an action for negligence, the judge can pompously state, 'Well, we told you so. Now sod off and don't stick your fingers in the teapot again.'

Signs also provide well-intentioned amateurs with scope for displaying their ignorance of the English language. *Battery's, Spark Plug's, Oil Filter's* reads the board outside our local motor spare(')s shop. That is forgivable. The poor man running the business against all the odds that the district council can summon to thwart his efforts, probably never learned the correct use of apostrophe(')s. What should not be tolerated are the official notices which abound, such as the one which accompanies contraflows on the motorways: *'In case of brake down* [sic] *use the hard shoulder'* instead of *'In the event of...'* The second will have the desired effect, whilst the first might have every well-educated Swede on the M25 quite justifiably bumping along the hard shoulder. One wonders what would transpire in court if one chose to appeal against three penalty points awarded for doing precisely what the sign ordered the traffic to do.

Whilst on holiday, Mrs D and I visited a very pleasant village and lunched at the Knightley Arms. As we left, we saw a beautifully prepared sign-writer's notice in the car park: *'Welcome to the Knighley Arms'* it proclaimed proudly. Notwithstanding, we enjoyed two very good shepherd's pis. Without doubt, the best notice we have ever seen was posted in the window of our local builders' merchant on the day we went to choose our bathroom suite. They are a great bunch and I would not wish to offend them, but this is what was written: *'Please bare with us. Most of the sales staff are out of the yard today attending the manager's funeral; we are operating a skeleton staff'.*

4

I left the boys to clear up after their 'breakfast', or whatever youngsters call it at three in the afternoon, and went outside to mow the lawns and make the most of the remainder of the day. As I walked out of the front porch, the ivy tried to throttle me again and, feeling that not only were my children against me but the local flora as well, I gave it a good tug. Nothing happened. The second time I pulled at it, I gave it my best effort and something then gave way accompanied by a loud 'crack'. Had I not been so annoyed with my charming offspring, I might have been a little more conservative in my efforts to rid the front of the house of the worst excesses of the monster vine; I might have gone to the shed and fetched the secateurs and pruned it properly or, at the very least, I might have looked up in an attempt to discover what had given way. Had I done so, I might have noticed that it was not the vine which had broken, but the ancient plaster rendering which faced the front of the house. Thoroughly invaded by ivy ingress, it had been further damaged by my blunt efforts. I didn't notice this crucial fact. I gave the branch, by now hanging mockingly at waist height, one more vicious tug.

At this point, I should explain that *Cromwell's Retreat* is not just any old, run-of-the-mill Suffolk cottage. It is what the Department of the Environment, that government organisation full of busybodies with nothing better to do than make life difficult for ordinary law abiding citizens, describes as a *Listed Building*. There are several sorts of *listing* by which civil servants can not only tell what you cannot do to your own home, but can also insist

24

on what you do do. Be warned; if you have thoughts about owning an old cottage in the countryside, check first. Don't, not even for a second, be tempted to feel flattered that they appreciate the qualities of your chosen house. If you have found what is referred to as a *Grade Two Listed House* count yourself very lucky. This particular form of bureaucratic nonsense only restricts what you may or may not do to the *outside* of your period dwelling whilst leaving you entirely free to do whatever you wish to the interior. If you should wish to convert your low-beamed seventeenth-century living room into a gaudy, multi-coloured imitation of a night club, with a stainless steel and chrome bar counter built within the William III inglenook fireplace, then you can do so. You may affix rows of gaudy flashing lights across the beam above the hearth, and then proceed to jiggle the night away ... if that happens to be your thing. I am not, of course, suggesting that you would wish to do so, but if you did, you could, and nobody could do a thing about it except turn up their conservationist noses and make tut-tutting noises at your extreme choice of décor.

And here is the rub. Because Oliver Cromwell, once MP for Huntingdon, in a moment of extreme weariness in 1648 decided to put his feet up and stay for a few days in our Suffolk cottage (a piece of local folklore for which there is no historical substantiation whatsoever) we have the privilege of abiding in what is now registered as a *Grade One Listed Dwelling*. Not wishing to bore you with the details of the regulations which govern what we may or may not do to our own home, which incidentally is paid for lock, stock and barrel having discharged my debts to the Saffron Walden and Basildon Building Society, suffice it to say that we have to notify a clerk at the Department if we wish even to put a picture hook on the wall. The point being that this particular form of listing does not only apply to the *outside* of our home, but it determines what may happen on the *inside* as well. It is preposterous. If I were to suggest that in two hundred years time, another house, currently occupied by a certain ex-Member of Parliament for Huntingdon, were listed for no better reason than *John* and *Norma* happened to have once lived there, you would immediately grasp how ridiculous the whole affair is. To put it bluntly, who will give a bugger? I am just glad that my garden is not listed. If it was, doubtless, each week I would have to suffer a myriad of lawn experts descending on us to tell me not only which bits of grass I might be allowed to cut (probably with nail scissors honed by a genuine, registered Craft Council endorsed blacksmith), but I would also have to preserve the grass clippings between layers of acid-free tissue paper in case a passing horticultural historian chose to research the origins of our daisy-infested lawn.

The reason for indulging in this little preamble is to be certain that you will understand the full consequences of what transpired after that fateful, final tug on the ivy. Had I known the financial and domestic misery which would ensue, I would certainly have been a little more circumspect, for, as the trunk-like woody tendrils of that voracious climber came away in my hand, so did a very considerable proportion of the front of the house above the porch. There was a rumbling, bouncing noise not unlike that made by Mrs D when she inadvertently lost her footing last year and the poor dear tumbled down our sixteenth-century caracole staircase. The only difference was that this time I found myself standing in the middle of a storm of dust, slabs of plaster and rending ivy stems as the whole lot collapsed into the front garden. I stood staring in disbelief at the exposed inner substance of the wall of the house, that part which one is never supposed to see; at the lumps of clay and straw which now protruded in a particularly unsightly fashion where only hours before Mrs Dudgeon's favourite Albertine rose had mingled aromatically with the ivy on the wall.

Greg's head appeared tentatively around the front door; his eyes gazed at the swirling dust clouds and piles of rendering. 'Uh, I thought you were going to cut the grass,' he muttered, surveying the debris of mangled rose now essentially buried under hundredweights of sixteenth-century plaster. 'When's supper?'

After an hour of stacking fragments of ancient rendering into a wheelbarrow and trundling them to an old pit at the bottom of the garden, I managed to stand Mrs D's rose up again. It had something of a curious stoop about it, as though it was finding the burden of life too much to bear. I was admiring my efforts when a voice called from the front gate.

'I hope you don't mind me asking, Mr Dudgeon, but I trust you are not planning to do anything too disastrous to *Cromwell's Retreat.*'

Before I even turned to address the speaker, I knew full well who it was. Madeleine Gascoigne, self-styled village busybody and author of *Smoke Bays and Early Chimneys of Strumpling Green, Suffolk* which, as one might expect, was a riveting read and at the last count had sold all of forty-seven copies. It occurred to me that I might play deaf, slip inside and make a much-needed cup of tea. Unfortunately I did not.

'I'm thinking of putting a large double-glazed picture window in the front actually, Miss Gascoigne. Of course, this ghastly little porch will have to go, to make space for it, but it will be lovely. I'm so fed up with all these ridiculously tiny windows. It's so *dark* inside.'

'Mr Dudgeon! You can't! The village won't stand for it. You are, after all, *only* a guardian of one of the area's outstanding examples of sixteenth-century vernacular building, and any attempt to interfere with the structure will be reported at once to . . .'

I knew the moment I had made my quip that it had been a mistake. 'Meddling' Gascoigne, as Mrs D refers to her, had one major failing – a total absence of any form of sense of humour.

'Just some repairs Miss G. It will all be put back together again soon. We need a spot of rendering.'

I struggled wearily to push the last barrowful of plaster to the tip, but, as I passed Miss Gascoigne, she flung open the wicket gate and seized a piece of the debris. She pushed her glasses to the top of her head and held it close to her eye for inspection, as though it might have been a nugget of gold from a riverbed.

'Aha!' she cried. 'I thought so. My goodness! Would you believe it? The original sixteenth-century pargetting, Mr Dudgeon. The real thing. See here,' she said, splitting the piece of plaster with her fingers to expose a subsidiary layer, which appeared to have been combed with an old garden rake. 'Stunning! Where are you putting all of this for safe keeping, Mr Dudgeon?'

'Oh, in a tidy pile round the back, Miss G,' I replied, realising that I had tipped about five hundredweight of priceless archaeology into a smelly old pond at the bottom of the garden. 'It will be fine, don't you worry. Very safe.'

'Good job, because it ought to be reassembled and recorded.'

Reassembled? Recorded? 'Over my dead body,' I muttered, as I took my leave, pushing the barrow to the tip with renewed gusto.

Having sunk several cups of tea, and finding that my irritation with the children had subsided somewhat, it occurred to me that the evening presented an ideal opportunity to enjoy a decent meal with the older ones, and I set about roasting chicken, peeling home-grown potatoes and preparing other fresh vegetables, knowing how they relished a good family nosh. It couldn't fail to improve the atmosphere. A little later Angelica came down looking remarkably presentable, wearing dark clothes and minus all the ironmongery she normally wears in her nose and ears.

'Going out tonight? You look nice.'

'Gotta job.'

'Really! Since when?'

'Since last night. At that new nightclub in the old cinema. Waitress.'

'Ah . . . and what exactly do you have to do at the club?'

She stared at me. 'Be a waitress, Dad. What else do waitresses usually do?'

I peered at her over the top of my spectacles. 'All sorts of things actually, Angelica. I didn't realise that there was a restaurant there.'

'There *isn't*. Nightclubs don't have restaurants, Dad. Why are you so out of date? I serve drinks at tables. People go there to, like, drink and dance. I get paid commission for all the drinks the clubbers order at the tables.'

'*I see*,' I said, in a way which wasn't intended to have quite such heavy overtones of disapproval attached to it. She stared at me for the second time in forty seconds.

'Anyway, I'll be off. First night. Mustn't be late. Neil won't like it.'

'*Who* is *Neil*?'

She looked at me again; that adolescent 'are you trying to be difficult or are you just an effortlessly stupid parent?' sort of look.

'The boss.'

'*I see*.' Bugger! I'd done it again.

She stared at me. 'See you later, Dad. I'll be late, and don't worry, I won't bring Bones back again. Ever.'

'Right. Well, I hope it goes well. I'm sorry you won't be here for supper. I've . . .' but the door banged closed before my words were out.

'Dad. Where's Mum today?' Stevie asked from the kitchen doorway, with his crash helmet tucked under his arm.

'Mum? Stevie, Mum is in America for three weeks. Remember all that fuss last night? Passport? Fond farewells? All that "see you in three weeks" stuff? That woman was your mother, and she was carrying the suitcase round the house because she was going away first thing this morning. You can't really have forgotten.'

He stared at me. 'Chill, Dad. All I wondered was, when she would be doing the washing? Three weeks, huh? Do you know how to do the washing machine stuff? I've sort of got some clothes, like, you know, a pile, like.' He stretched his arms wide indicating a mountain of laundry. 'Mussgo now. We'll sort it, yeah? Cheers, Dad. I can hear Phil outside on his bike.'

'Ah, Phil. Yes. Listen, Stevie, I've cooked a decent supper. I thought you'd enjoy it. I . . .'

The door closed and, seconds later, a motorbike could be heard revving as it rearranged most of the gravel on the drive.

29

The phone rang.

'Hello. This is the Dudgeon household.'

'Eh?'

'Duncan Dudgeon speaking. Whom did you wish to speak to?'

'Er . . . is that Greg?'

'Um, no. This is Duncan Dudgeon. Would you like to speak to Greg Dudgeon?'

'Er yeah. Cheers.'

I called Greg from the foot of the stairs. 'Greg! One of the nation's intelligentsia on the phone for you.'

Greg bounded down the stairs taking six or seven steps at once and grasped the phone as I stirred white wine into a thickening sauce on the Aga.

''Lo. Yeah. Stonky! How yer doin', mate? Yeah, long time no see, like. Cool. Yeah. Sure thing. Wicked. In ten. By the post office. Cheers. Cool. Ciao.' He tossed the phone back onto its charger in the way that only youngsters who have not paid for phone repair bills know how to do. 'Hey, Dad. Guess who that was?'

'Ah, let me see . . . Stonky?'

'How did you guess that? He's coming by and wants to meet up for a pizza.'

'Don't tell me . . . in ten minutes.'

Greg stared at me. 'Yeah, in ten minutes. How did you know that as well?'

'Years of practice, Greg . . . years of practice. You're off out then?'

'Yeah. Must dash. Catch up with you later Dad.'

'Greg, there's a roast chicken here that . . .'

Fido stirred himself in his basket and stretched. He padded over and stood beneath me as I carved a single portion of chicken, served out crispy roast potatoes and fresh vegetables. He looked at me in that opportunist way that only dogs can manage, then his gaze moved to the chicken carcass as he did his utmost to levitate it from the carving dish.

'Stick around, dog,' I said, sitting down to a table laid for four. 'I think you might be in with a fair chance tonight.'

5

'Mr Brownlea? Duncan Dudgeon here. Do you remember me? You very kindly came down last winter and put a new cistern in the outside lavvie ... that's right ... yes, and the pan. I'd forgotten that. Yes, after Mrs Dudgeon's little accident. Yes, you're right ... it was quite funny I suppose ... at least afterwards. Anyway, I've got a smallish job down here. A bit of rendering on the front of the cottage has come away. Interested? Good, good. Well, why don't you drop by at lunchtime on the way to the Pig and Whistle? Yes, have a look and see what you think ... fairly quickly because I don't want the rain getting into that old clay lump wall ... yes, I know, the forecast is awful. Until lunchtime then ... thank you. Bye for now.'

Archibald Brownlea & Sons ... *Sons* being the least reputable part of the operation – were the local builders. They were not renowned in the vicinity for their house-building skills but did a jolly satisfactory line in repair jobs and, most important of all, they were cheap to employ. Poor old Archie, a builder all his life, and a good brickie at that, was well over retiring age and left most of the serious work to his two sons, Seth and Barney. Archie must have cringed sometimes, when he looked at the quality of work the two 'lads' turned out. The 'lads', as he called them, were in their forties and had left a trail of sinking, cracked house extensions, leaking roofs and dripping pipes all the way from Strumpling Green to Thackett Corner. Not that they could do much damage to a few square yards of rendering.

Archie dropped in as promised and agreed that the lads would

32

come by the next morning and fit the job in before the weather changed. Meanwhile, the new bathroom, to be established in a tiny spare room next to our bedroom, awaited my attentions. Mrs D and I had decided that this piece of work was no longer an extravagance, as our six children had the capacity between them to jam the bathroom solid for hours on end, when they were all at home together. Admittedly, this was now a rarer occurrence as the older ones were at university, and the younger ones were less inclined to spend three hours under the shower, or to take the latest copy of *Loaded* into the loo. Mrs Dudgeon's little accident had been occasioned by her finding the bathroom, the upstairs WC *and* the downstairs cloakroom all occupied first thing in the morning, with the result that she hurried to the garden, in dressing gown and slippers, in order to use the outside privy, a curious affair apparently built in what was the old pigsty. Not realising that the icy cold weather had frozen the water in the ancient iron cistern, she had given the chain one of her hearty little tugs. Nothing had moved ... except the entire cistern, which parted company with the wall and then crashed into the vintage lavatory pan, which in turn disintegrated into thousands of china fragments, leaving the broken pipe discharging a jet of very cold water all over the occupant of the privy. Meanwhile, I was lying peacefully in bed savouring my first cup of tea and, on hearing the crash, assumed, perfectly reasonably, that Mrs D was doing some early morning weightlifting and had dropped one of her sets of weights. When she appeared, she had the general appearance of someone who had been prepared for the closing scenes in *Titanic* by an over-enthusiastic make-up junior. She was white-faced with dust, her dressing gown was covered in shards of china and dubious looking seaweedy stuff, and the poor woman was completely drenched from head to foot.

'Duncan, my dear,' she said calmly, 'I think we may need to call on the services of Archie Brownlea. The privy isn't quite what it was.'

Personally, I have always had a great fondness for the privy, particularly in the early morning when it is possible, given the privacy of our enclosed garden, to sit on the throne with the door open in order to answer the call of nature *en plein* while enjoying the sights and sounds of the local marshes. It reminds me of my camping days as a boy, and I find it a most uplifting experience. Archie was as industrious as ever and managed to acquire a turn-of-the-century vintage replacement pan and seat, and the cistern was restored to its original lofty position. I always think that you really can't beat a high level flush. However unsightly they may be, all that water falling from such a great height ensures that one never has those little problems with things failing to go round the bend.

Anyway, Mrs D and I had been to our local builders' merchant and, as it happened, had chosen the very afternoon when they were burying their late manager. We selected a new bathroom suite that had then been delivered and was in the garage awaiting installation. The appropriate permission had been granted by the building inspectors at Tolworth Rural District Council, subject to running the new soil pipes inside the house so as to avoid spoiling the half-timbered rear elevation of *Cromwell's Retreat*.

I began work not long after Archie had taken his leave, en route to his lunch at the pub. I pride myself on my plumbing skills and had intended to fit the new bathroom myself – a straightforward matter of installing a bath, WC and basin, and making the appropriate connections to the drains and the water supplies which were conveniently close at hand. I enlisted the support of Greg and Stevie to move the new bath upstairs, which they willingly did just after they got up at two o'clock on the Monday afternoon. Despite our best efforts, the apparently simple task defeated us. Sixteenth-century stairs, which turn through a hundred and eighty degrees in six feet six inches of rise were, of course, never designed to accommodate new bathroom suites and, having turned the bath this way and that, we realised that it was going to be extremely difficult to navigate the sharp turns involved. This is something of an understatement as, after half an hour of pushing and shoving, the bath stuck fast in the stairwell and would neither go up nor down. We left it there, jammed quite safely, and went to have a cup of tea. At least, Greg and I went to refresh ourselves while Stevie sat on the landing, as the teapot was on the wrong side of the imprisoned bath, and the only way for him to reach it was out of an upstairs window. Eventually, using a hammer and chisel, we gouged enough plaster from the wall thereby creating adequate tolerance for the bath to proceed upstairs, and Stevie was duly reacquainted with the teapot and the biscuit tin.

The second problem became apparent when the new bath was offered up to the corner of the spare bedroom and it was immediately very clear that the room was far from square. A three-inch gap loomed large at the tap end which would have made it impossible to ensure a watertight seal between tiles and bath – an essential feature as Mrs D and I intended to have a shower over the bath. Why on earth the builders and carpenters who constructed the cottage couldn't have done their job properly in the first place, I cannot imagine. Surely they must have realised the house wasn't square! It was clear that the wall would have to be built out to meet the bath before tiling commenced, and I phoned Ralph Jones, the tiler, and asked him to call by. Ralph produces exquisite tilework and I thought it worthwhile to pay to have this portion of the fitting done professionally. Any Tom, Dick or Harry can tile these days, given the foolproof systems available, but we had chosen 'Victorian' tiles with deep mouldings on them and when, in the past, I have attempted to cut them, the level of wastage was so great that it would have paid me five times over to engage a professional.

'Duncan,' Mrs D had said, 'don't be so stingy. Get Ralph to do it. Every day I look at the results of your tiling above the kitchen sink. I'd much rather the new bathroom tiles were level, without all those nasty broken bits around the light switches.'

I am sure I don't know what she can have meant. It looks perfectly all right to me.

Ralph dropped by on his way home and agreed that he would

first build a false wall before tiling commenced. 'It happens often in these old cottages . . . never square. Not a problem, though. You carry on and I'll work round the bath when you're done.'

I worked late into the evening, telling the boys to put sausages and jacket potatoes into the Aga. Angelica was going to *Neil's house* for supper, before work. I narrowly avoided saying *'I see'* when she told me, but I asked instead how old *Neil* was.

'Thirty-two,' she had replied, in a 'just dare to challenge me' sort of way. I didn't, despite the fact that Glic was only eighteen and, as it later transpired, *Neil* had a wife and children abandoned somewhere as he had roamed the country managing rather dubious nightclub ventures. Not exactly the sort I might have chosen as a suitable potential boyfriend for her. It was actually *Neil's fault* that I ended up at the cottage hospital. Well, as far as I was concerned it was. I was unpacking the bath and fixing those ridiculous, 'super no-fuss adjustable legs' at the time. I was ruminating on what I would do to *Neil* and his C-reg BMW if he laid so much as one finger on my daughter, when I ran *my* fingers under the bath and winced as I sliced them to the bone on the razor-like edge of the metal frame. Our primrose-coloured bath suite took on a new, interesting sort of random polka-dotted colour scheme as I searched desperately for tissues with which to wrap my fingers and staunch the flow of blood. Later, having managed to drive the Lada into Tolworth, and having acquired a number of stitches around the tips of two fingers, I was sponging debris from the new bath when Angelica came in from work.

'Ohmagod,' she said affectionately, 'wassappened?'

'I cut myself on the bath frame,' I said, waving my bandaged fingers.

'Ohmagod, Dad. Gruesome. I'm never bathing in *that* bath. It's disgusting!' And with that, she went to bed. *This* is the girl who is going to be a *doctor*.

Barney and Seth arrived the next morning and, under Archie's guidance, erected a small scaffold tower, mixed a huge quantity of gluey-looking stuff and daubed it all over the clay lump wall.

They set up a concrete mixer and assured me they would be back later with sand and cement and that the job wouldn't take very long. To be fair, it didn't, and they made a reasonable job of it, assuring me that when it had had a 'lick of paint' no one would ever know. What took a little longer was extricating Barney and his lorry from the remains of our five-barred front gate after he had misjudged the curve and slope of our drive whilst reversing in.

When Archie arrived later to inspect the lads' efforts, he stood looking aghast at the mangled gate and the drunken post.

'I'm terribly sorry, Mr Dudgeon. We'll repair it of course. You'd think he'd be able to back the truck after doing it for twenty-odd years.'

Poor man. He scratched his head and sighed, looking for all the world as though he might have been tempted to shove Barney's head unceremoniously in the concrete mixer which, having completed its afternoon's work, was being cleaned with two bricks clanging around monotonously in it.

Plumbing progress was slower the next day but, by lunchtime, despite two bandaged fingers, most of the pipework was in place and I was working away under the bath connecting the taps when the phone rang. Stevie appeared in his wet suit again to say that it was 'Mum'. In fifteen seconds of conversation, he had inadvertently managed to convey a garbled version of what was happening: 'Blokes, like, putting some sort of stuff on the front of the house' and 'Dad didn't get back from the hospital until late last night'. I suppose I should have thanked my lucky stars that adolescents being spectacularly unobservant meant that Stevie had ridden in and out of the front gate several times and not noticed Barney's carnage beside the drive.

'Hello, my love,' I greeted Mrs D, rubbing my head from where it had just collided with the underside of the bath as I had attempted to extricate myself hurriedly from the cramped space, aware that she was making an expensive transatlantic call.

'Duncan. Is everything all right? What's all this about hospital?'

'Oh, nothing much ... I nicked a couple of fingers last night. Perfectly okay today. How's Winifred?'

'She's fine. Wonderful to see her again. She sends her love and thinks you are marvellous to cope with everything at home *and* fit a new bathroom too.'

'Ah well, all in a day's work. Just as well I'm a teacher and have long holidays.'

'Duncan.'

'Yes, love?'

'What did Stevie mean about the front wall?'

'Ah, yes. Um ... well ... Archie's boys had a slack period ... you know, between jobs and ... er, I got them to come round and put a bit of mortar in that little crack on the front wall. It's needed doing for some time. Just above the rose, do you remember?'

'I see. How is the rose? Still looking as beautiful as when I left?'

'It is ... remarkable. I've er ... never seen it looking quite as it is at present. Considering. It's fantastic.'

'Considering? Considering what, Duncan?'

'Oh well, you know, a long spell of dry weather. Albertines don't bloom for long under the best conditions. A real survivor that rose is.'

'Well, darling, do take care while you are so busy. I'll keep in touch. Are the children being helpful?'

'They are. Their usual cheerful, considerate selves ... you know.'

'I do,' she said doubtfully. 'Just make sure they pull their weight. I'll phone again at the weekend. Winifred and Arthur are having a big barbecue tonight. Should be fun. Bye bye, my love.'

'Bye bye, sweetheart.'

No sooner had I put the phone down than it rang again.

'Mr Dudgeon?'

'Yes, speaking.'

'Ah, Tolworth RDC here. Wigglesworth, chief listing officer.'

I was sorely tempted to make a quip about having his shoe built

38

up so that he didn't lean to one side as much, but I didn't. 'How can I help you?' I asked obligingly.

'I've had it drawn to my attention that you have been effecting some repairs to your house. I wondered if I might come around and just check that the work is up to scratch. Just for the record you understand.'

Miserable, officious little bugger. 'Just for the record' my backside. I made a mental note to put my foot down hard on the accelerator next time Meddling Gascoigne's cat wandered across the village street in front of the car.

'Of course. Feel free. Any time. I'm here. Goodbye.'

While I was by the phone, I called Ralph and told him that my plumbing was nearly complete and that he could begin tiling as soon as he wished. He told me he would look in to measure up for the extra bit of bathroom wall. During the afternoon, Wigglesworth from the RDC rang the doorbell. I imagine he was surprised to be greeted by Stevie, still adorned in his wet suit, but by that time with a fistful of Marmite on toast. Wigglesworth strode across the front garden, clipboard in hand. He hummed and scratched his forehead with his pen.

'You've replaced this very recently,' he said, scraping at the drying mortar.

'Yesterday.'

'It doesn't match, of course. You realise that?'

'Really? I thought it had gone in very well. All it needs is a lick of paint.'

He stared at me. People seem to have a habit of doing that these days.

'Hmm. No, I don't think so. I'm afraid it will have to come out.'

'*Come out!?* You have got to be joking, Mr Worgleswipe.'

'Wigglesworth. I'm not joking. Can I see the rendering which came out, please? Miss . . . I was told that you had stored it.'

'Miss Gascoigne was absolutely right. I have stored it . . . in a particularly deep and smelly pond at the bottom of the garden. Feel free to help yourself.'

He emerged several minutes later with his neatly pressed corduroy trousers smeared with black, foul-smelling slime, whilst he held out a sample of plaster.

'Don't tell me,' I said 'a particularly fine example of sixteenth-century pargetting, which nobody knew about for several hundred years until it chose to fall off the wall and Miss Meddling bloody Gascoigne happened to be passing.'

'Mr Dudgeon. There's no point in adopting that attitude. The historic building stock of the country must be preserved and properly repaired. Are you insured?'

'Of course I'm insured. Always have been. What do you think I am?'

'Well then, they will pay; I am sure of it, and the work will be VAT exempt.'

'And what exactly are they supposed to be paying for?'

'A decent repair. A repair based on this mixture of materials,' he said, crumbling some of the old plaster in his palm. He took a magnifying glass from his pocket. 'Local river gravels, fine straw, horsehair and well-decomposed dung.'

'Horsehair and well-decomposed dung! Is this some form of practical joke, Worgleswipe? Have you got a camera team hidden behind the hedge? Who, pray tell, is going to come inspecting the front wall of my house with a bloody magnifying glass to check if my dung is adequately decomposed?'

'Wigglesworth. It's not a joke. There are significant fines for inappropriate treatment of Grade One Listed properties. I suggest you contact your insurers. I can recommend some *reputable* conservation experts and restorers. Good day to you, Mr Dudgeon.' Clutching his clipboard and notes, he strode off down the path in a manner faintly reminiscent of the goose-step.

'Excuse me, Mr *Wigglesworth*.'

'Yes?'

He turned to face me. I pointed at the piece of plaster he held in his hand.

'If it is as valuable as you say, I would like that piece of my

40

house back, please. You never know, there could be a significant market for that sort of thing.'

6

At nine o'clock the next morning, I telephoned the offices of *Serendipity Insurance*.

'Thank you for calling Serendipity Insurance...'

'Hello. My name is Duncan Dudgeon...'

'... all of our operators are busy at the moment. Please hold and your call will be answered in...'

I put the phone down. I have an intense dislike for phone queuing systems whereby one's call is put into an electronic stack while the businesses concerned often get a rake-off from the telephone company for the artificially extended call. In particular, I have also developed a dread of being played an appalling electronic version of 'The Flight of the Bumble Bee' whenever I telephone the railway enquiry number. It just doesn't feel right. They should be offering Brahms' 'Lullaby' ... or 'Autumn Leaves', if, that is, they wish to play customers anything at all.

I picked up the paper and made a cup of coffee, intent on enjoying a few moments of peace and quiet. Was it my imagination or was the silly season causing the media to sink into new and untold depths of summer mediocrity and irrelevance? There was nothing of consequence reported at all. The most interesting article concerned a piece of research carried out by supposedly reputable psychologists who had discovered that if you are called Tracy, Sharon, Wayne or Shane, you are unlikely to have been so successful in life as if your doting parents had called you Octavia, Cordelia, Charles or Gerald. Well, blow me down. I would never have guessed that. It couldn't possibly have anything to do with the fact that if you are named Ophelia, your father might well have a seat on the board of Sotheby's or Fortnum and Mason, and conversely, if you are called Gavin, your father might have spent his life working his socks off in the local paint factory? The most extraordinary aspect of it was that somebody – and they ought to be given a set of sheep shears and sent out to the Falkland Islands for a year – somebody agreed to finance this work. Here we are surrounded by a desperate need for serious and formative research into mental illness, and some august body directs thousands into a basin full of old eyewash like that!

I flung the newspaper down in disgust, swallowed my remaining coffee and dialled the insurers again. That time I got through. Or nearly.

'This is *the Serendipity Insurance Group*. If you would like to speak to someone about an insurance quotation, press One. If you would like to renew your car insurance, press Two. If you would like to report a crime against your person or property, press Three. If you would like to speak to the Motor Claims Department, press Four. If you would like to discuss your House Insurance Policy, press Five. If you would like to make an enquiry about loans or endowment policies, press Six. If you would like to apply for life insurance, press Seven. If you do not know what you want or have forgotten because of this crass phone system . . .'

Quick! Press Three! No! Four! Which was it? Help! Five!

'Hello. This is *Serendipity Insurance Claims Department*. Thank you for calling. Sharon speaking. How may I help you?'

Sharon? I felt myself blush.

'Yes. Hello, Sharon. My name is Dudgeon. I have a buildings policy with you. Its number is HCD101/9337889/9953862518/017625A.'

'Sorry. I missed that. Could you repeat it, please, Mr Dungeon? It's just the last five numbers that count.'

'You mean 17625?'

'Yes. Got you on the screen now. Here we are. For security

43

reasons, could you please tell me your wife's mother's distinguishing feature?'

'My wife's mother's what? I have absolutely no idea.'

'Oh dear, Mr Dungeon. We aim to please at Serendipity; perhaps you could tell me your postcode.'

I told her my code and pointed out that I did not call to play Twenty Questions. I also asked Sharon who else was likely to phone pretending to be me in order to get the front of my house fraudulently rebuilt.

'Could you repeat that please, Mr Dungeon?' the squeaky voice echoed on the other end of the line.

'No. Not now. Listen Sharon, my name is Dudgeon. D-U-D-G-E-O-N. I have to make a claim for my sixteenth-century front wall to be rebuilt by conservation experts who are familiar with things like horse hair and well-decomposed manure.'

'When was your house built?'

'It's a sixteenth-century cottage.'

'Yes, Mr Dudgeon, but when was it built? I need to complete the details.'

'I don't know, Sharon. Sometime between fourteen ninety-nine and sixteen hundred I expect.'

'I'm sorry. The computer can't accept that. Is it covered by a Building Guarantee, Mr Dudgeon?'

'What sort of guarantee?'

'Did the builders give you a guarantee covering you for faulty workmanship or failed materials?'

'Sharon, can I try to explain something to you? I live in a house that was built over four hundred years ago. Four hundred years ago they didn't even know what a guarantee was. The front wall collapsed and I had it repaired. The repair is not good enough so I must pull it all down and start again. It must be repaired by specialists.'

'You're going to pull your wall down so it can be repaired? Mr Dudgeon, I don't think even Serendipity can cover you if you do things like that to your house.'

'No, Sharon; I've been told to. By the conservation officer. It doesn't come up to standard. Listen, let's forget it has been rebuilt, all right? My front wall has just fallen down. It needs repairing by a special team of conservators, ones who work with horse manure, lime and such like.'

'Right. I understand, Mr Dudgeon. Now, let's see. What was the date of the building?'

That afternoon, Ralph appeared, measured up and went off whistling chirpily in his van to buy some plasterboard and timber. He didn't reappear that day and actually didn't do so until twenty-past nine the following morning when he drove into the drive. He spent some time twiddling something under the bonnet, and then went up and down stairs carrying bags of tools and materials until about ten-thirty when he called out that he was off to have a coffee break. He then jumped into his van again and roared off amidst a battery of shattering backfires. At the same moment, the *loss adjuster* from good old Serendipity arrived.

'Good morning. Mr Dungeon?'

'Dudgeon. Yes. How do you do?'

'I'm Merrick Linton-Forthworthy.'

We shook hands. He was a chubby chap who looked as though he might have enjoyed a good few lunches on expenses. He looked at his notes, and mopped his rosy face with his handkerchief. He explained that he was engaged by Serendipity to provide an insurance estimate and that he would report back to them as soon as possible.

'What I don't understand,' he continued, 'is how this horse got into your conservatory in the first place.'

'I beg your pardon?'

'Your conservatory wall has been damaged by horse manure?' he ventured, then he showed me the computer printout, courtesy of our Sharon. I read it.

'Mr Dudgeon appears to have a problem with well-decomposed horse manure in his conservatory front wall. He has forgotten to pull it down. The builders didn't leave him with any guarantees because they didn't know what they were. Adjuster required'

'Ah, no. Not quite right. I don't even have a conservatory, let alone a horse'

I explained to him about the front wall, the repair which had proved unsatisfactory to the conservation authorities, and the requirement to re-render it using authentic materials such as river gravels, horsehair, lime and dung.'

'Ah! Ha ha. Sharon strikes again, eh, Mr Dungeon?' he chuckled to himself.

'Dudgeon.'

'Pardon?'

'I said *Dudgeon*. Not Dungeon. My name is Dudgeon.'

'I beg your pardon.' He scribbled on his pad. 'No horse, no conservatory...' he did more scribbling and began to make his own notes. 'Right. I can see the problem. I am sure Serendipity will contribute. Is your property insured for a sum commensurate with its listed status?'

'It's insured for its market value, or a little more.'

'Good God, man. This should be covered for its likely rebuild costs.' He scratched the inside of his ear with his corporate image pen. 'About two and a half million, I should think,' he said, glancing knowledgeably around the cottage.

'*Two and a half million!*' I spluttered. 'But it doesn't need rebuilding.'

'Ah, but if it did, imagine the cost after, say, a fire.'

'But if it did burn down it would be impossible to replace it anyway. It's a sixteenth-century cottage. Where are you going to get one of those from?'

'No, no. That's not the point. Take this wall. It may cost say, twenty times as much as usual to repair it. What did this cost you?' he asked, jabbing at Barney and Seth's handiwork in a less than appreciative manner. 'A hundred and fifty quid?'

I nodded, reluctant to tell him it had cost me thirty-five quid and a twelve-pack of lagers.

'Repaired by conservationists, it will probably set you back about ... a grand.'

I staggered back and sat on an old tree stump in the front garden, feeling the colour draining from my face. Why the hell hadn't I just left the ivy flapping in everyone's faces? I began to wonder about getting a grant from the Society For Socio-Psychological Research; they might be interested to investigate the psychotic behaviour of sixteenth-century houseowners and what happens to people called *Merrick* when they make loss adjusting visits.

'You can see the problem. If any bit of your house needs repairing at that sort of cost, well, *big* bills. Suppose all the rendering fell off the whole house? At these costs ...' he shook his head. 'Who knows? A hundred grand just for that.'

'But all the rendering has *not* fallen off. It's not going to. It's just a little bit. There's nothing wrong with the rest of it.'

He smiled. A long, patronising smile. I thought about him falling head first into that filthy old pond at the ...

'Mr Dudgeon. We calculate claims awards on the basis that a certain proportion of your insured sum is for rendering ... say, a twentieth, and that this little bit of wall here is say, about a hundredth of all your rendering.' He tapped on his calculator. 'What's your total sum insured?' he asked. More tapping of numbers. 'We'll measure up properly in a minute but it will be about 0.00156 of your sum insured. About a hundred and twenty quid, I should think.' He snapped his calculator shut.

'*A hundred and twenty quid?* But you said it would cost about a thousand!'

'Yes, at a guess. It's the problem with under-insurance. Let's look on the bright side; we'll have a measure up.'

Ferrick, or whatever his name was, (a name which had no doubt helped him to get on in life, which is why he was in my garden instead of Sharon) took a long tape measure and asked me if I would be kind enough to escort him and hold the end. I felt inclined to tell him what my hourly rate for holding tape measures

47

for insurance nerds was. We measured all the way round the cottage and then he gazed up at the house and estimated the height.

'I'd say that was about nineteen hundred square feet and your patch is about seventy square feet.' He chuckled and tapped away and then exhaled noisily between his teeth. 'About three hundredths of the total. Hmm. Not so good.' He looked at me, and then his gaze fell on the privy.

'Ah. That yours as well?'

I turned to look. 'It's the barn and the privy...'

'Oh dear, oh dear. We'll have to measure those as well. It's all rendering, you see, Mr Dudgeon. Suppose it all fell down.'

'But it hasn't ... it's perfectly all right, it's ...'

'As I explained, we've got to take those *totals* into account; you know, *if it did* all fall down.'

For the first time, it dawned on me why these people were called *loss adjusters*. That's exactly what they did. Adjusted *the company's losses*. Loss *minimisers* would be more like it. It was institutionalised daylight robbery! We trudged around the barn, the privy, the garage, the workshop and the old apple store. Ferrick spent several minutes tapping away. I wondered whether to make him a cup of coffee, whether to butter him up and make him feel at home, when he whistled loudly and tapped the pen on his teeth.

'About seventy-five quid. Sorry. Lots of rendered walls here.'

'But that's preposterous. It's legalised robbery! I have paid my premiums for about twenty-five years, never made a claim before, even when the privy exploded all over Mrs Dudgeon, and you've got the cheek to come in here and ...'

'Big garden this,' he said thoughtfully, gazing around. 'How much land?'

I shrugged my shoulders. 'I don't know, about an acre, why?'

He tapped some more figures.

'Your house and outbuildings are the subject of a substantial proportion of the sum insured. But a big plot like this is also insured for quite a part of it.'

'My *garden is insured*?' I asked incredulously.

'Oh yes, the land is, definitely.'

'For *what*?' I could feel my temperature rising now. 'What can you possibly be insuring my garden against ... wait, wait; don't tell me ... earthquakes. It might be swallowed up in a seismic blast, sucked down into the fiery bowels of the earth, only to be spewed out and scattered into ...'

'We don't cover you for that,' he said, shaking his head.

'Forest fires, even though the nearest forest is twenty-five miles away?'

'Maybe.'

'Flooding, even though we happen to be on the side of a hill?'

'Yes.'

'Well, that's very reassuring. Tell me, Mr Finton-Munchworthy ... how much now, you know, taking into account the buildings, the garden, the trees, Mrs Dudgeon's gnomes – you haven't mentioned the air above the property, somebody could steal that of course – how much, when you have done your swindling, festering worst?'

'Linton-Forthworthy.'

He tapped some more figures into his calculator. 'Thirty-five pounds, twenty-seven pence.'

7

Angelica reminded me that I had long promised her another driving lesson since she had acquired her provisional licence and taken me for her first hair-raising drive. She had managed quite well, everything considered. Admittedly, never before had I needed to grab the handbrake when teaching Greg, who, on reaching the 'STOP' sign, usually paused before driving out into the traffic at the end of our sleepy country lane. Angelica had a slightly more cavalier attitude to the cars which raced across the marshes on the mile straight. At the blind junction onto the main road she had slowed beautifully, and then, before I could prevent it, had accelerated, spluttering and hopping her way straight out into the path of the oncoming traffic. The parking brake had brought us to a stalled halt in the middle of the central reservation, where I took a tissue from Mrs D's box on the dashboard and mopped my brow. Recalling how the juggernaut, loaded down with thousands of bricks, its air brakes squealing, had passed behind us leaving pretty swirling patterns of rubber on our rear bumper as its mudguards side-swiped the back of the Lada, did not fill me with enthusiasm for our next outing. In my dreams, the driver's anguished face, contorted with a thousand expletives, still plagues my sleep.

My elder daughter has always had difficulties with her coordination, a source of considerable frustration to her. At an early age, most children, when confronted with those plastic spheres with variously shaped holes and corresponding pieces which have to be matched and then pressed home, can, after a little practice, differentiate shapes. Not Angelica. At two years-old, Greg was sitting in the middle of the floor with my ratchet screwdriver and the Black and Decker drill, managing to put screws into a piece of wood (not that you would know it now). At about the same age, Angelica was still sitting, usually in a furious rage, trying to smash the round shape through the square hole, totally oblivious to the idea that the round shape passed effortlessly through the round aperture and the square piece through the square one. After a few minutes of this, she would toddle over to one of us, present us with the infuriating toy and watch spellbound as we demonstrated once again that the shapes slipped easily into the sphere. Two minutes later she would be found, once again red-faced and angry, as she tried to force the cross through the triangle.

She did improve a little as the years passed but we felt for her when she went for interviews to train as a dentist at university. The enthusiastic candidates had been told to sit down at a bench where they were each given a cube of dental wax and told to use the tools provided to fashion a symmetrical pyramid. The aptitude test did not play to her strengths. Something about Angelica's spatial awareness prevented her from being able to visualise the required shape, and, as she chipped and scraped away at the wax, she told us afterwards that she could see her chosen career path slipping from her grasp. At the end of the twenty minutes allowed, the technician overseeing the exercise called time, and gathered up the collection of superbly shaped offerings, labelled them and placed them in a tray. When he reached Angelica's work bay he was met by a tear-stained face, thousands of shards of wax and no pyramid. Never mind. She applied to study medicine and was immediately accepted. No doubt she will one day make a very fine neurosurgeon.

We gathered up the accoutrements of a second driving lesson: L-plates; obligatory bottle of mineral water ('I get so thirsty Dad'); my pipe and several ounces of tobacco; and, having checked my certificate of insurance once more, we got into the car.

'Okay, love. Let's go through what we learnt last time. Pedals. Which is which?'

'Um. Okay, okay. Don't rush me. Wait. Yeah, right. The, like, one on the left,' she said, peering down and pressing the accelerator with her right foot, 'is the go-faster one. Yeah? Hang on. Hang on. I mean right,' she said, watching my face.

'Good girl. And the one in the middle?'

'Crutch.'

'Not quite.'

'Er ... the brake-thing.'

'Good. And the other one?'

'Crutch!'

'Clutch.'

'Yeah, that's what I said.'

'Okay. Let's start up. Stop! What do we do first?'

'Wiggle the, like, stick thing.'

We eventually got onto a normally quiet country road and I suggested that we try changing into fourth gear.

'Okay. Okay. Right. Look in the mirror. Check there is no one behind ... there's a car with a caravan, Dad ... in fact there are millions of people behind us.'

'It doesn't matter, darling. You can change gear without looking behind ... smoothly now ...'

There was a great cacophony of crashing and grinding metal, and the car decelerated rapidly as she went into second gear, and a happy band of holidaymakers and their caravan nearly parked in our boot. Thank heavens we have a Lada. I think their gearboxes must actually be made for armoured patrol cars. They seem to be able to stand up to a great deal of abuse.

'That was second gear, love; try fourth.'

'Ohhh! I'll never be able to do this!' she cried, letting go of the steering wheel and tugging at her hair with both hands.

'Don't let go!' I shouted, trying to grab the wheel to return the car to the carriageway as it mounted what was, fortunately, a soft grass verge. 'You must keep your hands on the steering wheel ...

52

unless you are changing gear. One hand *always* stays on the wheel. Okay? Always.'

'All right, Dad. Chill. Don't shout at me. I can't do it if you shout at me.'

'I'm not shouting at you. I'm being very ... level. Let's take the next left turn.'

Anything to get away from this main road. I pointed to my left, just to be sure.

'Mirror. Indicate. Slow down smoothly ... SLOW DOWN, ANGELICA!'

Without any change of speed at all we careered around a right-angled corner, narrowly missing Archie Brownlea's truck which was about to pull out of the side road.

'Darling. That was too fast! You have to match your speed to the road conditions. Cars aren't made to go round junctions at thirty miles an hour.' I reached for my third tissue and wiped my brow. 'Okay. Now, there's a humpback bridge approaching. It's narrow and you need to be sure there's nothing coming the other way. Slow down. Good. Good ... ah, now you've stalled it. No, no. Don't worry about the car behind. He can wait. Parking brake. Neutral. Hang on. I'll just fold the wing mirror back a bit. It's stuck on this tree ... okay, let the clutch in gently, a little more accelerator ... well done. Second now!' I hollered above four-and-a-half thousand revs of screaming engine.

We eventually pulled up in the drive of *Cromwell's Retreat*. It was just as well that Barney had already widened our gateway for us, because otherwise I am certain I would have had a nine-inch oak gatepost resting in my lap by the time we lurched to a halt in front of the garage.

'Well done, love. That felt a bit better, didn't it?'

'No, it was crap.'

'It wasn't ... that bad.'

'I could do it all right if you didn't get so stressed out, Dad.'

'Stressed out? I'm not stressed, darling. I never get stressed.'

'You are. You make me forget how to do it. You start shouting when I do anything wrong. Midge says her driving instructor is cool. *He* doesn't get cross with her all the time.'

'Angelica, all I can say is that you had better save up your pennies from *Neil*, and book some lessons. I'm not sure you realise how often we have brushed with almost certain death in two driving lessons. Never has my life flashed before me as many times in thirty minutes. Please don't talk to me about getting stressed out any more. You must pay attention if you want to drive. I don't think I can cope. Mum might be able to. She is trained in torture resistance techniques. I am not. I'm just a teacher. I think you should have a lesson or two with "ABC" ... they have dual controls. It's safer. They can slow you down sometimes ... on corners ... and at stop signs and traffic lights.'

Angelica did book some lessons, not with *ABC* but with *U-Pass Quick*; she certainly does that. When the oikish-looking chap called at the door, I noticed that he had no less than six earrings and a nose stud. Good company for Angelica. They can rattle their way round the lanes of Suffolk together. I introduced myself.

'How yer doin' Mr Dudgeon? Mickey Rafferty,' he ventured in reply.

When Angelica came downstairs she was wearing one of the shortest and most unsuitable driving skirts I have ever seen, and she hadn't any money.

'Daddy, darling.'

'Yes, Angelica? How much do you need?'

'What! You're so rude to me. That's a terrible thing to say.'

'It is. Forgive me. How much do you need?'

'Thirty-five pounds, please. It's a two-hour long introductory bargain lesson.'

I wondered if Mr Earpiece, outside on the doorstep, knew what he was letting himself in for. Two hours! I'd rather be shut in the broom cupboard with Mrs D's obnoxious sister, Dorothy, while she smoked twenty Marlborough and gave me a non-stop summary of her most recently read Mills & Boon books.

Needless to say, Angelica breezed in two hours later with her instructor man, both looking as cool as cucumbers. Sycophantic little ...

'Ah, Mr Dudgeon. A good lesson. Well impressed I was. Your daughter drove exceptionally confidently. One of the most promising students I have had the pleasure of taking out. You have obviously given her a good grounding in the basics. I think she should pass fairly quickly.'

'How quickly?'

'Hmm ... about twenty lessons. I'll book her test today.'

'Twenty lessons! That's about ... four hundred pounds!'

'Oh, we can better that. We've got a special offer on this month. Book and pay for twenty and get three free. Yeah? Good, eh?'

'No. That's not good. You just said she needed twenty. Why pay for twenty-three?'

'But they're free.'

'They're not free if you don't need them in the first place. Where's the saving in that?'

'Ohmagod, Dad! Please don't embarrass me in front of Mickey.'

'I'm not embarrassing you. Business is business ... or have you got four hundred quid to spare?'

'No, but ...'

'Three hundred and fifty quid for twenty lessons, *Mickey*. Take it or leave it.'

Rafferty did some revolting piece of finger work with his nose-stud, and then offered me his hand.

'Okay, Duncan. It's a deal.'

Duncan? Duncan? I looked at him in the most deprecating manner which I hope conveyed that I was old enough to have taught his mother. I don't know what these youngsters are coming to. When did trade start to call their customers *Duncan*?

'To whom shall I make the cheque payable?'

'*U-Pass Quick*, please,' he said, and did a little jig as though we might have been his first ever customers.

'Have you been doing this long?' I asked.

'Oh yeah, like, ages.'

I gave him one of my penetrating stares. The dog glanced at me and immediately slunk into his basket.

'How long?'

'I er . . . started on Monday, but I've got a lot of . . .'

'Monday? This Monday? But it's only Wednesday today.'

I stared at him again. 'Twenty lessons young man and that's your lot, and you, young lady, can start learning how to mix three hundred and fifty pounds worth of sixteenth-century well-decomposed dung and horsehair rendering. Go and put your jeans on.'

8

I tiptoed across the landing, the sounds of my stockinged feet drowned by the incessant burble from Radio Two and Ralph's less than tuneful accompaniments.

'My, my, my Deelilaaaah, la la la la la ...'

Hoping to see some progress, I peered stealthily around the bathroom door, desperately wishing that Ralph would not see me and begin one of his interminable time-wasting conversations. I have never known a tradesman pass so much time doing absolutely nothing at all. It must be exhausting *trying* to be *that* slow. The previous morning, he had greeted me, risen from the floor, and sat on the edge of the bath in order to continue a discussion which I can only assume had been going on somewhere inside his head, and which I had no chance of joining in any meaningful manner.

'I think it's shameful, but as my Jocelyn says to me yesterday, Mr Dudgeon, "What else do you do?" I mean we ain't got no choice really, have we? We pay up or we lose it ...'

'Absolutely, Ralph ... Buggers all of them. Er ... how's the false wall going?' To date, there was no sign of anything remotely resembling a wall.

'I'm just going into town. I could have sworn I had some plasterboard nails in my bag, but I can't see 'em. It won't take me a jiff, then we'll have it up in no time.'

Up until that moment, Ralph had spent part of one day moving in, the next day, after getting his van going, he had laid out his dust-sheets, gone off for coffee, returned, gone off to get some filler, scraped said filler into a few cracks for about ten minutes before going off again to 'his Jocelyn' for a 'spot of tucker'. He then returned at about two and spent an inordinate amount of time practising laying tiles out on the floor. At about four o'clock he cleared them all up, having written his tile sequence hieroglyphics on the bathroom wall, and gone home ('to fetch Jocie from her mum's, yer see'). The next day he arrived just before Mickey Rafferty did, and began to saw some lengths of batten for the wall. By lunchtime he had fixed the board which constituted the new shower wall and, in doing so, had covered the notes he had pencilled on the wall the day before. He then spent most of another afternoon again laying out tiles on the floor and recreating a new set of measurements only nominally faster than he had done it the first time. It was exasperating to watch his comings and goings; in particular his need to go home for coffee breaks.

After forty-eight hours of this, I tentatively enquired as to whether or not he had ever considered using a Thermos flask in order to avoid journeying to and fro. I also felt like asking him point blank if he had considered the possibility of making progress on the wall before Christmas ... but I didn't.

'It's my Jocelyn's nerves, Mr Dudgeon. Her nerves. I goes 'ome to steady 'er a bit.'

And that was that. Tea and coffee breaks remained major features of his day, and I was left doing my utmost to prevent my blood pressure going through the roof. I was just glad that we had agreed a fixed price for the job. The next morning, tiling commenced in earnest and, to give Ralph his due, once he started progress was rapid. In fact, it was a little too rapid. Mrs D had selected a few bold chrysanthemum tiles to be dotted in among the 'Victorian' royal blue ones, and we had had to wait a very long time for our order of two boxes of imported tiles. I visited Ralph and stood listening to one of his little chats which, as far as I could determine, was about their poodle's visit to the vet (if it wasn't, Jocelyn was having some very unusual treatment) and I noticed immediately that something was very wrong. We seemed to have a bad case of the wilts on our hands. The flower heads were most definitely all facing downwards in a very sulky fashion.

'Ralph,' I interrupted him, as he scraped adhesive across another chrysanthemum. 'Have you noticed how the flower tiles don't look quite as perky as they might do?'

'Well now, Mr Dudgeon, it's funny as you should mention that. I was thinking to meself that they weren't quite as chirpy as they had seemed before, but I thought it was because they had all been spread out all over the floor.'

'I think, Ralph,' I said, perhaps a touch too frostily, 'it's because they are upside down.'

Ralph stared at the tiles, slowly turned the one in his hand and stared at me. Then he stared at the tiles, slowly turned the one in his hand, and stared at me again. 'I think you might be right,' was all he said, and he tried, without success, to prise one of the offending tiles away from the cement which had dried exceptionally quickly in the warmth of the summer morning.

'Brenda Fortesque? It's Duncan Dudgeon here. I don't know if you remember me? Yes, that's right; Angelica's father ... yes. Dear, dear. Yes, she used to get into quite a paddy with the horse, didn't she? The reason I'm phoning you, Mrs Fortesque, is that I need some horsehair and I thought you might be the person ... Yes, I thought you might have some at the riding school ... It is, is it? How expensive? Goodness. That's worth more than mine is. I'm not sure how much a pound of horsehair is. I can't quite visualise it. Perhaps I could come and see? Yes, I will. I take it a few bags of well-rotted manure won't be beyond you? No, quite. Shit everywhere ... coming out of your ears ... I see. Well, Angelica and I will pop over, if we may. No, no. She's far more placid than she used to be, but I will keep her away from Cherry Blossom. No, I'm sure you don't want her upset. I'm sure they *do* have long memories, yes. Right. Until this afternoon then. Goodbye. Thank you.'

Angelica and I spent the afternoon with the old trailer hitched on the back of the Lada. To her eternal delight we went to the estuary with sacks and a shovel, and gathered bags of course sand and fine gravel. Then with the trailer groaning and creaking under its load, we went to Mrs Fortesque's stables.

'I'm staying in the car, Dad. I don't want that old cow to see me. She gives me the creeps,' Angelica said, as we pulled up in the yard where numerous plaited little girls were leading ponies back to their stalls.

'Ah, Mr Dudgeon!' a hearty voice hailed us. Angelica slid so far down into her seat that she was almost under the glove compartment.

'Hello, Mrs Fortesque. How nice to see you again,' I called, as I slipped out of the car and made my way towards the larger-than-life figure who was once described by her ex-husband as, 'being about eleven hands and a bit of handful, with a backside the size of Suffolk'. Bernie Fortesque had once taught with me, and would regale the staff with over-intimate lunchtime accounts of married life with *Brenda*. To my surprise, Mrs F embraced me and kissed me on both cheeks with a loud smacking, sucking sort of noise; an experience which was not improved by the powerful aroma of horses which followed her wherever she went.

'Eet's such ah long time since I saw you, Mr Dudgeon. Duncan isn't it? How are you? And Mrs Dudgeon?'

I explained that Mrs Dudgeon was well, but away in the USA for a few weeks. I thought I detected a certain gleam in her eye as she crossed the yard. It was confirmed when she gave me a hearty nudge, and said, 'Haw, haw. While the cat's away and all that?' and squealed with laughter as she led me to the tack room and began to rummage about in her cupboards.

'I suppose you don't fancy coming to the barbecue tomorrow night, in aid of the steeple repairs at St Crispin's?' she said, as she lifted out numerous horse clippers and various instruments of equine torture. Then she suddenly withdrew her hand and, in some considerable anguish, said 'Eow, eow!' and waved her finger frantically in the air. 'Ay've got a splinter in my finger, Duncan.

60

Can you see it? The bally thing's gorn right down behind my nail. Ah! Ouch! Such pain. Could you get the first-aid box down from the wall? There's a pair of tweezers in there. Oh! Do hurry, Duncan!'

Brenda sat on her desk and I leaned over her, taking her hand in mine and peering at it.

'I'm terribly squeamish, Duncan. Don't mind horse blood, but mine, ugh! Just do the bally job, but don't let me see.'

I twisted around so she couldn't watch, whereupon in one swift movement she pulled me from my perch on the edge of the desk, by my trouser belt, and sat me on her lap.

'There! That's far more comfortable. Ha ha! There have to be some perks for the casualty.'

I'm not sure how comfortable Brenda Fortesque was. Bernie had been right; she was a well-upholstered thing. I, however, was feeling distinctly uncomfortable, and squirmed with embarrassment at the thought of anyone finding us. Goodness knows what Miriam Whippleford thought when she came across the yard towards the tack room for a bottle of Neatsfoot oil.

'Brenda! Coo-eee Brendaaah!' her voice could be heard trilling outside.

Brenda meanwhile, without wishing to be uncharitable to the unfortunate woman, was making something of a fuss about her splinter extraction.

'Ah, Duncan. Oh, Duncan. You've no idea what it feels like. Ah! Oh! Yes! I can feel it coming. Yesss! Ah, Duncan. Oh, Duncan. The relief . . . oh my goodness!'

'Eh hem.'

There was a polite cough, and Mrs Whippleford's head appeared around the door as I held the splinter up in the tweezers.

'Ah Brenda. I . . . oh, sorry,' she flushed. 'I do hope I'm not interrupting anything . . . Oh, Mr Dudgeon, I . . .'

I slipped off Brenda's rather ample lap, told her to wash her finger with antiseptic, and smiled innocently at Mrs Whippleford. She happened to be the mother of one of my fourth form boys.

'Well, Mr Dudgeon. Fancy. I say. How are you? I didn't know you rode.'

'I don't. Not at all. Can't stand horses. Just wanted some hair for patching my front wall.'

'I see . . . Yes. Of course. Your front wall. Hair. Right.'

She looked at me as though I might have taken leave of my senses. 'Anyway, I'll be off now,' she murmured. 'I just wanted some oil for my harness. Bye for now ... um, have fun.' She winked at Brenda Fortesque as she turned and disappeared into the yard.

'Thank you, Duncan. What would I have done without you?' She flung her arms around my neck and gave me another of her kisses, except that this time it was slightly more lingering and, in the confined space of the tack room, the smell was almost overpowering. 'Now, where were we, Duncan?' she said, dreamily, if such a term could possibly be applied to Brenda Fortescue.

'Horsehair is exactly where we were. Perhaps you could see if you have any? I have someone waiting in the car, and I shouldn't be too long. If you could show me where the rotted dung is stored, I will pick up a few bags.'

'Took you long enough,' said Angelica, as I returned to the car bearing a sack of hair which Fido cringed away from when I flung it into the back of the Lada.

'Brenda got a splinter in her finger and so I had to do my first aid bit and ...'

'I see,' she said, moving away from me as she lowered the window. 'You smell of horse ... or Brenda.'

When we returned, Ralph had managed to prise away the chrysanthemum tiles, not to mention a considerable amount of the wall behind the hand basin. A sizeable pile of broken flower tiles lay scattered on the floor. Wearily, I recalled the extreme difficulty we had encountered with the ceramic supplier, who purchased directly from a little known peasants' workshop in a remote part of

Portugal. I thought about the seemingly interminable delivery period. Perhaps we should have left them to wilt, upside down.

9

Taking full advantage of the bright summer morning, first thing the next day I went out into our garage and took out the ladders, hammers and chisels which I needed to remove Seth and Barney's patch of rendering.

'Thirty-five pounds twenty-seven pence,' I muttered, as I recalled the pathetic offer from the man at *Serendipity*. How spectacularly inappropriate a name that was. Where, pray tell, was the *fortunate discovery* there? The only fortunate thing about it was that the insurance company had stumbled upon a good-sized proportion of the population who were damned fool enough to part with several hundred pounds every year on house and buildings insurance cover only to discover that they had insured their *gardens*. I made a mental note to while away an evening studying the small print of my *Serendipity* policy. Frankly, my thoughts about it all had been made far worse when I learned that the likes of Linton-Forthworthy generated their incomes by earning a percentage of what the insurance company saved! The more he swindled the client, the richer he became. Anyone who knows me will tell you that I am not the vindictive sort – far from it; I think I am basically a generous-hearted chap ... usually. As I arranged the ladders however, I confess it did occur to me that the thought of one of those sacks of ripe horse manure being tipped through the sunroof of Munchworthy's three month-old BMW did have a certain sense of poetic justice about it. Perhaps he would like to claim on *his* insurance. Bastard!

I placed the ladders against the wall and tied various boards together, wishing as I did so that I had Archie's scaffold tower. Looking at my watch, I decided that eight-thirty was plenty late enough for the younger inhabitants of *Cromwell's Retreat* to sleep in, and commenced vigorous hammering. Before long, I had a good proportion of the offending material removed, although it seemed to be securely bonded to the ancient clay lump wall by the gluey substance that the Brownlea boys had applied. I developed a remarkably efficient sequence of operation: chisel the outline of a square, insert the jemmy beneath it, give a good heave and prise the mortar away. Nothing to it! Another chunk fell into the rosebed below. I wiped my brow. Only a few more pieces to go.

Those of you who are not foolish enough to be deceived by the roses-round-the-door image of old country properties will know that a certain law comes into play whenever one so much as picks up a screwdriver to adjust a curtain rail. The precept decrees that the smallest job will inevitably mushroom, until what began as a five-minute task with one of those super little pocket-sized multi-headed screwdrivers from Woolies will, by steady degrees, escalate into a major civil engineering project replete with a tower crane, a workforce of twenty-seven (living on site in caravans), mobile toilets and a bulldozer. For the duration of the work, it goes without saying that most of the services, which one relies upon for comfortable everyday life will, of course, be out of action.

There was a ferocious *bang*! and seconds afterwards, as the remaining and somewhat stubborn piece of rendering came away, I caught a whiff of that smell one associates with sparks and hot electrical components. In a more poetic moment, I might even be tempted to describe it as a *blue smell*. A muffled voice could be heard muttering, 'Dad! What the hell are you *doing*?'

I stood on the ladder and peered around the garden to see which of my sons had risen so early, but saw no one. Not a soul was in sight. A trickle of sixteenth-century clay lump wall skittered down the rungs of the ladder. I pulled at the remaining piece, which came free very readily and then twirled before me... apparently attached to an electricity cable. I stared at it.

'Dad!' (louder and clearer now) 'What are you *doing*?'

I looked at the hole in the wall and, to my surprise, found myself gazing into Greg's face which was, somewhat surrealistically, still in its bed, on its pillow.

'Dad. It's freezing! Why don't you come in the door as most reasonable people do?'

Whatever other deficiencies I may have, I am not known to panic in a crisis and, having climbed down the ladder, I entered the house, this time by the back door, and exchanged early morning pleasantries with Stevie who was slumped in front of a particularly inanimate television screen.

'Telly's gone off,' he muttered, through cereal and milk.

Upstairs in Greg's bedroom, the 'blue smell' was more apparent, but what was more remarkable still was the stunning view across the fields through a hole in the wall near the head of his bed. His bed cover, a pretty, cottagey affair run up by Mrs D on her Singer sewing machine, was littered with plaster debris from the bedroom wall. It reminded me of those photos taken during the Second World War depicting cheerful sooty faces peering from the rubble during the morning after an air raid. They are usually captioned: 'Londoners in the Blitz'. Greg coughed and stretched.

'Any chance of a cup of tea, Dad?'

By the time I had traced the blown circuit and replaced the wire which had been torn from its fixing, all the youngsters were up and about, hours earlier than usual of course, and in turn were demanding to know why the toaster, the kettle, the television, the mobile phone chargers, the hairdryer, the cordless phone, the cooker, the shower, the computer (and therefore e-mail) and the seventeen stereos were not working. Ralph appeared and went to the bathroom carrying his tool bag. He came down a few moments later to report that his electric drill wasn't working.

'I know it isn't, Ralph,' I hissed from the depths of the fuse cupboard. 'I'm just making a few adjustments to the house's wiring.'

When Parcel Force arrived and the delivery man explained that he didn't think the door bell was ringing, the poor man got a more hostile reception than he really deserved when I poked my head out of the hole in Greg's bedroom wall and shouted that I was well aware that it wasn't. He took no offence until I added that the next person to point out that the power was off was likely to get the two prongs of my circuit tester shoved up their nearest available orifice. I understand we are now blacklisted by Parcel Force until I make an abject written apology.

When the electricity came on again, the house was filled with a cacophony of strangled noises as every appliance the children had tried during the power failure bleeped or came on at full volume. At times such as that, it strikes me afresh that we are ecologically shameless about our total reliance upon electricity and, indirectly, upon fossil fuels. Nearly every item we use requires power. Even the huge dogflap, bought for me last Christmas by a cooperative of children, needs a low voltage supply to recognise the coded chip which Fido wears in his collar. Quite why *I* was given a dogflap for Christmas, I'm not sure.

I've always respected an ex-colleague of mine who, on deciding that his children were watching far too much television, bought a twelve-volt caravan set and wired it to a dynamo, which he then fitted to the family exercise bike. Not only did the whole contraption have a satisfyingly 'green' aspect to it, but it had a dramatic and healthy effect upon the children's viewing hours, which plummeted as they drew lots to pedal before they could watch *Blue Peter*. I take my hat off to him. Where did *I* go wrong?

Dreading the possibility of Meddling Gascoigne passing by and observing the new opening in the wall, which would doubtless have filled her with righteous indignation prompting her to call the conservation officer again, I found some old bricks and shoved them in the hole. As soon as I could, I mixed up some mortar and completed the repair. I have to say that the environmental quality of the air in Greg's room had been greatly enhanced by the added ventilation, and I very much regretted having to seal up the hole.

When Angelica was suitably clad, we left the boys to clear away lunch and went out to prepare our sixteenth-century rendering mixture. I gave the child a pair of scissors, and a pound of horsehair, and asked her to snip it into short pieces.

'It's *disgusting!*' she said, tipping it out at arm's length and viewing it with great disdain. I have to say it looked a good deal more wholesome than her own hair which, some weeks previously, she had persuaded a friend to plait into thousands of tiny ringlets, *Rastafarian-style*. The whole job was then covered with a malodorous concoction that caused hundreds of excited flies to pursue her all day long. I said so.

'I'm not working for you. You're so rude to me. It's, like, child abuse; that's what it is.'

I pointed out that she was eighteen, that Child-Line would no longer have the remotest interest in how her father chose to describe her haircare and that it would only take one phone call to Mickey Rafferty to undo the driving lesson deal. As a result, she snipped horsehair in an exaggerated, sulky silence while I shovelled grit and lime. Together we then tipped bags of well-rotted horse dung into a pile and I found myself unable to resist the temptation to cause further assault to Angelica's senses.

'I just need to consult the chapter in the library book I discovered. It's great; all about mixing this stuff.' I returned bearing the tome which I pretended to study as I strolled around the front garden. 'First,' I quoted, '"any remaining straw must be cut to very short lengths". That's your job my sweet, as you have the scissors. "And then", wait for it, "the whole mass must be thoroughly compressed by treading on a hard surface". How waterproof are your trainers, darling? Not very? Hmm. I suppose you could always do it in bare feet . . .'

'Oh yeah, right. I'm on strike. That's it.'

'I'll tell you what, love. You go and make a pot of tea and I'll do the nasty bits. I don't mind. I'm used to this sort of thing. It's just as well I wasn't so fussy about your nappies when you were small.'

'Yeah, well. I'm never having smelly babies . . . ugh!' she said.

And with that she stomped off to make tea. I threw the whole lot into a pile and mixed it with my trusty old shovel. When she returned, bearing a tray of tea, she was immensely grateful and gave the glutinous-looking heap a wide berth.

'We're going to stick that lot on the wall?' she enquired, incredulously.

'That's what all the fuss was about, yes,' I answered, wishing that Worgleswipe was there to inspect the consistency of the mix at close quarters . . . very close quarters.

When we had drunk Angelica's tea, or at least after she had been back to the kitchen to bring some tea bags which she had omitted to put in the pot the first time, we drank the tea, and loaded the first bucketful. I tied a rope to the bucket handle in order to haul the suppurating mass onto my temporary scaffolding. To my surprise, the mixture stuck to the wall like the proverbial . . . I suppose that's the point; it was, or at least a good proportion of it was, courtesy of Brenda Fortescue's four-legged friends. Before long, we had the rhythm going and the patch of wall was covered with the first layer which I then combed with an old garden rake just to satisfy the bloody purists. Another pot of tea, this time with tea bags, was followed by the application of the second layer. I climbed down the ladder to admire our work. It looked fine, it really did. Admittedly, there were hundreds of tiny spiky bits of hair and straw protruding out of the otherwise polished surface but, as far as I was concerned, that only added to the authenticity of the job. Eat your heart out, Worgleswipe.

We cleared up, washed the buckets and tools under the garden tap, and returned to the kitchen where Greg and Stevie were still sitting at the untouched lunch table reading *The Times*.

'Guys,' I said, impatiently, 'I thought you were going to clear lunch away.'

They both looked at the table with its piles of crockery, cheeses and breadcrumbs, as though it had all suddenly sprung at them from nowhere.

'Sure, Dad, sure. Chill,' said Greg.

'But it's nearly supper time!'

'Is it? Oh shit!' said Stevie, leaping up from the table and dumping the sports' page in the tub of cholesterol-free spread. 'I'm supposed to be meeting Chloe. Dad, listen. I *really* did mean to do it. I *will* do it, tomorrow. I've just made a *serious* miscalculation on the time. I must *dash*.'

'Hey, Stevie,' said Greg, alarmed. 'Quit joking about, mate. You can't seriously expect me to do *all* of this by myself! There's like *mountains* of it.'

'Greg,' I remonstrated. 'Four of us had a bread and cheese lunch. You have a dishwasher to hand. You're being ... pathetic. Just do it, please. Like now.'

'Humph. Okay Stevie, you owe me one,' he shouted up the stairs at his brother's retreating back. 'A *big* one. This is purgatory, man, purgatory. Where does the cheese live, Dad?'

I pointed. 'In there. It's called *the fridge*.' I sank into a chair, looking forward to a hot bath and a quiet evening with a book. At that moment the phone rang. Angelica, who was closest, answered, and a grin spread across her face.

'Yes, he's here. Tonight? No, I don't think he's doing anything. I'm sure he'd *love to*. Hold on ... Dad, it's for you. A woman. She wants to know if you'd like to go to the church barbecue. She thought you might be lonely,' she said, with something approaching a malevolent smirk. She covered the mouthpiece with her hand. 'I think it's Mrs Fortescue. That'll teach you to make me shovel shit all afternoon.'

10

Given a completely free choice, I would rather gloss over the hazy and somewhat dubious twenty-four hours which followed that telephone call from Brenda Fortescue (now referred to among my children as 'Brenda Fortescrew'). Unfortunately, they have threatened to shop me to my publisher if I dare to omit it. Suffice it to say, I woke up on our settee, still fully clothed, at ten forty-five the following morning. I had the vague impression that there were people in the room.

I opened my eyes, but immediately closed them again as the narrow streak of sunshine, which prised its way through the gap in the closed curtains, bored a hole in my head. I have to confess that, at least initially, I thought I was dead. It had been a good few years since I had experienced a hangover such as the one which possessed me that morning. Although I wasn't up to making objective comparisons or analyses, I would say it produced more or less the same symptoms as I had experienced when, as a student, I managed to fall off the platform of a number 89 bus in south London. I was doing my level best to impress a young lady at the time, but my elbow, casually crooked around the grip, was not up to the centrifugal forces exerted by a London Transport double-decker negotiating a roundabout at high speed, and I suddenly found myself hurtling through the air heading for a municipal flower bed on a traffic island. On that occasion I came to with the mother and father of headaches, closely scrutinising a clump of African marigolds. On this more recent occasion, I opened my eyes and, having taken the precaution of shading them,

I found myself staring into Stevie's face. Behind him I could see Greg and several people I had never before set eyes on.

I closed my eyes and sank back. A hushed conversation was taking place, snippets of which reached my consciousness.

'Do you think he's all right?'

'He looks terrible...'

'He smells of horses!'

'Should we get a doctor perhaps?' someone said sympathetically.

'Get a life!' another added. 'He just got pissed. Pissed as a bloody fart. Leave him to sleep it off...'

That did it. Determined to show the gathered company that I was not suffering from any ill affects after a quiet night out, I sat upright and swung my legs towards the floor.

'Steady, old man!' said a voice I did not recognise, as the floor rushed up to meet my nose. I sat, unable to comprehend what was going on. My mouth felt like the shed roof. I gestured towards it with my finger.

'He's asking for a drink! Get him a drink. He's probably dehydrated.'

Someone came into the room.

'*Awesome*,' I heard Angelica say. 'Bloody amazing *awesome*. If he ever has the neck to give me a hard time again...'

The barbecue at the vicarage was a sedate affair. They had really pushed the boat out for the occasion and, rumour had it, the summer fruit punch had brandy in it. Not that one could tell. Mrs Slitherby, the vicar's wife, had arranged tables and parasols throughout the vicarage gardens, and as dusk settled strings of fairy lights lit up the sylvan scene. The Reverend Hereward Timothy Slitherby, preferred name, not surprisingly, Timothy (never Tim, please) was making ineffectual fannings at the barbecue when I arrived. Not long afterwards old man Mace, the retired butcher, arrived having spent a little too long in the George and Dragon at Thackett Green, and he took over the desultory barbecue with gusto and a half a pint of lighting fluid. Hereward Slitherby leapt backwards in an attempt to avoid the resulting conflagration and afterwards he confined his parochial activities to discussing the forthcoming marrow growing competition with some nominally younger members of the local WI. They looked enthralled.

There is something terminally depressing about fund-raising barbecues for which one pays an exorbitant sum for a sausage, a dried-up bun and a spoonful of coleslaw. To give Harry Mace his due, he had procured some decent steaks and several hundred of his home-made sausages. The crowning moment came when I surrendered half of my ticket for a drink – *the* drink – and the opportunity to enter the raffle. Just as I was sipping the punch from the obligatory plastic cup, a booming cry echoed across the garden.

'Duncan! So glad you could come. How's your front thingummy? Done it yet?'

It was Brenda Fortescue with her stablemate, Rosalind Hamthwaite. There was, frankly, little to choose between them.

'Duncan's front thingummy, Brenda?' she screeched, just in case anyone had missed it first time around. 'It sounds wonderful. Can I join in? Haw, haw, haw.'

I could see the evening was going to be one not to be missed. How I longed for my armchair and a glass of whisky.

'What are you drinking, Duncan? Not the WI witches' brew, surely? Stroll on man. Have some of this.'

Brenda produced a glass flagon from her shoulder bag, tipped my punch onto Mrs Slitherby's nasturtium bed, and refilled my beaker. The drink she poured had a curious, almost fluorescent hue in the half-light.

'What is it?' I ventured, passing it beneath my nostrils.

'Birch leaf wine.'

'I see. Birch leaf, hmm.'

It tasted of . . . well, very little actually. The sort of flavour one might discover if, in a desperate moment, one decided to drink the

water left over in the saucepan after blanching the runner beans ...
sort of thin and greenish, but it was all right. In fact, after a few
mouthfuls I decided it was quite palatable; warming and enabling,
exactly the sort of social lubricant one needs at the vicar's
barbecue. Before long, I do recall laughing heartily at Brenda's
horsey jokes, despite having heard most of them before courtesy
of Bernie, her ex. She refilled my cup and hid the flagon as
Hereward joined us and she asked him, unnecessarily
provocatively I thought, how his prize marrow was swelling. I
have to say that I would not normally have laughed so mirthfully
at that sort of humour, but I did, particularly when Rosalind asked
him whether Mrs Slitherby was also pleased by the size of it.

'Oh yes,' he replied, seemingly oblivious to the tenor of the
question. 'I think I might be in with a chance this year,' whereupon
Brenda and Rosalind nudged each other and collapsed in helpless
laughter. I was aware of the evening becoming steadily warmer,
which struck me as a little unusual, and Brenda's jokes seemed to
become funnier, which, on reflection, strikes me as even less
likely, particularly as she was screaming with laughter and telling
everyone that Hereward might be in with a chance this year ... 'if
it kept swelling'.

I do remember staggering a little uncertainly round the garden,
partially supported by Brenda who seemed, for some inexplicable
reason, to be far more steady on her feet than I was. Every so often
the flagon would appear from Brenda's shoulder bag, my cup
would be refilled and I continued to enjoy the pale mysterious
nectar. There seemed to be a corresponding diminishment in my
capacity to hold a lucid conversation. At one point I stumbled
across a familiar-looking chap standing with his wife, although
initially I could not for the life of me place him. When he asked me
if I had been in touch with my insurance company, the penny
dropped. It was bloody Worgleswipe! His wife was a grim-
looking affair dressed in a lurid pink trouser suit. I probably
shouldn't have told him that if he had not yet had her listed as an
ancient monument he should do so as soon as possible, but I don't

think it justified his somewhat over-emotional reaction. I think he was offended, because he started ranting and raving and, before long, Brenda came and somehow steered me away just as I was telling him in no uncertain terms where I might deposit a shovelful of my horse dung mixture.

I sank into one of Mrs Slitherby's folding wooden chairs at one point and watched as the lights and parasols flew around the garden as if they might have been affixed to one of those terrifying rides at the funfair. I also asked Rosalind what Brenda did to give her birch leaf wine such a kick. Apparently, she fortifies it: 'half and half' Rosalind said, 'you know ... fifty-fifty.' She winked and told me to 'watch out for Brenda'. It transpired that the other half, the lethal component, was Russian vodka.

I have hardly any recollection of the rest of the evening. I know I was driven to Brenda's house, and I vaguely recall her showing me her sizeable improvements round the back, all achieved since Bernie had left, but quite how I arrived back on my own sofa I will probably never know. It's a mystery to me, and, quite frankly, I'm not sure I have the stomach to enquire further.

When I finally managed to stagger to the kitchen to make coffee, the place was full of kids. They were frying bacon and mushroom sandwiches and, although normally I am passionate about a full-blown cooked breakfast, the smell sent nauseating ripples through my insides. I felt my way to a shady seat in the garden where a nice young thing, who said her name was 'Midge', brought me my coffee. Sympathetically, she patted my shoulder and said 'Poor Mr Dudgeon' in such a kind way, and then proceeded to tell me that she was used to dealing with hangovers as her father also got *rat-arsed* every Friday night. Charming.

I felt, on balance, that the constant ribbing and sarcasm to which my children subjected me for the rest of that day was slightly uncalled for. I was not, as Angelica chose to put it, 'breaking-out' or 'revealing my true suppressed inner self' in the absence of Mrs D. Why I ever let her do psychology A level I cannot imagine. At one point, the three of them sat in the kitchen

75

singing a smug and highly disrespectful little chorus which began, 'Leg-less in Strumpling Green...' to the tune of 'Come down O Love Divine', not that one of them would have ever sung it in church. It was most unfair. When all was said and done, I had only been to the vicarage for a spot of supper.

11

At the end of the week, Ralph arrived to complete the bathroom tiling. Looking at me somewhat smugly over his mug of coffee, he produced a glossy catalogue.

'You know them tiles, the ones you got from Portugal?'

'I do, Ralph.'

'The ones you waited ages and ages for from that chap in Chelsea who ships them over...'

'I do, Ralph,' I returned, munching on my digestive biscuit.

'The ones you paid the earth for...'

'Yes, Ralph, I do. Get on with it. You are, I presume, talking about the ones you managed to stick upside down on the bloody wall?'

'Yeah. Them ones.'

'Yes, Ralph...'

He slurped his coffee noisily and grinned.

'Yes, Ralph! Are you going to tell me something about them or is this just a ploy to while away yet another morning?'

'They're in here.'

'In *where*?'

'In this 'ere catalogue.'

'Well, blow me down! Whatever next?'

'Don't you want to know where they really comes from?'

'Don't tell me. France. No, wait, Taiwan? Bognor Regis? I don't know. Where?'

'Mardlington.'

'Mardlington?'

'Yeah, Mardlington in Yorkshire.'

'Ralph, I do know where Mardlington is. I wasn't doubting that Mardlington is in Yorkshire. I was just surprised that the tiles come from there. They must be imitations of the peasant-crafted Cantalucian ones we bought from Portugal.'

I think if we had been sitting somewhere other than in the kitchen, Ralph would probably have spat on the floor.

'Nah! I rang them. They supplies them to that nancy shop o' yours in London.'

'Are you *sure* about this, Ralph?'

'I am,' he said, looking like a cat who has just caught a mouse with cheese still on its whiskers. 'Certain.'

He passed me the catalogue. The tiles certainly *looked* the same. I looked at the price list. 'They're about half the price!'

Ralph gloated. 'You've bin 'ad , Mr Dudgeon. 'ad.'

Furious, I rummaged for the receipt and picked up the phone.

'*Piles o' Tiles, Chelsea Limited.*'

'Oh, good morning. My name is Dudgeon. I purchased some Portuguese tiles from you a little while ago and we've had a few breakages. Is it possible that you have one or two in stock?'

'Unlikely, sir, but I'll check. As you know, we import the Portuguese tiles to order from the Cantalucian folk craftsmen and they are very difficult to acquire. We tend to have long delivery dates as you will know, but ... if you want an outstanding, authentic product, the envy of your discerning friends, that's the price you pay I suppose.'

'I appreciate that. Well, we may have to order some then. On the other hand ... I could drive up to Mardlington, this afternoon, and get them for myself ... couldn't I?'

'Mardlington?'

'Mardlington in Yorkshire.'

'Yes, sir. I wasn't for one second questioning where Mardlington was, merely that you might buy the tiles from there.'

'Well, let's just say that if I can buy the tiles there, I imagine your local trading standards officer might be interested to read about the Cantalucian "folk craftsmen" you write about so effusively in your *Piles o' Tiles* literature.'

'Trading standards?'

'Yes, trading standards. Goodbye for now. I'll be in touch soon.'

It's quite a long drive from Suffolk to East Yorkshire, but by evening I was on the outskirts of York, and a little later I was driving slowly around the streets of Mardlington looking for a bed and breakfast for the night. As there was a bank holiday coming up and, being at heart an obstinate old sod, I was determined to get the tiles myself, before the weekend. Above all else, I wanted Ralph to finish the tiling so that I could complete the bathroom for Mrs D's return. Frankly, I also wanted to get rid of Ralph. I had a feeling that if I had to sit and listen to him talking about 'our Jocelyn's nerves' once more, I was likely to do Ralph's fingers a mischief with his own tile guillotine. To give the man his due, with the exception of the upside down flower tiles, his work was second to none, and the new bathroom tiling looked magnificent. It's just that it had a few chrysanthemum-free zones in it.

It was surprisingly difficult to find a house with a vacancy sign, and several which did have them displayed turned out to have no vacancies, a deception which seemed to serve no purpose at all, except that it allowed the landladies of Mardlington to recommend their friends.

'Ah, now lad, if yer goes t' end of street and turns left and goes to number fifty-three, Mrs Randolph might be able to take you in, or, if yer goes a few doors further to Mrs Fenwick at fifty-nine, she may help.'

Mrs Randolph didn't have any vacancies, and, neither did Mrs Fenwick but it was, potentially a very cunning marketing ploy. Apparently, the famous Mardlington Summer Fair was due to take place the next day and, as a result, all the town's B and Bs were fully booked.

Mrs Codley, who opened the door and offered me the remaining room *with facilities* (on account of her son, John-Junior, being away in't Navy) looked suspiciously over my shoulder as though I might have been concealing a dozen illicit bed and breakfast clients outside her front porch.

'Is it just for you?' she enquired, which seemed a particularly pointless question as I had very clearly, only ten seconds before, asked for a room for one. 'Got children?' she asked, and when I told her I had six, she glanced at me even more inhospitably and looked outside again, just to be sure. I went to the Lada to collect my bag, then locked it, leaving it safely under a street lamp, around the corner in a leafy square. It was slightly disconcerting to notice a motionless policeman just across the road in a shop doorway; he was watching me in the most intense manner. One way and another, the town's welcome did not live up to the reputation which Yorkshire folk have for their famous hospitality.

Mrs Codley led me up the stairs past a series of particularly charmless paintings of buxom Tahitian girls with flowers in their glistening hair, to a room at the top of the house which, I am sorry to say, was in even worse taste than the portraits. The whole room had the appearance of being a loft conversion constructed of stout cardboard. The walls reverberated with every movement, and the large sloping wavy ceiling was covered in that ghastly form of heavily textured plaster which has apparently been applied with the hand; sort of pseudo-Spanish wine bar in Welwyn Garden City style. The whole lot was crowned with artificial, nailed-on beams which were not very carefully picked out in gloss black.

'We had this done up special for my son for when he comes home from sea,' she told me.

I bet he can't wait to come home on leave, I thought to myself. I surveyed my *on sweet*, a loosely divided cupboard with louvred doors; the sort of thing one finds at the back of a betting shop to separate the punters from the office, only in this instance they barely concealed the WC and a shower. As for their sound-baffling qualities, they must have scored one-and-a-half on a scale of ten.

'Make sure you keep shower curtain in't tray,' she said gruffly, in a forty-Woodbine-a-day voice. 'Otherwise it drips through our bedroom ceiling.'

As my children would say, *'Nice'*.

There's nothing quite like really grotty lodgings to make one miss home. I thought about the kids, their cheerful faces lit in the evening lamplight as they gathered around the table in the living room enjoying a good old family game of Monopoly. Then, a little more realistically, I thought about the piles of undealt with washing-up, the sandwich toaster left with melted cheese and baked beans solidifying down the sides, and the dog pacing in endless circles by the back door because no one had thought to let him out. At that very moment, my mobile phone rang (Mrs D and I keep one for emergencies). It was Stevie.

'Hi, Dad. Oroight? Listen, no probs. I'm just, like, cooking this pizza, and you know all that, like, plastic stuff, basically, do you take it off before you put it under the grill thing?'

'I do, Stevie. Definitely, yes. And I think you should as well.'

'Cool. Wicked. Bye,' and he was gone. As they say in the adverts, 'It's good to talk.' Even the 'Bye' was abbreviated to a brief 'B...' owing to the rapidity with which he hit the 'off' button. It sounded as though he might have been suffering from chronic indigestion. I mustn't be unfair to him; he probably *did* have chronic indigestion, still lingering on from lunchtime.

Thus relieved of all feelings of homesickness, I plugged in my kettle to make a cup of tea. The socket wobbled; its fixings were loose in the wall. When it had boiled, I held the socket firmly before I pulled out the plug. Bearing in mind my recent experiences with walls and electric cables, I had no wish to black out half of East Yorkshire. I changed my mind about tea, and made coffee instead, as there were only two tea bags, which I would have to eke out for several cups in the morning. I swear that if I ever run a hotel or a bed and breakfast I will, on a point of honour, provide copious amounts of tea and coffee-making materials. Beside each kettle, I will place a tea caddy stuffed full of tea bags, a huge jar of sugar and about a hundred or so of those little milk cartons. There is no better way to make people feel welcome. I have yet to stay in a hotel where there are adequate numbers of these basics left for the guests. Even the very best establishments, those charging exorbitant sums for a night's stay, can't seem to take it on board that we Brits like to *drink* tea, and that if one arrives at say, three in the afternoon, it is impossible to survive until breakfast time with only *two* tea bags and four sachets of sugar.

Having risen early, as is my habit, and sat reading in hotels for several tannin-free hours, I now make a point of asking at the reception if I could have more tea, milk and sugar provided. I do this on principle, even before going up to my room. The extraordinary thing is that the necessary components then arrive at one's room in prodigious quantities, courtesy of those wonderful chamber ladies (I hesitate to say *maids*) who run *their* corridor and who would rather perish than think of one of *their guests* going short. Without exception, *they* always understand these things. Why can't the management just do it in the first place? Are they afraid that if they put too many out the guests might do something whacky with them? Or steal them? By contrast, down in the dining room one is plagued by obsequious waiters who ply the teapot with a monotonous over-zealousness which ruins that special communion the Englishman develops with his full breakfast. Why not put the bloody tea bags in the bedrooms instead? If any hotel managers are reading this, I say to you, 'Be bold! Break out! If you must economise, then skip the shower caps and four tiny bars of soap in the bathroom and please, instead, stack in the tea bags!'

I savoured my coffee with half-rations of sugar, and sat in the chair, which immediately sagged towards the floor with a groaning noise which made me think my neighbouring guest's stomach was rumbling through the wall. Realising that to remain there was to court a bad back, I took my cup to the bed and lay down with my book. Fortunately, I had put my coffee down on the bedside cupboard (purchased I think from 'Eddie's Home Clearance Bargain Centre' which was just up the road from Mrs

Fenwick's) because, quite involuntarily, I rolled over three times and ended up in the middle of the double bed. Some beds just dip in the middle. Dipping is tolerable. It demonstrates that the mattress has that lived-in, cosy feel about it. This one *caved in.* Caving-in is not acceptable. There should be a Health and Safety regulation governing such beds. This bed caved in with a roaring vengeance. I swear that it was determined to annihilate me. It was as though the mattress might have suffered from some sort of glacial erosion which had scoured out the middle of it, leaving a crevice which was nigh on impossible to climb out of without the aid of crampons and climbing ropes. For a few moments the sparse light above me from Mrs Codley's forty-watt bulb was lost as the bedding slid down the precipice and engulfed me. It was nearly black within the deep chasm which had swallowed me ... it was like being trapped in an over-stuffed blanket chest. My hand, protruding from the mass of bedding, scrabbled around in fresh air and found a handhold on the bed head. I clawed my way out, panting and shaken.

When I eventually regained my composure, I ventured to peer under the bed. It was difficult to see in the gloom, but it seemed there was a case of terminal spring failure. This bed was dead. The springs were actually sagging so far down that they rested on the floor. One doesn't see many spring bed frames these days, and I could only imagine that this was part of Mrs Codley's job lot from Eddie's. No wonder John-Junior had run away to sea.

I slid the armchair into the corner, moved the bedside cupboard to one side, and pulled the mattress onto the floor. Tentatively, I lowered myself onto it and found that it was possible to lie nearly flat if I crooked my knee over the side to hook myself near the edge. At least arranged thus, my well-being was not threatened and I stood a chance of returning to Suffolk and seeing my children again. I imagined Mrs D receiving a message in Arizona: 'Your husband been lost in a B and B in East Yorkshire. We haven't yet given up hope. Rescue teams have gone down into the mattress and are still optimistic that he may be trapped in an air pocket...'

Mrs Codley needn't have worried about the shower curtain failing and water leaking onto her bed. The shower dribbled pathetically from a loose fitting without the remotest chance of it splashing onto the floor. The only way to get wet was to sit in the tray with the shower balanced on my head. This arrangement seemed to spur the plumbing on to the point where it delivered a half-hearted stream of lukewarm water.

Exhausted from my long drive, not to mention the near calamity in the bed and the resultant furniture moving, I sank onto my new bed, on the floor, and fell asleep.

12

At four-thirty the following morning, a piercing buzzer sounded. It was a very loud, insistent buzzing which broke into my sleep. My first thought on waking, when I remembered where I was, was that Mrs Codley's house might be on fire and that in the attic I was in a strategic position to receive a really good toasting. The buzzing continued its barely wavering note. Unable to get a bearing on where the sound was, I struggled to my feet, from the bed on the floor, and began a stumbling, bleary search of the room. Nothing. As sleep drained away from me I realised that the persistent noise was actually in the room next door and that it was the paper-thin walls that gave the impression that it was nearer. I put my ear to the wall. It was definitely in the next room. It sounded like an *alarm clock!* The question was, why didn't the occupant silence it? Surely no one could sleep through that! Perhaps given time it would exhaust itself and stop.

It continued unabated for *ten minutes*. I sat wondering about sacrificing one of my two tea bags and enjoying an exceptionally early cup of tea, then I decided against and opened my door. Out on the landing in the darkness the noise seemed more muffled. I tapped on the door.

'Hello. I say, erhmm, excuse me. Hello.'

The buzzing continued.

I tapped on the door again, more loudly that time, and tried the handle. It was locked. Surely nobody could possibly sleep through that infernal din. I knocked loudly. No response. I went back to my room. The noise was definitely louder there. For a second or two I wondered whether to drag my mattress onto the small landing where I might get back to sleep, and then I dismissed the idea as quite ridiculous. I was *paying* for this bed and breakfast nightmare! No! Action was needed. Someone would have to get up, open the room and turn off the alarm. I found a light switch and crept downstairs in my night-clothes.

I have, in my time, had to deal with a number of night-time incidents while pyjama-clad. I have, for example, trudged out into a muddy field with secateurs in order to free sheep hopelessly entangled in brambles. At a boarding school, I entertained parents at two o'clock in the morning, albeit under slightly strained circumstances, politely chatting whilst holding their inebriated son's head in a bucket while he vomited. There was even the occasion when a coach load of Italian holiday makers were mistakenly dropped at our door, in the dead of night, because their guide thought *Cromwell's Retreat* was the *Cromwell Hotel.* As far as I am aware, however, I have never had to wake a landlady in the middle of the night because the neighbouring room possessed an irrepressible alarm clock. I must admit, it posed something of a problem, not least because I did not know which room Mrs Codley was sleeping in. I climbed the narrow flight of stairs and tried the door once more. Perhaps I could force it open. Wait! What had she said? 'Keep curtain in't tray because otherwise it drips through our bedroom ceiling.' Well, that was one answer. If all else failed, a lukewarm dribble of water between the floorboards would certainly do the trick. I looked at the door beneath my room. No question about where to knock...

Right then. I raised my knuckles to the door. Right! Ready! I lowered my trembling hand. 'Dudgeon,' I told myself, 'get on with it. What are you afraid of?' Think, think. What should I say, if and when I managed to wake her? 'Ah, Mrs Codley. I'm sorry to bother you but ... Mrs Codley! I just wish to make it clear that this is the worst bed and breakfast it has ever been my misfortune to...'

Try as hard as I might, I could not quite raise the necessary to...

86

'Waaaaah! Aaaaaaah! Jo-Jo!' a female voice screamed. 'There's a man on't landing!'

Whether it was the unexpected shock of the door suddenly swinging open as if by magic, or whether it was the absolute terror which overtook me, occasioned by Mrs Codley appearing in the half-light in a full set of curlers and an ankle length nightdress, I am not certain. The effect was the same. I leapt so far backwards that I stumbled on their landing and before I knew it, I was falling backwards down the first flight of stairs.

Fortunately for me, the house was furnished with a series of short staircases and half-landings which meant that I did not fall too far. The most calamitous part of the whole escapade was that I happened to collide with Mrs Codley's rather pretentious dinner gong which, for most of its existence resided fairly quietly on the first turn of the stairs. There was a booming noise as I hit the gong, followed by a crash as it fell from its bracket and hit the floor, followed by very loud echoing alternate booms and crashes as it bounced down the remaining stairs. When it reached the hall it rolled along the linoleum until its progress was impeded by the front door, whereupon it spun like a pirouetting dancer, finishing its solo with a protracted, excruciating drum roll.

I looked up from my cramped position on the stairs and, upside down through the banisters, I viewed a large balding chap, in a string vest, with more tattoos on his arm than a matelot in Gibraltar on a Saturday night.

'What the fook are you up to?' he asked menacingly, which I suppose, however uncouth, was a perfectly reasonable question under the circumstances. I felt that my reply, indicating that the alarm clock in the next bedroom was keeping me awake, was probably less than adequate.

'Wot's goin' on?' said a voice from another door, which opened presumably in response to the hubbub on the landing.

'Can't we be allowed to get any sleep? Some of us have got to work in the morning,' said another voice, a woman's this time.

'All of you, go back to bed,' said the bald one. 'I'll deal with this little Peeping Tom. I'll give you creep round t' house in t' middle of night. What are you? Huh? Some sort of pervert?'

I tried to explain that all I wanted was a key to the next room, but it was difficult because by then Mr Codley Senior was holding me by the scruff of my pyjama jacket and the tightening constriction around my throat made the words come out in a strangled squeak. Eventually, he put me down.

'If you'll just come upstairs with me for a moment I'll show you the problem. It's really very simple. I woke up and . . .'

'I don't go upstairs with no perverts. Gladys, call the police.'

'Oh no, Jo-Jo. I'm not doing that. Whatever'll the neighbours say? Keeping an unruly house. It'll put me out o' business. Ever since the police went to Mrs Harbottle's they've not had a single traveller stay there.'

'Right you. Upstairs. Now. Keep your 'ands to yerself. Go on. In front of me where I can see yer.'

We climbed the stairs to my room.

'If you'll just listen for a moment you'll hear why I needed to . . .'

The silence was punctuated only by the sound of Jo-Jo's heaving chest.

At five-fourteen, the sun was just breaking through the early sea mist as I trudged, breakfastless, around the corner with my bag. To my surprise, not only was the policeman standing stock-still in the doorway, his attention still riveted upon me, but my little mustard coloured estate was not there. Instead, in its place, stood a sea of partially erected market stalls, funfair rides and shuttered candy-floss huts. I stood as if frozen, unable to believe the transformation that had overtaken the quiet square in the course of the all-too-short night.

My car was nowhere to be seen. I walked to the lamppost where I was sure it had been. Nothing. It had vanished. Relieved that there was a police officer on hand who was bound to know something about the car, I crossed the street. As I approached the doorway, he stood quite still, calmly watching me. Not a flicker of response crossed his face.

'Excuse me, Officer, I . . .'

I'm not sure what first gave me the idea that I was speaking not to a real policeman but to a life-sized photograph mounted as a cutout but, believe it or not, that was what confronted me. No wonder he had been able to stand sentry-like all night long. 'Ah,' I said, taking a step backwards feeling rather foolish, but nevertheless conscious of the fact that it seemed less than respectful to just turn and walk away. At that moment a police van pulled up and an officer jumped from the passenger seat, picked up my cardboard bobby and stood him in the back with about twenty-seven others. I gaped in astonishment.

'Everything all right, sir?' the officer enquired, meeting my quizzical gaze.

'I . . . I've lost my car. It was left there under that street lamp,' I said, pointing across the square.

'It'll be round the corner in Josamund Street,' he said. 'We always put them round there when folks park in t'Square.'

'You've moved my car?'

'Aye. Traders just pick them up and carry them out of harm's way.'

'I see. Pick them up and . . . yes. Right. Thank you. I'll go and find it. Um, officer, are these . . . are these serious?' I asked, pointing to the van full of two-dimensional impersonations.

'It's chief inspector's idea. Deterrent, you see. While the force is under-strength. Criminals see the cutouts and think twice before they break the law.'

'They see a cardboard replica of an officer and . . . surely you are joking.'

He fixed me with a stare. I resisted the temptation to make further provocative comment.

'I'll be off then, Constable. To find my car . . .'

He watched me intently as I crossed the road. When I turned to glance at him he was still there, quite motionless.

One of the great disadvantages of being thrown out of a bed and breakfast by a brawny Yorkshireman with a surfeit of tattoos at five in the morning is that one then needs a cup of tea and a decent breakfast. Having found the car and dumped my bag on the back seat, I set off at a brisk pace along the promenade where a gang of street sweepers were cleaning the tarmac. I paused for a while to light my pipe and watch as one drove a mechanical pavement cleaner, one squirted a spray at lumps of squidged chewing gum, and another followed a few minutes later and methodically scraped up the offending goo. It struck me on that misty morning that their chores, in some curious way, represented something of life in microcosm. Despite their menial jobs, they were a cheerful bunch and, after I'd told them about my early and somewhat forceful ejection from my lodgings, we had a hearty laugh and they recommended a café which would open at six. I continued my promenade, watched the sun rise over the Dogger Bank, and ordered myself a staggering full breakfast in a greasy spoon of a place imaginatively called *Barry's Breakfast Bar*. I can commend it to you, but would suggest that before you order and *Barry* puts your eggs on the griddle, do check that he is not suffering from one of his sneezing fits brought on by the pollen blowing off the moors.

By nine I was waiting at the door of the Mardlington Tile Company, where I bought two dozen chrysanthemum tiles, and shortly afterwards, I was back on the A1 driving south to Suffolk, vowing never to visit East Yorkshire again.

13

The day after I returned from Mardlington, Ralph finished the bathroom tiling. He arrived in his van, which, rather like Ralph himself, was still suffering from retarded ignition, walked into the kitchen and took the tiles from me with a sort of 'I told you so' look.

'Are you going to ring them *Piles o' Tiles* people?' he queried, settling down at the table where I was eating a late breakfast, and where I presume he thought he might also share my coffee pot.

'I am Ralph. I am. All in good time. Now perhaps if you would like to fix the missing tiles, you could then get cleared up and I will be able to finish the plumbing, the woodwork and the hundred and one things I need to do before Mrs Dudgeon comes back. Coffee at the usual time?'

Unexpectedly, I had managed to wean Ralph off his trip home at ten-thirty by the simple expedient of percolating a pot of 'real coffee', as he called it. His desire for a cup of freshly ground coffee had overtaken that for being at home and providing whatever steadying influence Jocelyn's nerves received from his presence. The aroma drifting towards the bathroom was like a magnet and, within seconds, his head would appear at the top of the staircase.

'My, my. Is it half-past ten already?' he would say, looking at his watch in surprise, as if his furious activity in the bathroom might have proceeded at such a cracking pace that he had completely lost track of time. As my children would say, 'You wish...'

Children are funny (and I use the term in its loosest possible sense). Their comments and observations about Ralph were absolutely spot-on, but there was a certain sense of irony about hearing Greg or Angelica holding forth about the shortcomings of the British craftsman.

'...He never does any work, Dad. You know that, don't you? You're paying him for doing nothing.'

'...Yeah, he's so *lazy,* and when you're not here, Dad, he slips off home early.'

This, from two of the idlest little buggers the earth has ever known, while they sat slumped in kitchen chairs, still dressed in nightwear at midday, their bare feet adorning the table. One was conducting an experiment with a piece of junk mail and a pair of scissors which, as far as I could see, involved meticulously snipping it into as many minutely thin strips as she could manage and leaving them spread as far as possible across the kitchen floor. The other was excelling in his efforts to chase a puddle of spilled breakfast milk into the maximum acreage of patterns on the tabletop. Not satisfied with making a disgusting mess that a two year-old would have been chastised for, he was doing it lazily at arm's length using, of all things, the aerial of the cordless phone.

'Greg. I don't want you to think I am getting at you, but I don't quite understand how you can sit there and criticise the likes of Ralph. I mean, have you looked at your bedroom recently? Even the dirty socks are heading for the door in an escape bid. The only thing tidy in there is the ceiling. You came home from university about four weeks ago and your bag is still sitting in the hall, just as your mother left it when she carried it in for you. When I came back from Yorkshire there were seventeen plates on top of the dishwasher, fourteen mugs and glasses scattered around downstairs, and the dog was looking like an anorexic teenager because he hadn't been fed. It also happens to be ten-past twelve and you're still sitting here in your pyjamas. Whatever you may feel about Ralph, presumably he got up at seven-thirty *am,* like the rest of the world, and has been reasonably conscious, and probably vertical too, throughout the morning. You on the other hand have . . .'

Greg looked exceptionally shocked. Stunned is the word. He stared at me, then at his own attire. I had obviously hit the mark. Bedroom cleaning here we come!

'*Pyjamas*?' he said incredulously. '*Pyjamas*? Since when have I worn *pyjamas*? Pyjamas are for wrinklies and seriously sad people.' Abruptly, he turned to his sister. 'Hey, Glic. I've had this wicked idea for my art submission. Got a camera? Photograph this lot in close-up,' he said, viewing his milk dribble creation with his eye at tabletop level. 'It's *awesome!*' and with that the two of them left the room, probably in search of my spare films. When they did return with Angelica's camera, as predicted, it had no film.

'Gotta film, Dad? I'll replace it. Must do it now. This is just phenomenal. Don't touch it! Don't move a thing!'

Feeling as though I was in danger of becoming an accomplice in this nonsense, I fetched a film. With the camera loaded, he began to crawl around *on* the kitchen table in his boxer shorts, using vast quantities of my expensive professional film.

Ralph came down for some detergent, glanced at Greg kneeling with his camera focused inches above a puddle of milk and sugar on the table, looked at me and raised an incredulous eyebrow.

'Holiday snaps?' he asked.

'Modern art,' I replied, half-defensively.

'Silly arse, more like,' said Ralph, as he left muttering. 'Bloody conscription, that's what they need. A good dose of the army . . .'

'There. See what I mean?' said Angelica. 'What's he doing wandering around wasting time again?'

A year previously, at the end of Greg's first year of art study, the foundation course had held an exhibition at which he and all of his fellow students displayed their work. I attended, having a genuine interest in art and my son's work. That was my first mistake. I should have stayed at home. I should have been wise enough to remain in blissful ignorance, imagining that he and all of his

93

friends had been usefully engaged stretching their creative little beings thereby justifying the exorbitant fees and millions of pounds of taxpayers' money which had been spent on them. I should have known when I set eyes on the untidy pile of scrap metal in the forecourt. I thought someone had mistakenly tipped up a lorry bound for the dump, until I noticed a title at the base. 'Lonely on an Autumn Morning' it read. *Lonely on an Autumn Morning*? No wonder the artist is lonely. I'm not surprised he hasn't got any blinking friends if he's in the habit of doing that sort of thing! People probably give him a very wide berth. You may well chuckle. But this was no beginner's piece. The individual practising this monstrous piece of 'artistic' self-delusion, was none other than the college's Professor of Three-Dimensional Art. *He* was teaching them! God save us all from artists who have learned to brandish a welding torch.

The first thing that struck me was that the entire campus was a mass of dreary rust-stained concrete and glass, like some inferior imitation of the Barbican which, in my opinion, wasn't worth trying to emulate in the first place. It was such a depressing environment. The second point of note was that it was all locked up, except for an entrance at the back which necessitated walking half a mile in one direction, going through the door, and walking half a mile back again. The lack of organisation did not exactly convey any sense that the college wanted to welcome visitors. It was like trying to break into the local Securicor depot. I happened to be on crutches at the time and the excursion through endless corridors covered in scruffy posters, most of which seemed to be advertising various thrashes for the gay fraternity, was most decidedly not what I needed. Why, we all wondered, couldn't they have simply opened the front door?

When Greg and I arrived in the Foundation Department, we found ourselves in the middle of several hundred Marlborough cigarettes wedged in the mouths of an equivalent number of half-washed, shaven-headed young people, most of whom had more metal fixed to their faces than I have attached to my bath plug.

94

'Oroight Mick?'

'Oroight Greg?'

'Oroight Nick?'

'Oroight Greg?'

'Oroight Lindy?'

'Oroight Greg?'

'That was one of my lecturers, Dad.'

'Who was?'

'Lindy.'

Lindy? Lindy with the festering eyebrow ring? You mean *'Oroight Greg,' Lindy?*

I turned to look at her. 'I don't believe it, Greg,' I said. 'I thought the lecturers were supposed to set some sort of example, you know, be people to look up to . . .'

Greg looked at me as though I might have just landed from a different solar system. 'Yeah, right, Dad. Whatever you say.'

As we passed through the courtyard filled with even more 'sculptures', everyone milled around a table where refreshments were being served. I say 'refreshments were being served' – what was actually happening was that a couple of the great unwashed were handing out cans of lukewarm beer or, for those who wished to cling to some semblance of civilisation and were prepared to wait for it, a glass of red wine.

The work displayed ranged from a few pieces of the genuinely intriguing to the majority which was appalling rubbish that looked as though it might well have been the cast-offs after a morning session of the local play school. A hammock swung from fluorescent cords with a half-dozen bricks suspended within it. I think it was called 'Mother's Heartbeat'. An airless blacked-out cubicle with space for a sweaty twosome showed an interminably long monochrome film which, as far as I could tell, involved wobbly shots of a youth lying on a bare kitchen floor or standing by a sink muttering things like 'So much washing up, er. . .' and 'So much to do, er. . .'

What was most noticeable was the reaction of the guests who

wandered from piece to piece giving partners and friends little tell-tale shrugs of the shoulders, as if to say 'How the hell should I know ... I haven't got a clue'. The show was a revelation which filled me with despair for our artistic future. As one elderly lady remarked to her friend. 'Yes dear, I understand that, but what have they been *doing* all year?'

Searching for a glimmer of potential at the exhibition gave me the same sort of hopeless feeling that I used to experience when correcting the work of the least able children in 5Z. I would sit at home with a stack of marking, desperately seeking a sign, even the tiniest indication, that one of the children might not only have been *present* but actually *heard* something, *anything*, that I had said in class. Then, suddenly, it would be there like a jewel amidst the dross, and one would feel so uplifted by the discovery, that it was possible to believe that life was worth living again, and that there was *purpose* in the universe after all.

Thank heavens there was *one* piece, near the exit, which had this fundamental quality, and to prove to you that I am not a prejudiced old fart without any interest in modern art I must tell you that it was a heavily painted white canvas, but not quite so. Beneath the white was a hidden landscape which was allowed to emerge in one small area only where the white had been very subtly scraped away. It was absolutely compelling, and the promise contained within it demanded a response from the small crowd which stood spellbound before it. Move over Damien.

And I went home a happier man.

14

Knowing that the three younger children were all due back home within a few days, I dedicated the first part of the morning to changing their beds and tidying up. By about ten o'clock, the washing was all drying on the line, and I was enjoying a cup of coffee. The forecast was good although summer storms were predicted.

I think it is fair to say that I am no longer one to become obsessed by the state of the house. I would go as far as to say that I once had the *potential* to be, but no more. What has changed me? Six children and a dog. It's that simple. I now offer courses for folk who need to be weaned off their obsessions. They are one hundred per cent effective. Money-back guarantees are all part of the deal.

The first and sometimes only 'treatment' necessary involves sitting in Greg's bedroom, equipped, it goes without saying, with the necessary latex gloves and other protective provision. We begin by encouraging clients to tolerate a minute a day and gradually increase the exposure on a daily basis. We have seen remarkable successes including one lady who, very bravely, removed her gloves, mask and coverall after only fourteen days and actually managed to be present just after lunch at the great waking-up. We refunded her course fee immediately on the simple basis that even I have not yet achieved that degree of conditioning.

Phase Two of the therapy, if it is necessary, takes place on Sundays and involves tidying the entire house by ten-thirty a.m. at which point coffee is served and the client is encouraged to rest.

97

The younger children begin to stagger from their rooms into the pristine kitchen where cereals, milk, Marmite, peanut butter, tuna paté and toast crumbs are then liberally distributed over every work surface and cupboard door, not to mention the floor. They grunt at each other imbecilically and then gravitate to the living room where the said foodstuffs are further distributed over the television, the video player and the settee. Glasses of fruit juice are stood to leave rings on the french-polished sideboard, a third of the video collection are removed from their cases and flung across the floor in a desperate bid to find the long-lost *Lion King* tape, and the dog, ever optimistic of a tuna-flavoured crust, slobbers all over the carpet. The client, meanwhile, is restrained in the doorway and forbidden to make any sort of protest. Indeed, marks are awarded to those who can coo lovingly as the mayhem unfolds. Then, it is back to the kitchen to clear the debris, wipe down surfaces and mop the floor.

Just before lunch, the assembled company vacate the dishevelled room, the dog cleans a few pieces of discarded crockery and it is time for the client to clean the living room (again). While the vacuum and rubbish sacks are being employed there, the second contingent, the late-teens and twenties, awake and descend, grunting with even more polished imbecilities, upon the sparkling kitchen only to slosh around a few more breakfast goodies and even more exotic drinks. Meanwhile the first three are doing their worst in the bathroom, shower and their bedrooms.

The second contingent then gravitates towards the living room to repeat the process, the only difference being their proclivities for more adult videos which involve horrendous noise, less pleasant lyrics and greater violence and bloodshed. The kitchen can then be cleaned again and, if there is time, this might be accomplished before the younger children arrive chorusing 'Wos for lunch?'

If there is an interval, the client may be taken upstairs with a spade in order to prise a layer from Greg's new eco-laundry system which involves *composting*, rather than washing, his dirty clothes. On the way, it may be possible to gather up a few of those fermenting glasses of old orange juice with the thick blue rime of mould growing upon them.

This scenario is, of course, only a brief résumé of the beginner's version for those with moderate disorders. We encourage clients who have major obsessions to be present not only for a full day in the holidays, finishing at about midnight, but to do it when the children all have their *friends* present. It is far more lively and much more likely to deal with the pathologically house-proud. Most clients leave us rejoicing in the token clutter and filth which abounds in their own homes and live happily ever after.

To encourage you and provide you with a little perspective, Angelica had a somewhat revealing misadventure last summer. For some reason, which escapes me now, Mrs D and I agreed that, having earned some money, she could travel to Hawaii with a girlfriend for a two-week holiday. All went swimmingly well (or at least, that's how the official account went) until the last couple of days when the girls returned to their hotel room and found that the door had been forced and all of their belongings of any value had been stolen. Poor things, they must have been beside themselves with worry, although, thank goodness, their passports were safe. Far from seeking to elicit your sympathy, the point of relating this tale is that when the police arrived, the first officer in the room was so horrified by the scene of utter devastation that he radioed back to base asking for crime scene backup.

'Jeez,' he said to control, 'you've never seen a hotel room trashed like this. It's just unbelievable Jed. We've got some real screwballs at work here.'

Angelica, later, safely back in Suffolk, related this conversation to Mrs D and I. 'The thing was,' she said, 'we didn't like to tell them, but no one had, like, trashed the room at all. It was *exactly* as we had left it.'

I very much hope that will be a source of comfort as you seek to come to terms with your own adolescents and their delightful little ways.

With regard to running our house, I have several principles that I commend to you for the sake of your general sanity and wellbeing. My rules of thumb are:

a) That I do not ever venture into the older children's bedrooms unless I have first attached a safety line to myself. The sort of thing the Fire Brigade uses is most suitable. It at least guarantees I will get out again.

b) That I never venture into any bedroom in darkness. I once had an unfortunate accident with a discarded skateboard when I was on crutches.

Broadly, I maintain that what they do in their rooms is more or less their own affair, unless the noxious vapours begin to creep across the landing, in which case I will take remedial action. Under crisis conditions I have been known to open one of their windows. I like the kitchen to be healthily clean with the majority of the waste-food in, or at least aimed approximately at, a bin. The living room should be passably tidy with less than, let's say, a dozen pairs of discarded trainers scattered over the floor. About fifty per cent of the chairs should be visible to the naked eye – that is, free of carelessly flung-down clothes, copies of *Hello!* and empty bags of Chipsticks. Healthy compromise is the key to happiness. Good old fashioned give and take. You give and they take.

I hope that you will agree that I adopt a reasonable attitude to it all. I confess to beginning with something of an advantage. Having been a boarding school housemaster with no less than a hundred and thirty adolescent boys in the building, nothing, but *nothing*, can ever compare with the sheer horror of that massed testosterone-driven mayhem. There, one existed from term to term in one of three phases: the first was. 'We're still unpacking, sir' which lasted for about four weeks after term began; the second phase was 'I've been so busy in the middle of term that I haven't put anything away'; and the third was 'It's nearly the end of term,' (four weeks before the Christmas holidays began) 'so it's not worth clearing up sir'. The heroic cleaning ladies who ventured into the boarding house each morning had a standing instruction before hoovering: 'If it moves, stamp on it, and if it doesn't, dump it on the bed'.

Believe it or not, there were occasions when some youngsters were so unspeakably antisocial and untidy that other adolescent boys would actually present a petition *begging* not to have to share dormitories with the offenders. Take a moment to dwell on that thought. When the full impact of that ghastly possibility has sunk in, I trust you will go back to your own chores, and your delightful kids, with a happy tune on your lips. Years after I gave up that particularly masochistic means of earning a living, I can still find extreme solace in the memory, as I delve under my children's beds with the garden rake in one hand and a laundry basket in the other.

When all is said and done, there is one final retribution at your disposal: The Fine. It should be used only sparingly, possibly only once in a child's lifetime, but when appropriate, use it decisively and without any sort of mercy. Hit hard and imagine as you do so all those pints of Newcastle Brown which, as a result, will not be swilled down their guzzling little throats. I would restrict its levying to those occasions when one of the children goes away, say to university, and through sheer gracelessness and ill-planning (which usually means too many nights in the pub) does not leave adequate time to clear up. I believe that at that point my rule of thumb breaks down. They *know* that either Mrs D or I will have to move in to give the offending room a going over. No parent can tolerate the possible complications of adolescent bedroom fermentation and the subsequent risk of spontaneous combustion. I once spent two hours cleaning one of the youngsters' rooms after a bad case of 'jumping ship' in this way. It was *disgusting*. Old sandwiches, half-eaten bits of toast and two month-old underclothes were among the more savoury items hauled from beneath the bed, caught whistling in the end of the Hoover tube. It gave me great pleasure to drag out my 1923 Olivetti typewriter (the one with the missing 'h') and write:

101

January 19t
Dear (I won't name him/her, it's not fair)
I ave just finis ed clearing t e ovel you call your bedroom. I enclose one or two of t e c oicer items found festering beneat your bed. You mig t need t em. I also attac notification t at your bank account will be £25 (twenty-five) lig ter t is term as a result of t e FILT FINE I ave levied being stopped from your allowance t is mont .
  As ever,
  Your loving Fat er
  XXX

It worked a treat. Ever after, I only had to wander around the house just before the beginning of term muttering 'Twenty-five quid...' to provoke a mad scrum at the Hoover cupboard.

All parents should be encouraged by the following account, supplied by a reliable friend, of a visit to a newly married son in New Zealand. I have no reason for believing that it could not happen here. Whilst the story is not concerned with filth and squalor *per se,* it proves that however hopeless your indolent, exasperating offspring may be, all things are possible. Our kids can and *do* change!

My friends, who we will call Harry and June, had spent about fifteen years following their son around the house, clearing up, performing laundry duties and generally acting as unpaid skivvies until they were more or less tearing their hair out with frustration. One of the boy's most annoying habits was to roam from room to room and, as he did so, he would switch on every light until the house was glowing like a power station in meltdown. This would happen several times each evening. Nothing seemed to change him. Harry tried sticky notices on the light switches, reduced-wattage bulbs and even pulling selective fuses from the main switchboard. It changed nothing. The wasteful and expensive behaviour continued.

Harry and the boy's mother were delighted when he married a

lovely Kiwi girl and settled down in a coastal house perched high on some spectacular cliffs. Not surprisingly, at night, the house could be floodlit to enhance its position. When Harry and June visited, they had a beautiful meal on a terrace overlooking the sea and afterwards they both offered to help clear up. Harry's son told them to remain on the terrace while he showed them the floodlit scene, and disappeared inside to switch on the lights. Suddenly the whole hillside was lit up and everyone present was deeply moved by the beautiful landscape that spread out before them. The lad then disappeared indoors again and the illumination faded after about thirty seconds, as he switched off the lights.

'Oh no!' Harry and June cried. 'Don't turn them off yet. It's so beautiful!'

'Mum, Dad,' the boy replied, 'have you any idea how much those lights cost to run?'

Harry spluttered over his beer in the half-light, and managed to avoid his wife's eye.

Later, in the kitchen, their son proudly wiped down the new electric cooker and, reaching across Harry, he turned off the appliance at the main switch on the kitchen wall. The boy winked at his dad.

'You never can be too careful. It just might leak . . .'

15

Having tidied the house, found the settee and sorted the laundry into approximate piles, I took the family diary from the wall and tried to imagine how the next few days might pan out:

Tuesday 2.30pm: Dad due at Phil's camp, Blixworth
Tuesday pm: Aga man. Service. Phone Wigglesworth?
Wednesday: Ring Granny to arrange collection of Mel and Ed on Thurs.

That seemed in order, not that I was looking forward to phoning Wigglesworth; not after my vodka-fuelled brush with his luminous wife at the vicarage. I decided I would leave it. He could ring me. Top of my immediate list was to seal the new bathroom floorboards, and repair the little blemish above Greg's bed. Given that it was probably better to do the latter when the lad was up and about, I took the sandpaper, varnish and brushes up to the bathroom and began to prepare the floor.

By noon I was hoovering up the dust which, if not done exceptionally thoroughly, appears out of the cracks in the boards and gets fixed in the varnish. Ever after, it looks and feels as though someone has thrown sand across the floor which, even in these days of the popular 'distressed' look, I cannot quite bring myself to accept as satisfactory.

Angelica appeared at the door, as dishevelled as I have ever seen her, shading her eyes against the light. She was wearing one of her favourite T-shirts, a black number with '*If you think I'm a bitch, you should meet my mother'* emblazoned across the front. Fortunately, Mrs D has a fine sense of humour and has never taken offence. Yet. I silenced the vacuum cleaner.

'Dad! D'you have to do that *first thing* in the morning?'

'Afternoon love. Rough night was it?'

'The club was so busy. Nightmarish. It was booked by all these wrinklies from the round-something. They just stayed and stayed and Neil wouldn't let me finish.'

'Round-something?' I queried.

'Yeah, like some charity thingy,' she said, scraping her hair back.

'Oh, you mean *Round Table.*'

She looked blank.

'You know, The Round Table? Arthur?'

'Arthur *who*? Dad, I really can't be expected to know all your friends. I'm going to eat something. I'm starving.'

I finished cleaning and opened the tin of varnish. I actually intended only to paint the perimeter of the room with the small brush, but I was carried away as the beautiful colours of the pine began to glow as the sealant took effect. I treated all around the door and then worked backwards towards the bath and lavatory.

'Dad! Do you have to make that *revolting* smell first thing in the morning? I thought I was being embalmed when I woke up. It's disgusting.'

'Afternoon, Stevie. Sleep well, old son?'

'No I didn't. Can we do something about the birds?'

'Which birds?'

'I dunno,' he said, waving his hand in a vague gesture. 'The ones out there. They keep, like, singing and waking me up and stuff.'

'Stevie, what am I supposed to do about the birds in the garden for goodness' sake?'

He looked at me. 'Okay. Okay. I just thought I'd mention it. I thought you might get someone in to see to them ... something, anything.'

105

At that moment I stood up and realised that in my rush to see the floor sealed, I had made the classic mistake and managed to maroon myself with a vast amount of wet varnish between myself and the door to the landing. How embarrassing. I hoped Stevie wouldn't notice. He wouldn't. He was still half-asleep.

'Do you want me to bring you your lunch?' said Stevie grinning. 'Or are you planning on demonstrating your Tarzan capabilities by leaping for the light fitting and swinging out of the door?' and he disappeared downstairs chuckling to himself.

I sat on the WC and contemplated my predicament, finally deciding that the best thing was to stretch as far as possible, place my heel on a spot near the middle where we planned to place a rug and where a mark wouldn't matter, and from there grasp the door frame and vault through the doorway. Unfortunately it didn't quite go to plan. My heel slipped on the wet varnish and shot away from under me, with the result that I did a fair impression of Rudolf Nureyev, and landed heavily, sitting on the floor. Doing the splits is absolutely fine if you are young and athletic and pliable ... but not if you have had a hip replacement, which I happen to have had. I hadn't extended my titanium-steel bits quite so forcibly before and was suddenly aware that every muscle and ligament in my hip was screaming in protest. I was reluctant to attempt to stand up. I put my hands down on the wet varnish and lifted and turned myself until I was able to crawl to the door. I lay on the landing, massaging my shrieking hip and studying the backside-shaped mark, the hand impressions and the skids where my knees had chafed the wet sealant.

'Hi, Dad. How you doing? Having a break, huh? Oh, you've done the floor. I thought I could smell something ... There's a lot of, like, marks and dust and stuff on that paint. Did you know?'

I looked at Greg and counted to ten.

'Hello, Greg. I did know actually, yes. I slipped on the varnish and I've given my hip a bit of a jolt.'

'Oh no. Dad, are you going to be all right? You said you'd help me to do the brakes on my van today.'

'Er, yes. So I did. Well, we'll have to see.'

'Yeah. Okay. Take it easy, yeah? I'm going down to have some toast. I'm *starving*,' he said, as he disappeared downstairs.

Blixworth Common, where I had to drive to collect Phil who had been camping with the Scouts, was about twenty miles away. I studied the map, sitting in my study with my left leg stretched out, wondering how to get there without changing gear too many times. Sod's law dictated that the only route was cross-country, on C roads and in particular those with '*Gated road*' marked on the map.

I arrived just before three, having negotiated countless bends with the car grinding along in fourth gear, far too many gates across common land, and finally, a succession of cattle grids; those ones which Ladas, with their 'firm' suspension, excel on. It was not a comfortable ride. I pulled up amidst a sizeable gathering of cars, and an excited Phil ran up to the car.

'Hi, Pa. You're a bit late. Everyone else's dad arrived ages ago. They've all gone off to the trout farm.'

'Sounds great. Any chance of a cup of tea, or is the billy dry?'

'Er yes, but I think we ought to get going. I've got a map and everything. Dad . . . where's all your stuff?'

'What stuff, Phil?'

'Well, your sleeping bag and eating things and a rucksack and boots?'

'Sleeping bag? Eating things? Phil, *what are you talking about*?'

'The Sons' and Dads' Night, *Dad*! What did you think we were doing tonight?'

It took a moment to take on board the fact that I had totally and utterly forgotten about something that Mrs D had signed me up for about a year previously. It had eluded even my faintest consciousness that we, no *I*, was supposed to be camping for a night, having previously thrown myself into the rigours of a wide-game, preceded by going out and shooting and cooking our own supper . . . or something.

Phil leant on the car door and I did my best to swing my leg out. I was desperate not to let him down. This was what the American psycho-babble books all refer to as my opportunity for *quality time* with the lad.

'I could go home and get the gear, Phil. I mean it wouldn't take long. I could be back by...'

'Oh Dad! Everyone else has set off. We've got to go *now!*'

'Okay, let's go,' I said, in my best Clint Eastwood-camping-in-the-desert-with-son-voice. 'Sure we'll manage, Phil. No sweat.' I ruffled his hair. 'Hop in old thing. Got the map?'

'Dad; we're supposed to be *walking there*!'

'Walking?'

'Yes, look, it's here.' He pointed a very grubby finger at the map. 'See? We have to go up over this ridge, through the woods until we get to that place, where they say it's possible to wade across the river as long as you hang onto the rope the leaders have put up, then you scramble up the old quarry and when you get to the top you can see the way down through the fields to the trout lakes where we catch our supper and the minibus brings us back here where we cut enough wood for our fire and cook the trout and after that there's loads of games organised ... Dad? Are you all right?'

I have, in my time, been on quite a lot of expeditions, including those required by that most excellent scheme for young people, The Duke of Edinburgh's Award Scheme. I have humped fifty-pound packs across the Brecon Beacons, leapt out of aeroplanes above Somerset, tackled the peaks of Snowdonia and even survived for a week on worms, fungi and stolen eggs. What I have not done is scramble through woods, waded through fast-flowing rivers and scaled the sides of scree-covered disused quarries in my decorating slippers and a pair of varnish encrusted, holed and paint-spattered old trousers. Fortunately, I had kept a walking stick in the car for just such an eventuality ever since Mrs D and I went to the local Marks and Spencer super-store not long after my hip operation, a venture which puts twenty miles across Dartmoor

108

well and truly in the shade. Thus armed with stick, slippers and wallpapering T-shirt, not to mention an old paint scraper and a plumb line I found in my pocket, we arrived eventually at the trout farm.

I was totally wrecked by the time we staggered into the car park, and I collapsed on a wall, my leg throbbing with pain. A far-too-jolly Scout leader with a bristling moustache, which looked as though it had not been trimmed since he left the Army in the Fifties, strode up and grasped my hand.

'Wilkinson.'

'Dudgeon. How do you do?'

I looked him up and down. He was wearing a ridiculous pair of shorts, which only covered small portions of a pair of rather bandy legs, long socks with a knife handle protruding from one calf, and around his neck a scarf with one of those woggle-things which, I have to say, I gave up wearing when I was about ten years-old. He looked absurd. He looked me up and down.

'Always tell the lads to dress for the job,' he said quietly. 'Can't tackle the great outdoors dressed like a ... decorator.' He leant close and murmured, as if to prevent Phil hearing, 'Not up to it, old man? Eh? What? Don't be afraid to say if it's all too much for you. Can't all be as fit as I am. Fifty miles a week I always aim at. Anyway,' he said in a louder voice, 'report to the office and they'll fix you up with a couple of rods.'

We walked to the trout farm office, my still-wet trousers slapping against my soft-shoes. I thanked my lucky stars that we didn't have to go out and secure supper with a couple of rabbit snares. It took two minutes to catch a pair of decent trout. They were so used to jumping for food that they leapt onto our hooks as if competing to end their days in the pot.

'I never realised fishing was so easy,' Phil said. 'It's a complete doddle!'

He grimaced as I bludgeoned the two fish with the club provided by the farm.

'Right. Now let's get a cup of tea.'

It took about three and half minutes to drive back to camp by road because the particularly daunting, circuitous foot-route they had devised in order to inflict the maximum misery upon the ailing and infirm parents was nine-tenths of a circle with the road forming the final leg. When we arrived there was a huge black, iron kettle steaming over the fire, and we were soon gathered around drinking wonderful mugs of sweet tea.

'Drink up, Dad. That's my mug you've got there. I want some tea in a minute.'

'Have you forgotten your mug, Mr Dudgeon?' said an unspeakably strapping femaleish Akela, accusingly.

'He has,' Phil said, under his breath '. . . and his sleeping bag, his wash kit and his boots.'

He turned away as if to disown me.

All around, Dads sat in the latest no-sweat-fabric shorts, snazzy gaiters, bush hats and a stunning array of boots and all-terrain trainers.

'Like 'em?' one of the fathers enquired, seeing I was eyeing up his boots. 'The latest technology from *Snerker*.' He tapped the sole. 'Tough as shit, mate. Take a look.'

He unfastened his super-fast *Snerker* lace-up system, and levered off a very hot, sweaty boot which he passed to me.

'You're right,' I said, examining it, 'Just like ... shit. Thanks,' and I passed it back to him.

'Personally, I prefer the casual approach,' I continued airily. 'I don't believe you need all this clobber for a saunter in the English countryside. It's a rip-off. All unnecessary. Now, when I crossed the Brecons in January, living on my wits, well, that's a different matter. Then you need the works: helicopter surveillance, high altitude thermal gear, the whole lot, but, today, no. Nice sunny afternoon, good forecast ... no problem. I sleep under hedges in this weather. Get to grips with the countryside, commune with nature...'

'Dad,' Phil whispered, '*please* shut up. None of my mates will talk to me again if you carry on like that.'

'There's nothing wrong with sleeping under hedges, why, when Mum was training with the SAS she did it for weeks on end...'

Phil nudged me. 'It's not the hedges I'm worried about. It's your shoes. The bottom's falling off this one.' He tapped the bottom of my right moccasin. Sure enough, the sole was flapping on the ground. 'Can I have my mug now, please?'

I passed it to him and stood up. 'Right. Well, thanks for the tea, Akela. I'm off to have a nosey around ... find a place for the night, you know ... a spot for the old bivouac.' I kicked off my crumbling moccasins. 'Mother Nature's way, huh?' I nodded to a dad who was equipped from head to toe in clothes, compasses and Everest-expedition map pouches from the latest survival catalogues, then sauntered nonchalantly off into the clearing doing my best to avoid the worst patches of brambles and stinging nettles.

'Does your dad really sleep under hedges, Phil?' enquired a little voice as I walked out of earshot.

'Uh huh,' I heard Phil say. 'He does, but he's a softy. You should see my Mum.'

At about ten-thirty that night, an hour after the wide-game had finished and everyone was counted back into camp, I sat on a log near the flickering flames of the camp fire, chatting to a small group of Phil's chums, wishing that the inferno in the soles of my feet would abate.

'You have to use your wits to survive out of doors but, you know lads, you're surrounded by everything you need. Take this,' I said, drawing the old paint scraper out of my pocket and tapping it on my palm. 'With this, you can do anything. With a trusty blade and ... a length of good string,' I said, taking the plumb line from the other pocket, 'you can catch your food, build your bivvies ... the lot.'

Half-a-dozen admiring eyes looked at me in the firelight. Next to me, Phil's looked slightly less certain. A little later we all turned in.

'Goodnight, Dad. Are you sure you're going to be all right?' asked Phil, as he headed for his tent where his mates were waiting with bated breath to hear more tales of Mrs D and her escapades in some of the most inhospitable areas of the world.

'Of course I will,' I chuckled, heading for my bivouac. 'Don't worry yourself about me. Sleep well, old son,' I called softly, behind him.

'Sleep well Dad.'

It began raining at about one forty-five in the morning. At first, the neatly arranged pine branches, needles all sloping the same way to shed the rain as I remembered seeing in *Look and Learn*, did their job magnificently. Even so, it was still quite spooky, what with the undergrowth crackling as creatures made their nocturnal way through the woods and an owl shrieking to its mate overhead, but it was passable. I wrapped myself up, as best I could, in the small tarpaulin that usually covers the car windscreen in winter. The bracken under my head wouldn't stay flat and, once or twice, a sharp frond jabbing in my right ear disturbed me. I lay dozing under the stormy sky, listening to the gentle patter of rain, musing on how those little lads had looked on admiringly at Phil's dad as we sat around the fire. Then the drops of rain increased in size, and what began as an insignificant shower became a steady downpour, and the thudding on the tarpaulin echoed in my tiny shelter. By the time the streams of water were rushing along the side of the hedgerow my wrap had become an irrelevance. I was wet through.

Sleeping curled up in the back of a small car is not for the faint-hearted, nor is it in any way beneficial for those who have artificial hips; but I did doze and then awoke at first light. I had the distinct feeling that I had been incarcerated in a damp old fridge. I let myself quietly out of the car and crept across the deserted campsite. The sky had cleared and it promised to be another fine day. At the firewood cache I helped myself to some dry kindling and before long I was ensconced in front of a decent fire outside my bivouac. I was just balancing some logs against the fire when footsteps crunched on the undergrowth.

'Ah, Wilkinson,' I called. 'How are you my friend? Good night's sleep? Got a kettle and a few mugs to hand?'

When Phil emerged from his tent with a couple of chums, 'Wilkie' and I were enjoying a good natter over our second brew, and lighting our pipes.

'Hello, boys,' I said. 'Come and join us. It looks like we might have had a spot of rain in the night judging by the damp ground. Slept like a log myself. That's the great outdoors for you, eh, Wilkie?'

16

Needless to say, when I arrived home with Phil we were both tired and a certain sort of post-camp mildewy aroma pervaded the house until we changed and loaded our clothes into the washing machine. I saluted the passing of my trusty moccasins and lowered them reverently into the dustbin.

A few minutes later I furtively retrieved them, covered the bottoms in glue and left them under two heavy encyclopaedias. You never know, the soles may stick and the shoes might live to tell another tale. I don't approve of the throw-away mentality which seems to be rife these days. It is ecologically unsustainable. We do not have the global resources to discard items that have so much life left in them. I admired an elderly friend who recently reached inside his 'demob' sports jacket and produced his 1939 RAF-issue pig bristle toothbrush. It was still in daily use. Good for him, I say. In a similar vein, I am still using the same slippers that I bought from a car boot sale when Greg was four! Mrs Dudgeon has hinted more than once that she thinks I verge on being a little stingy. The last time she said it I had just spent *two hours* rebinding the blade of our potato peeler with best quality Danish shoe thread. It had given seventeen years of faithful service and is as good as ever again as a result of my efforts. Stingy indeed. I am a great believer in make and mend. 'Waste not, want not' my mother used to say.

I contemplated using the afternoon to plaster the little blemish above Greg's bed, but in the end I elected to have some time off and retired to the study to rest my leg and go through the mail. We keep a wire basket just inside the door and all the mail, other than personal correspondence, is deposited there. It was nearly brimming over mostly, I have to say, with unsolicited post. I do find myself wondering if every household in the country receives as much junk mail as we do. You will probably think me something of a pedant, and worse, one without enough to occupy him, but I once weighed our junk mail over a period of a week or two. The average daily delivery amounted to over 500g. This represents nearly two tonnes a year! Can it really be true that annually over fifty million tonnes of this unwanted rubbish drops onto British doormats? The environmental impact of manufacturing, printing, distributing and, finally, recycling such a huge amount of paper is quite unacceptable. It is not only arriving in the post. Newspapers, many magazines and, most surprisingly, environmental journals such as the RSPB's *Birds* also contain leaflets about three-piece suite covers, photo processing and various investments. I wrote to the RSPB and asked how they could, on the one hand, campaign for the protection of the environment to conserve wildlife, and on the other distribute this unwanted rubbish. To give them their due they wrote a very civilised reply, the gist of which was that junk mail earns them much needed revenue. Ha ha! Every man has his price! I did not renew my subscription. It's just not cricket. Principles are *principles*.

Having paid the electricity account, the coalman, Archie Brownlea and the garage, I opened the phone bill. I am glad I was sitting down at the time. The older children had only been home for four or five weeks and the phone bill had gone through the roof. It was in three figures again! What do they do with the phone, for goodness' sake? Bearing in mind that none of them can string together more than seven words without exhausting themselves, *and* they each have their own mobile phone, it beats me how they can run up bills for one-and-a-half-hour calls. If you could see them you would understand my amazement. If they wish to lie on the floor with the phone, grunting at one another like

Neanderthals, that's their business ... but for ninety minutes at a time?

While I was at my desk I responded to my publisher who had sent drafts of the cover of my book. I explained that owing to a substantial part of my house falling down and Mrs D being away (not to mention camping in an inhospitable part of East Anglia), I had not had sufficient time to evaluate their proposal. My first reaction to a half-naked woman draped across the front of a book about life as a schoolteacher was 'no'. Are they trying to get me struck off? Have they never heard of 'List 99'?

I was tempted to hurl all the polythene-wrapped catalogues straight into the recycling bin along with a fistful of leaflets which the Royal Mail now deliver for a small fee ... The Lonely Hearts Club Introduction Agency, and 'Paint your house in new *Silko* indestructible, guaranteed for a lifetime, plastic paint'. Can you imagine Worgleswipe's face? I must say, it was jolly tempting.

I started tearing envelopes open and have to admit that I became totally absorbed in the world of mail order – not that I had the slightest intention of buying such rubbish. Do you know, it is now possible to buy a tiny electric razor which you poke in your ears and your nose (presumably in that sequence) in order to trim unwanted hair? Seriously. There was one in the catalogue: '*Rid yourself of unsightly body hair in seconds*'. At the touch of a button you can plunge this disgusting little thing up your nose and 'zzzipp' ... no more nose hair. What for? I am rather partial to my nose hair. Don't they understand, that it's *not unwanted* ... that Mother Nature put it up there for a reason? That if you get rid of it you'll probably have every insect for miles about setting up camp in your sinuses, or wallowing around in your earwax? I mentioned this little gadget to Mrs D on her return and she said it sounded like a very good idea. She then asked me if I had looked up my own nose recently. How exactly, I enquired, am I supposed to look up *my own* nose?

Once I began on the catalogues, I couldn't put them down; it became something of an obsession to find the most imbecilic invention. They should award an annual prize for it, along with the Prince of Wales' coveted Design Awards. A strong contender would be the palm-held tabletop battery powered vacuum cleaner designed to rid the table of crumbs. It measures a few centimetres in diameter, and I calculated that the average table would require several dozen sweeps with this gadget. Assuming that it has to be moved quite slowly, I reckon that the chore would be about equivalent to cutting the lawn! Imagine that three times a day with our brood. I would spend most of my time picking bits of baked bean and globby cheese out of the nozzle. Does it occur to these people that the time-honoured damp duster is slightly more efficient? I have a much better idea: combine the nose shaver jobby with the table vacuum and ever after there would be no need to pick one's nose. If they ever decide to manufacture it I would like them to remember that it was *my idea*. I will certainly buy one for Stevie who seems to have had a bit of a problem in that direction ever since he was a small boy.

Who thinks of these things? It is mind-bending to realise that teams of designers presumably sit and think of all those little household chores that are so easily accomplished every day, and then dream up complicated, environmentally unacceptable gadgets for achieving the same end. They have them manufactured in Taiwan and shipped over here for our gullible public to buy. Everything you never wanted and more! No wonder our balance of payments is what it is. It's not the imports of cars, technology and washing machines that the Chancellor needs to be worrying about, it's those message recording key-fobs and pens, speaking weather stations, Alpine air-fresheners and cigarette lighters with dazzling diode light-shows that are the country's downfall. The latter, believe it or not, is billed as a *'wonderful conversation-opener'*. What?! I have to say that the day I need to rely on a sparkling display of flickering lights in my lighter to start a conversation with a friend will be the day that I ask Mrs D to take me out in the woods and shoot me. I just know I won't wish to live any more.

One of my favourites is the alarm clock that is equipped with a large trumpet on the top. At six forty-five in the morning you can be roused from your slumbers by a Yorkshire brass band playing 'Seventy-six trombones' or some other invigorating little number. Can you imagine that? Why not pour a little turps in your morning cuppa just to round off the experience? But wait, worse is to come. Having been assaulted by the Mardlington Mills Brass Band, you can then press a button to activate the snooze alarm which is a female voice repeatedly calling *'Good morning! Have a nice day!'* I cannot wait. As my daughter says when an eloquent, poetic turn of phrase descends on her, 'I'd rather drink my own...'

Waking people and telling the time provides these retro-designers with untold opportunities for excelling themselves. You can now buy a laser clock that projects the time onto the ceiling. Now, correct me if I am wrong, but it seems that the only time this will be effective is in the dark ... when most people are asleep. Only insomniacs can really benefit from this gadget. People with sensible sleep patterns will doubtless suffer immense frustration and have to reschedule their lives in order to get their money's worth from it. If you sleep as soundly as I do you will probably *never* see it working.

For the man who likes precision, there is a wristwatch accurate to *one second in a million years*. How, I wonder do they substantiate that? Time itself is not *that* accurate, but, more significantly, of what use is it to someone who commutes by train or car? During such adventures, accuracy to the nearest *hour* would be more appropriate and infinitely less frustrating.

There is an insidious side to this plethora of commodities: it is the notion that somehow you will not be complete, or beautiful enough, or the right shape, or sufficiently engaging, or *fast enough* without these gadgets. The truth is, these things do not save time *or* energy. They consume energy ... endless amounts of it both in manufacture and use. That little phrase, *'batteries not provided'* tells a story. Anyone who has ever made the mistake of buying battery-operated toys for the children (or themselves) at

118

Christmas, will know from bitter experience that one either spends the whole of the Christmas holiday leaping up and down putting batteries of batteries into chargers or one fails to buy adequate supplies of the damned things and has the children moaning throughout because the shops are closed. It is a nightmare which, without doubt, was at its worst with the invention of the hand-held electronic games which children would spirit away at bedtime and compulsively play with under the bedclothes, thereby mysteriously exhausting themselves. Where did most of these ideas come from? Japan. Say no more.

The advent of electronic 'babies', 'dinosaurs' and 'puppies' was hailed by a torrent of publicity. The media depicted long queues of parents camping outside toy stores to acquire the first imports. We were fortunate. The craze nearly passed us by because Melanie was more or less too old to be interested, or so I thought. We ended up with no less than *seventeen* of these creatures around the house and the *whole family* became involved with their 'upbringing' and 'survival'. For those of you who are fortunate enough not to have encountered them, I should explain briefly that they are nothing more than a bit of dastardly micro-chippery and a tiny screen in a plastic case the size of a cotton reel. The chip is programmed to imitate a growing organism which needs feeding, changing, tucking into bed, waking, educating, amusing and ideally *treading on* as soon as one can inadvertently contrive to do so whilst hoovering. We reached the stage where children would leap up from the table at the sound of the buzzer, and then be told to sit down again, prompting shrieks of 'Oh, *how* can you be so cruel? The Baby, he'll die if I don't feed him/read to him/change him/amuse him', etc. There were times when I couldn't think of anything more appropriate for the little tyke than for it to drown slowly in its own wee, whilst suffering terribly from indigestion and 'Famous Five' withdrawal symptoms. If you don't like the sound of that, I have to say you are a prime candidate for becoming a right sucker when the next rash of these ghastly things comes around. Take my advice: tread on them; feed them to the dog; reverse their polarity in the dead of night; anything, but *don't* give them houseroom. They will take over your home and *possess* your children.

Thinking of feeding things to dogs, I have had a revolutionary idea for a new burglar deterrent. It just came to me, in one of those fine moments when the old brain exercises itself laterally. I was imagining what would happen if Fido *ate* one of those detestable musical greetings cards. He had been amused by one that Stevie was writing to a friend, and the stupid boy put it on the floor for the dog to play with. Not surprisingly, Fido pounced on it and, in three seconds, shredded it. Suppose, I thought, just suppose he swallowed it. Would the dog sing '*Happy Birthday*' every time he stretched and yawned? Then the old grey cells raced ahead and I realised that if you were to feed Fido with a pre-recorded chip, one with a particularly menacing message, it would be possible to have a guard dog that *shouted* at would-be thieves as soon as he jumped up! Imagine their surprise when Fido came bounding round the corner and a deep tenor voice hollered, 'Okay you bastards! Which one of you wants your nads torn off first, then?' Spectacular! I will write to the mail order company and suggest it, along with Stevie's bogie-seeking vacuum cleaner.

Anyway, having immersed myself in mail order catalogues, I picked up the phone and ordered the following Christmas presents thereby saving myself a huge amount of legwork, not to mention petrol: Greg will receive an electronic bug-repelling device to be strategically placed about halfway between his bed and his laundry pile; and Stevie, on account of the longevity of his daily enthronements on the WC, will receive an FM/AM radio toilet roll holder with built-in snooze alarm just in case he dozes off and gets into difficulties.

I am not sure about the destinations of the following. I just became caught up in the whole business and it is *so* easy to order with a credit card; I will sort out who gets what later. The 'Bathroom Stationery Store' is a must because I have never heard of such a ridiculously coy euphemism for a pile of six toilet rolls.

120

A jar of 'super, amazing, effective spot-remover' (not the adolescent zit kind) 'as developed by the American Space Agency' for removing ... spots. I wouldn't have thought they had much time for carpet and upholstery cleaning on the way to the moon, but there you go. I decided to buy it because I had never read so many superlatives gathered together in a single paragraph about a jar of soap. It may well, if I am desperate, turn out to be quite a conversation piece, and it is on its way to Angelica who is the messiest person I have ever met.

Mrs Dudgeon is likely to receive a 'staggeringly meticulous, perfect, stunning Colt Forty-Five Replica Hand Gun' which doubles up as a compact make-up kit or a Virtual Reality Golf Game (batteries not included) depending on which way 'the easy-to-use switch' is operated. I thought this somehow reflected many aspects of my amazingly versatile (superbly constructed), authentic wife.

One of the children will definitely receive the 'Pan-Monster', an ugly little gremlin-like thing whose front feet one attaches to the underside of the loo lid with rubber suckers so that it rears up, if you will excuse the pun, as the seat is lifted. I cannot wait to see what sort of state it gets into when the lid is closed again.

The dog will receive a towel with 'Dirty Paws' emblazoned across it so that he might learn to wipe his own feet. I decided to have it *personalised* for only £4.99 so that nobody will think it is a tea cloth and wipe the coffee mugs with Fido's towel again.

For myself, not being one for gismos, I spotted a new pair of 'super comfortable' moccasins with tough-as-shit-elasto-propenane sure-tread soles which I can wear at camp when Ed has his Sons' and Dads' Night.

Finally, two of the children, probably Mel and Ed, will each receive solar battery chargers, and copies of *Ecologically Sustainable Technological Solutions for the Twenty First Century and Beyond* which, incidentally, did not come from a mail order catalogue. I just hope it is sunny on Christmas Day.

121

17

One of the most exasperating things about plumbing jobs is that at least ninety-nine per cent of the time they work, which leaves an unpredictable one per cent which can have the calmest blow-lamp wielder fit to commit murder. I was lying under the basin on the new, dry varnished floor in the bathroom. Judicious application of a little sealant to the impressions caused by my trousers, knees and hands had obliterated all but a few traces of my acrobatics. I watched the connection beneath the cold tap and concentrated, a sink spanner in my hand, as I willed the tiniest of seepages to stop. Nothing. I crawled out.

Drip!

Was that a drip, or my imagination?

I crawled beneath the basin again, this time wiping the joint with a tissue. It *was* damp. I tried to tighten the nut, but it was solid. Wait then. Was that a bead of moisture or a trick of the light?

A trick of the light.

Drip!

'Bugger!'

There is no doubt about it – it is far more satisfying to cure a proper leak than to drain a system for a less-than-piddling drip. At least with a gushing blast of water one is not left debating whether or not it is worth doing. Mrs D and I once lived in a house where the central heating seemed to be leaking and, eventually, having hammered her way through the concrete floors, a pastime she seemed to relish, we found the leak: two pipes which had never been soldered and had been cheerfully gurgling hot water under the house since it was built. It was hugely satisfying, not only because it cut our fuel bills by about eighty per cent, but because it also explained why a particular strip of the garden flourished in winter like the vegetation in a tropical glasshouse at Kew Gardens.

Up in the loft, I closed the stopcock and headed back for the stepladder, stepping gingerly across the joists, remembering the time I had once dropped a hammer with disastrous results. At the time, we lived in a row of old cottages which had a communal loft with only one access hatch that was from our house. I had been working in the attic, and the dear old lady next door, who was actually very unlikely to have scaled a ladder as she was quite sedentary with arthritis, asked me if she could have her own loft hatch. I agreed that she should have one, and offered to make it for her. The ceilings in the cottages were old and somewhat fragile owing to nail fatigue, but I was careful and at the end of a day's work a new frame and loft lid were in place, neatly plastered, awaiting a coat of paint. How pleased she will be, I thought to myself, when she comes up to her bedroom and sees the new construction all achieved with no fuss or mess. I gathered my tools together and stepped across the joists but, as I did so, a large hammer slipped from my grasp and, while I lunged at it, somewhat fearful of slipping and putting my foot through the ceiling, it did a couple of somersaults and I missed it. Rather than catching it, my bungled attempt to grasp the handle propelled it at high speed . . . straight through the floor. Not satisfied with making a hammer-sized hole, the weighty tool crashed through the lath and plaster, dislodging a sizeable piece of the ceiling. This would not have been so bad had there not been several hundred years of filth in the loft, and my neighbour's pristine white lace counterpane on her bed just below. Needless to say, I had just gathered up a huge dustsheet which until minutes before had covered the entire bedroom.

When I peered through the hole, cursing the day I had offered to help her out, I gasped in astonishment at the devastation below. Had I taken a sizeable sack of soot, bird dung and garden compost and shaken it vigorously all over the bedroom there could not have been more mess. It was everywhere: bed, dressing table, wardrobe and floor were covered in a thick film of dark-grey, gritty dust, seeds, leaves, birds' nest material and plaster. The gilt-framed photo of her late husband in Army uniform stared accusingly back at me from a dusty chest of drawers. I suppose I could, and should, have knocked on her front door and said, quite straightforwardly, 'Sorry, Mrs Pinkleton, but I've had a little accident and knocked your bedroom ceiling down' ... but I didn't. By a laborious process of lowering Hoover, rubbish sacks, buckets of hot soapy water, plasterboard and tools through her new loft hatch, I managed to clear up and replaster the ceiling before she went to bed that night. Never has anyone trodden a more careful retreat across an attic floor than I did that night. You live and learn.

Determined to fix the drip beneath the new bathroom tap, I headed for the steps and, as I stood on the top rung, I noticed a box with photograph albums protruding and pulled it towards me for closer inspection. Old pictures of a childhood Duncan Dudgeon looked back at me from the faded pages and, not having set eyes on them for years, I carried them downstairs for an evening's browsing.

The annoying drip was soon cured and, having restored the water supply, run all the taps and flushed the loo, I locked the door and sat on the throne for the first ever khazi ceremony. It is difficult to describe the immense pleasure to be derived from fitting one's own bathroom, and having one's first bath, the first shave, and the first ... crap. It may be a simple pleasure, and one that if examined on a world scale of indulgences may be questionable, certainly not ranking alongside building one's own yacht and cruising the Greek Islands for example, but it was enough for me. I was in raptures. It was an experience that would have been greatly improved by furnishing the room with the all-important 'Bathroom Stationery Store' which, at a certain point in the proceedings, became apparent as a significant omission. Fortunately, no one was about as I shuffled, trousers round my ankles, to the other bathroom in order to remedy the situation.

All that was then required was the work of a day or two to wallpaper and finish the paintwork. Mrs Dudgeon would be thrilled. That evening, I sat in my favourite armchair with the three older children out somewhere (probably enlivening the 'Pig and Whistle'), while Phil was upstairs reading his new fishing book. I browsed photo albums, smiling at snaps from the fifties depicting a little boy in school cap and short trousers, with a satchel hanging from his shoulder. I had never realised that my mother must have assembled all the mementos of my childhood, sealed them in a bag and placed them in the bottom of the box. I stared at the contents of the unwrapped package that lay on my lap. There were letters and cards, cuttings and school reports, certificates and medals; a veritable Aladdin's Cave of nostalgia.

On the top of the pile was a card, about me, not from me:

John and Deirdre Dudgeon are delighted to announce
the arrival of
Duncan Peregrine Dudgeon
on 16th June
Weight 6lbs 12oz
Mother and baby doing well

I've always thought the name Peregrine had a certain something about it. It brings to mind a bird of prey soaring effortlessly on the air currents above Snowdonia ... free-living, free-thinking, free-wheeling ... free. Most people who know me well will, of course, tell you that that this is fundamentally me. It was what you might call ... a well-chosen name. I do of course have a slightly irascible side to me ... on occasions ... when provoked, as Mrs D will tell you, but generally I am level, generous and extremely tolerant. Well ... reasonably tolerant. On second thoughts, perhaps I am not at all tolerant. I don't know. Who cares? Perhaps the Parcel Force man was right: perhaps I am a 'miserable old basket'.

Continuing through the pile, I found a gaudy display of scribbles, possibly some sort of flower with '*Happy Mothers Day, Love Duncan*' which clearly had been laboriously written over someone else's dots.) Then, Fathers' Day, probably 1958:

> *Dere Daddy Happy Fatters Day*
> *Here is some pip cleaners for your pip*
> *Love Duncan XXXXXXXX*
> *PS I love you very mush*

As Angelica would say, 'Sweeeet'.

That neat homemade card appeared to have been constructed with a Cornflakes packet. I noted that Mr Kellogg was at that time giving away 'Free Welsh Guards'. That brought the memories flooding back, I can tell you. Then there was a gap before I found a postcard from Southwold (Boys' Brigade Camp 1964):

> *Dear Mummy and Daddy,*
> *Having a fab time here. The food is grate. John and the other officers are really funny. The journey up in the lorry was bumpy but we got up here all right. The weather has been good. The camp is right beside a golf course. I got hit on the head with a golf ball and knocked out. Don't worry. Simon French kept asking me what my name was when I woke up and then asked me if I knew who he was! See you soon. Love Duncan*

And then a year later, a postcard from Reculver Towers:

> *Dear Mother and Father,*
> *The camp is great. We went to see 'Help' in Herne Bay. The weather has been a mixture. I'm afraid I have broken my arm. I went to Canterbury Hospital where there was a big fat farmer in the bed next to me and the nurse was picking shotgun pellets out of his bottom. I'm all right though. I did it*

126

watching football. See you on Saturday. It doesn't hurt. My
arm is in plaster.
Love Duncan

Watching football? 1966 can't have been a good year either, because in the New Year of 1967 I wrote the following to my aunt. Quite why mother kept it is not clear:

Dear Auntie,
Thank you for the book token you sent me for Christmas. It
was very kind of you. I have done lots of reading since I fell
out of the tree. I am feeling much better now. I seem to have
spent all the year going to hospitals and dentists. My teeth
are growing again after they fixed them all in and my nose
has only got a small bump where I broke it. The dentist says I
can have false teeth like you but mine will be fixed in. The
dentist was pleased when he unwired my jaw and Mummy
cried. Daddy says I must learn to tie a rope properly before I
swing upside down on it. My arm comes out of plaster on
Friday. My fifth broken arm!
Lots of love Duncan

Among the school reports, which dealt with the lack of progress owing to so much time off school on account of '*the accident*' was a little gem from the guitar teacher:

Duncan Dudgeon, 4Z Classical Guitar
Duncan, having spent nearly two terms in plaster (again),
was, once more, not able to progress his lessons on the
classical guitar.
Fernando del Plonco

Which seems an odd sort of thing to write to parents who had just spent weeks feeding their son with a teaspoon through his wired jaw. I am sure they needed to be told that I hadn't spent much time practising my fugues.

The back door crashed open and four youngsters came into the room, filling it with their chatter and laughter and rather dispelling my reverie.

'Hey, Dad. What's this then? A trip down memory lane?'

I closed the package.

'Oh come on. Let's have a look. Promise we won't laugh.'

I passed them the photo album.

'Hahaha hahahahahahaha! Look at that. Sweeeet! Dad we're going to town to get a few pizzas. Is that okay?'

'Absolutely. Please yourselves how you spend your evening.'

'You won't be lonely, will you?'

'Erhm, no. I don't think so. Thank you for asking.'

'Um, Dad . . . Can you lend us some money? We're all a bit, like, skint.'

I passed Greg a five-pound note.

'Ah,' he said looking at it. 'Like, very skint, Dad. I mean, like paupers.'

I passed Greg another fiver.

'Wicked! Cheers, Dad. Bye now.'

'Bye Dad. See you later.'

'Bye Dad. Don't go ringing that Brenda woman while we're out . . .'

'Goodbye, Mr Dudgeon.'

'Oh, goodbye. So nice to have met you.'

Who the hell was that?

18

'Mr Dudgeon?'

'It is.'

'Eric Wigglesworth here. The conservation officer from Tolworth RDC.'

Eric! Eric ... no wonder ... with a name like that.

'Yes, Mr Wigglesworth. What can I do for you?'

'I was wondering how you were getting on with your insurance company, and whether you needed the name of a good firm of conservationist builders.'

'I'm not getting on with my insurance company is the most apt way I can think of to describe my present relationship with *Serendipity Insurance Limited*, and an equally succinct answer to your second question is *no, thank you*. It's very thoughtful of you to offer.'

There was a silence.

'Is there anything else, *Eric*, or is it possible to return to my wallpapering? I happen to be standing here with seven feet, ten inches of wet wallpaper over my arm and it is rapidly taking on the texture of a rather soggy railway egg sandwich. But don't let that worry you if you want to have a little chat.'

'Mr Dudgeon, you will remove that rendering and replace it with a different mix based on the authentic composition, won't you?'

'No, Mr Wigglesworth. I have no intention of doing anything further.'

'Mr Dudgeon, I do hope you appreciate that I am, if necessary, able to raise an official order requiring you to complete the work to a satisfactory standard. That is the nature of the listed status of your house.'

'That, Mr Worgleswipe, will not be necessary. The work is complete.'

'Oh. I thought you said you . . .'

'I know what I said. You asked me if I *will* be removing the rendering and I said I would not. It is complete. Done. Finished. Nothing more to be said about it.'

'In which case, Mr Dudgeon, if you don't object, I would like to come and make sure all is well.'

'You may. Whenever you choose. The wall is awaiting your *inspection*. Good day, *Eric.*'

I returned to the bathroom carrying the over-pliable piece of wallpaper, thinking as I did so of the numerous occasions over the years when I have had dust-ups with surveyors and their ilk. What was it about them? Do they coach them in the skills of being thoroughly objectionable and bloody-minded as a requirement of their basic training? I cannot understand it. No matter how reasonable and level I am with them, they are always so damned disagreeable.

Mrs Dudgeon and I once found a house in the country that we very much wanted to purchase. It wasn't so much 'roses round the door' as 'crab-processing works next-door'. We felt that the small factory could have been something of a problem on a hot summer's day, but the advantages of the property, in terms of spacious accommodation for a growing brood, outweighed the possibility of noxious vapours issuing from the neighbouring cottage industry. Had 'Riddleton's Crab and Shell Fish Wholesalers' not been next door, the value of the house would almost certainly have been out of our reach. It was a question of 'smells and adequate space' or 'fresh air and cramped, irritable youngsters'. The choice was straightforward. Give me smells every time.

The estate agents' details told of the house's 'immense charm', its 'quaint features', which happened to include its own well beneath the kitchen floor, and 'a remarkable' set of outbuildings, loose boxes and other useful spaces which dated back to its days as a farmhouse. The whole sat on the edge of the 'famous and pleasant green'. The village, according to the blurb supplied by estate agents, Poxier, Poxier and Poxier (pronounced *Pox-ee-ay*, I'm told), was an 'up-and-coming corner of the county; a rural idyll, well supplied with buses, schools, shops, and possessing a strong social character' etc. etc. It sounded wonderful. This, of course, was in the days before the estate agents' pens were brought to heel, whereafter they were required to call woodworm woodworm instead of an 'abundance of local wildlife'. It was, in short, the most effusive, glowing description of a house one could possibly hope to read. Features such as the late-eighteenth century oriel window on the front elevation were described with gushing verbosity: 'a remarkable asset, typical of the house's unique wealth of architectural heritage, reflecting its fascinating and unspoilt period charm'. We imagined the bank manager tripping over himself in his anxiety to forward us thousands and thousands of pounds of mortgage advance.

A few weeks later we commissioned a surveyor's report, which unbeknown to us was duly prepared by one of the Poxier family members, a brother-in-law I believe, by the name of Nuggett, who, it transpired, *was also a director of the estate agency.* When the report arrived with its attached invoice for over two hundred pounds, Mrs D and I pored over it with bated breath. We expected to encounter the usual fatuous *caveats* ('I was unable to inspect the inside of the lightbulbs and am therefore unable to vouch for their soundness' sort of thing), but from the moment we began to read we questioned whether the man had surveyed the right house!

This run-down and uncared-for property on the edge of a village which has a questionable reputation as a result of housing many London overspill families will require considerable sums to be invested to bring its dilapidated structures back into good repair. The oriel window on the

131

south elevation has suffered from considerable water ingress and is beyond conservation and repair. Many similar decaying features should only be viewed as liabilities in terms of the specialist work needed to restore them ... the well, situated inconveniently in the kitchen, has not been tested and its water should not be assumed to be potable; connection to the mains water supply will almost certainly be necessary, again at some cost to the owner ... the village school is due to close ... the bus service is likely to be withdrawn or reduced ... the unattractive industrial unit next door is likely to expand considerably if permission is granted ... and the sun which has traditionally shone in the south may move, thereby throwing the house into deep shadows which will further exacerbate the mildew and dampness...'

And so it continued in that excessively gloomy vein for page after expensive page.

Needless to say, our bank manager did not don his bicycle clips, leap on his Raleigh and pedal furiously to our house bringing the mortgage forms with him tucked beneath his arm. On the contrary, the bank offered such a paltry sum, and required so many undertakings to complete 'urgent structural works' that we were unable to proceed, and the house was duly sold to another buyer.

Weeks later, we happened to make the discovery about the firm's somewhat confused professional loyalties when I was examining the small print at the foot of their headed notepaper. There, among the list of directors of Poxier, Poxier and Poxier, was our surveyor man: I.M.A. Nuggett. I wrote to one of the professional associations which purports to oversee the work of its members, expecting them to, at the very least, hang, draw and quarter Nuggett on the village green. Their grudging reply was a protective litany of phrases such as: 'whilst we can understand that the two descriptions of the property concerned do seem to be at some variance, and we accept that under these circumstances there does exist the potential for there to be some confusion of interests, we do not conclude that...'

A few days later, all hell was let loose when we visited Dumpton-on-the-Hillock, or wherever the property was, (we assumed that it had not, by then, sagged and collapsed into a mouldering heap of dry rot infested ex-architectural heritage) and then drove into the local market town. We visited the offices of Poxier, Poxier and Poxier and confronted them with the disturbing evidence of their ethical misconduct. Mr Poxier Senior peered at us over his thick-lensed spectacles, and his piggy little eyes watered as Mrs Dudgeon leant menacingly across his desk and explained to him in magnificent detail what she was planning to do to him. Nervously, he promised to investigate our allegations as soon as he could.

'How *soon* is soon?' asked Mrs D, toying with his letter opener.

'Oh, I'm sure we will be able to give the matter our most urgent attention in the next few days...'

Mrs Dudgeon inched closer and slowly shook her head. 'Today...' she mouthed at him across the desk, as she flicked his tie with the paper knife. '... Today.'

Setting up our best picnic table in their reception area and unpacking our flasks and sandwiches did cause them to become a trifle agitated. Thus ensconced, we patiently awaited the outcome of a meeting of Mr Poxier, Mr Poxier, Mr Poxier and their brother-in-law, Mr Nuggett, who was rapidly recalled from his surveying work in the town. Mr P Senior eventually emerged through the frosted glass door of the inner sanctum, sat down at his desk and delicately mopped his brow with his handkerchief.

'We have met,' he said, eyeing the picnic table and chairs, now joined by the ex-Army sleeping bags I had brought from the car as the afternoon wore on. 'We have come to the conclusion that the least we can do under the circumstances is to er ... refund the full cost of the survey and make some small recompense for the disappointment you have endured.' In his shaking hand, he fingered a cheque for three hundred pounds. 'And furthermore, should you wish to avail yourself of our services in the future, we will be more than willing to make special provision for the most advantageous rates to be applied to your account.'

I wouldn't have availed myself of the firm's services again if the obsequious little fat-boy had promised to come out on the pavement in the market square complete with a pig's bladder and dance a jig.

Several years later, quite by chance, we met some people who made mention of a man called Nuggett. 'Nuggett?' said Mrs D, catching my eye. 'A surveyor? I think we met him once.'

'It could well be the same one,' said our acquaintance. 'He lives in a delightful old farmhouse on the village green at ... now let me see ... where is it now? Dumpton-on-the-Hillock, I think. It has the most wonderful oriel window...'

I glanced out of the window at the darkening sky with its imminent threat of rain, just as they had forecast for several days. Recalling the vivid memory of Messrs Poxier, Poxier, Poxier and Nuggett, I slapped my wallpaper brush into the paste bucket with renewed vigour and generously applied it to the last piece of paper, the one which was to be fitted behind the cistern. Having tackled a number of jobs behind lavatories, I have now come to the firm conclusion that a) the shape of the average pan and cistern were not designed with maintenance or the human frame in mind, and b) despite being able to develop the high technology to send men to the depths of the oceans in nuclear submarines, we are still unable to construct a viable lavatory seat hinge. They always work loose and break, presenting the owner with a repair task with which only the most able contortionist can cope.

Wallpapering in this particular area is nothing short of a nightmare and I began to wish that I had decorated the wall before any of the plumbing had been fixed in place. It seems that no matter how one measures and snips, it is impossible to get one length of paper to begin at the ceiling, pass beside and underneath the cistern and then go around the soil pipe. It *always* rips. By the time one has made many repeated attempts to adjust the paper, it is either so soggy and stretched that it tears at the crucial moment, or it is bone dry and one is left prostrate across the toilet seat whilst desperately scrabbling behind one's back to locate the paste brush. It was as I was fastidiously trimming a circle for the soil pipe that a great roll of thunder clapped overhead and I heard the first heavy drops of rain on the roof.

I had just straightened my aching back, washed the glue from my hands, face, elbows, trousers, the cistern, the lavatory pan and the floor, when Phil called up the stairs.

'Dad!'

'Yes, Phil.'

'There's a lot of water outside the front door, Dad.'

'There will be, old chap. It's raining hard.'

'No. I mean, like, lots. Like a flood.'

Knowing the youngster's endless capacity constantly to make the most outrageous and preposterous exaggerations, I picked up the bucket and brush and sauntered downstairs. Phil was standing calmly by the front door watching as a veritable *tidal wave* of water torrented down the drive, foamed around the inadequate domestic drain and threatened to pour over the front door step and into the house.

'Why didn't you tell me?' I roared above the storm, horrified as yet more crashes of thunder boomed overhead and the pelting rain seemed to renew its efforts to wash *Cromwell's Retreat* away.

'I did, Dad. I said, *a flood.*'

'That's not a flood ... that's an ... an inundation ... it's like the end of the world ... it looks like a job for the Fire Brigade.'

Phil's eyes lit up. 'The Fire Brigade! *Wicked!*'

19

We tried everything to prevent the floodwater entering the house, including wading around knee-deep in water trying to dig drainage channels. As the house is situated in a natural hollow in the side of a hill, we might just as well have been trying to redirect the Thames. As a last resort, Phil and I packed bundles of waste newspaper against the front door.

Stevie appeared at one point and then disappeared, only to reappear in his wet suit. I think that boy may have a problem. The other problem, an equally wet one, had never occurred until the Highways Department, in their very great wisdom, had ordered the pot-holed lane to be resurfaced. This raised the level of the road sufficiently to shoot all the surface water straight down the steep slope of our drive. The old boy who did the work pointed out the folly of the alterations but was powerless to act contrary to the specifications of his work order.

'Like water off a duck's back,' he reported, having questioned it with 'them desk boys at the council'.

Our stacks of soggy newspaper stuffed with plastic carrier bags were all that stood between the water and our ground floor undergoing a dramatic conversion to an aqua-theme park, when sirens and flashing blue lights put in an appearance. The vehicle scrunched to a halt outside with such force that another wave shot over the threshold and came rocketing down our drive. A considerable number of feet could be heard jumping down and running around, doors banged, shutters rolled up and firemen came jogging down the drive unrolling a hose. A white-helmeted officer waded through the water to the door.

'Where's your water got to, mate?' he asked, and I showed him how our improvised defences were just about keeping the water at bay. He wiped the torrential rain from his brow. 'I'm afraid I'll have to put you down the list; you'll have to cope until we can get back to you. There's folk with two feet of water in their front rooms waiting for a pump out. Sorry, chum. I suggest you try Highways.'

With that, the firemen rolled up their hose, there was the sound of a considerable number of feet rushing around, rolling shutters and banging doors, and their departure signalled another wave of water down the drive.

'Hello. Is that the Highways' twenty-four-hour emergency service?'

'It is. Gavin speaking. How can I help you?'

'We have a flood, and the Fire Brigade have suggested I contact you.'

'Right, sir. Just let me take a few details, and we'll get a team out to you. Which road is flooding?'

'It's not. That's the point. There's no water in the road. It's all in our drive.'

'In your drive?'

'In my drive.'

'Do you mean it's not a flooded highway?'

'Strictly, no. The water was in the road, but now it has moved. Now it's in my drive.'

'I'm sorry, sir. We aren't authorised to send anybody unless the flooding is on the highway.'

'Look, wait. You don't seem to understand. The water is pouring in off *your* blinking highway and gushing straight into *my* private property. It's about to flood my house!'

'I understand your predicament, sir, but once the water is no longer situated on the highway there is nothing we can do.'

'But it's because of the level of *your highway*. You have a duty to come and do something. It is *your water.*'

'No. That's the point. I'm afraid it's not.'

'It's not what?'

'It's not our water.'

'What do you mean, *it's not your water*? If it's not your water, *who*, pray tell, does it belong to?'

'Water.'

'Who?!'

'Water. The Water Authority. Strictly speaking, the water is theirs. The highway is ours, but the water *on it* is theirs.'

'Sunshine, you have got to be joking,' I said, wondering which imbecilic department had dreamed up these crass regulations. 'Look,' I implored, plumbing the depths of my being for renewed patience, 'the water is coming off the road, across the pavement, and down our drive...'

'You mean there's a pavement?'

'Yes, sort of ... a small one. Why?'

'You want the District Council.'

'I beg your pardon?'

'The District council does pavements. You want the District Council.'

'Listen Shane ... Wayne!'

'Gavin...'

'Gavin. Listen to me very carefully,' I hissed. 'What I really *want* is some help, and frankly, I don't care if the Serengeti National Park turn up with an elephant, as long as it's a bloody thirsty one...'

'The District Council are responsible for the pavement,' he said flatly. 'The water left our jurisdiction and passed to the Council's when it crossed the pavement. I should try Water, if the Council won't help you.'

I put the phone down and counted to ten while I peered out of the window only to see Greg pushing Stevie across the drive on a surfboard.

'Greg!' I shouted. 'If you can't do anything more useful than that, make a blinking cup of tea.'

I dialled the District Council. I went straight into overdrive through gritted teeth. The time for pleasantries was over.

'Listen carefully, because any minute now I might well be washed away and I won't be able to repeat this. I have a flooded *pavement...*'

I gave my details and hung up. Then I dialled the Water Authority number. It seemed to me that a regional organisation would have more emergency resources at its disposal than the local council could have.

'Please hold the line, all our emergency operators are engaged at the moment. We will answer your...'

I put the phone down.

'Dad,' called Greg from the kitchen. 'Come and look at this.'

In the kitchen Greg appeared to be staring at the draining board. 'What is it?'

He nodded towards the sink. 'Look.'

I stared at the sink, unable to comprehend what he was referring to. Perhaps he had had a moment's mental aberration and cleaned it.

'Greg. *Please,* be fair to me,' I begged him. 'I'm not at my best, I'll admit that, but I've spent goodness knows how much on your education. Do you think you could just explain *what* I am supposed to be looking at!'

He shrugged. 'Water's off.'

'What!'

'Can't make the tea; there's no water.'

'No *water*! *I don't believe it.*'

I was beginning to think that I might suddenly be overcome with uncontrollable hysteria. I spun the top of the tap. He was right. A meagre drip appeared, hung indecisively from the tap, and then plopped into the sink.

I dialled the number. It rang. Wonders would never cease.

'Water Emergency Service. Tracy speaking. How may I help you?'

Tracy?

'Hello Tracy. I do hope you can help. I have a problem. Actually, I have *two* problems. I have a lot of water outside my front door. My flood ... no, *your* flood, is about to come into *my* house. It's run off the road, across the pavement, down my drive and soon, very soon, its about to turn my sitting room carpet an ugly shade of brown. The second problem is that inside the house, in the pipes, we don't seem to have any water. The water supply is *off*. Given a choice, I think I can live with that for a few weeks. In an ideal world, and I don't want to appear greedy, I'd like one lot taken away, please, and the other put back; preferably as soon as possible.'

'I see. Just let me take a few details. What is your account number?'

'My *what*?'

'Your Water Authority Customer Account Number. It's on the top of your bills.'

'Look, Tracy, I have about twenty thousand gallons of water outside my house. It is absolutely itching to burst through the front door. Not to put too fine a point on it, we are about to re-enact the story of Noah. Do you remember Noah? The address is *Cromwell's Retreat*. It's in *Fairweather Lane* in *Strumpling Green*. My name is Dudgeon. My wife's mother only had nine toes. Could you feed that into your computer and see if it's possible for a little man with a very big pump to come round? I promise you faithfully that I will give him my bloody account number when he arrives.'

'That's all right. I've got you now. You're in *Fairweather Lane* in *Strumpling Green*, aren't you?'

I gulped.

'Yes, I am actually.'

I thought to myself, if she asks me for the house number, I will scream.

'Mr Dudgeon.'

'Yes, Tracy?'

'What's your house number?'

*   *   *

To give the District Council their due, they responded within an
hour, and two cheery lads came tripping down the drive, soaked to
the skin, quickly assessed the situation and brought a dozen
sandbags from their lorry. We piled them tightly in the doorway.

'Haven't got a pump, I'm afraid, guv, but they'll keep you out of
trouble.'

I thanked them profusely and offered them a cup of tea.

'Love one. Just a quickie,' they said in unison, and their faces lit
up. 'It's a bit chilly this work.'

I turned to go inside, then I paused as I remembered.

'Lads,' I said. 'You're not going to believe this. We haven't got
any water.'

It stopped raining at dusk, and slowly, very slowly, the water
began to go down as it seeped away through our tiny drain. We
were just sweeping the silt and accumulated filth away when a
truck pulled up. It had a large trailer with a mobile tanker drawn
behind it.

'Water Authority. Would you be Mr Dudgeon?'

'I am,' I answered wearily. 'Tell me, are you delivering the stuff
or taking it away?'

20

First thing the following morning a white van man pulled up outside and delivered a box containing my new moccasins. These mail order companies provide such a wonderful service! I decided not to save the new shoes until Christmas as my old ones, although well glued, seemed to have suffered from their extended spell under a stack of Encyclopaedia Britannicas. They looked like two hairy flippers. A couple of volumes also seemed to have taken on an ethereal image of a furry new born lamb on the covers where the glue had seeped out, taking the woolly lining with it. I didn't think anybody would notice, as the twenty-four volumes had not emerged from the bookcase since Weetabix held a competition to construct the longest list of words that end in 'x'. That was about 1964. I did not win. The winner listed all the possible *French* words. I have not bought Weetabix since. French words indeed.

Angelica had invited one of her *friends* to stay. I just couldn't wait. His real name was Charles, which seemed a perfectly acceptable name to me, but she referred to him as *Jacko*. Why is it these children abominate perfectly good names? Their parents spend days, weeks even, poring over books of names, thinking of really original ones that kids can live with for the rest of their lives, and what do they do? Rush out and find the ugliest and most convoluted corruption of their surname or some other ghastly nickname. I can't remember them all ... *Bones, Knacks* (he is keen on horses and wishes to be a vet, *wishes* being the operative word judging by his academic record), Charlotte, who is known as *Vic* (because she lives in the vicarage at Thackett Corner), *Ming* because she *mings* (*ming* being the approximate Neanderthal equivalent for unkempt, smelly etc., what they call *rank*) and *Tool*. Well, your guess is as good as mine.

Jacko was due on the ten fifty-three train from London. Needless to say, Angelica was not up in time when I was ready to leave, to go via the builders' merchants to acquire the plaster for Greg's bedroom ceiling. Having called her no less than six times I felt I had discharged my duty and left without her. It never occurred to me that there would be very many young people getting off the train, or that it would be difficult to identify one of Angelica's friends. Had I known what it was going to be like, I might have written '*Jacko*' on a piece of card. No matter how embarrassing it might have been standing in the booking hall looking like an advertisement for a boys' comic, it would have been infinitely preferable to what happened.

Assuming that Jacko would have a fair collection of iron-mongery in and around his face, as most of *Glic's mates* do, I began to approach one or two likely looking characters. A young bloke with bleached blond hair, dressed in a scruffy denim jacket, was unnecessarily rude when I ventured to ask him if he was 'Jacko'.

'Piss off,' he replied. 'You dirty old git,' he called over his shoulder, as he ambled down the platform, so I assumed that he didn't want a lift to Strumpling Green. Another, who was tall and thin, carried a suitcase and looked like a vaguely suitable weekend boyfriend, turned out to be a girl. I think. I searched the remaining faces, but was feeling a little less confident about approaching anyone else for fear of reprisals which might have spoiled my weekend. I nodded to a chap dressed in a smart pin-stripe city suit, and decided that our Jacko had missed the train. Typical. Trust one of Angelica's friends to be dossing in bed instead of catching a train at Liverpool Street Station.

Outside, the suited figure was enquiring of a taxi driver.

'Excuse me,' I overheard him say in a remarkably well-spoken voice. 'I was due to be met by some friends, but they don't seem to be here. Is it possible that you might be able to take me to Strumpling Green? The address is Fairweather Lane.'

The taxi driver grunted, pushed a home-made cigarette around in his mouth and muttered. 'Cost yer though. It's bleedin' miles away.'

I looked the young man up and down. Surely not? It just couldn't be. But by the law of averages, it had to be. How many people were going to Fairweather Lane? But I couldn't just walk up and call him *Jacko*.

'Charles?'

He spun round. 'Yes, I am. I say, are you by any chance, Mr Dudgeon?'

'I am. Sorry to have missed you. I wasn't expecting ...'

What does one say under such circumstances? *Someone who looks clean? Looks tidy? Doesn't grunt? Someone whose tongue doesn't clack up and down with a disgusting great stud in it?* I introduced myself and shook his hand.

'Well, that's a bit of luck, sir. I was just setting off in a taxi. Where's Angelica, then? No! Don't tell me, still in bed.'

I laughed nervously. I have to admit it had been a long time since I had heard anyone under the age of forty-five refer to her as *Angelica*. I realised this chap could grow on me. I showed him to the car.

'She wasn't stirring when I left,' I said. 'I'm sorry, Charles. It's not very polite of her.'

'Don't worry one bit. Listen, would you mind calling me Jacko? Everyone does. Bit silly really. My father's called Charles as well. I'm Charles Jonathon, you see, hence Jacko.' He stifled a yawn. 'Terribly sorry. I've been up at six every morning; working in the City for a few weeks, getting a bit of experience under my belt before university. Commuting is very tiring. Hence the suit. Law office, you see.'

I smiled at him. This boy was definitely growing on me. *Up at six every morning?* I could see something of a clash of cultures in the offing here.

'Well, you can have a lie-in tomorrow. I'm afraid the children are not early risers.'

'Hmm.' He ran a hand around his face. 'I might, but I'm trying to get fit, so I go running every morning, you know, whenever I can. Work has scuppered early morning jogs.'

I smiled at him again. Did this immaculate, fresh-faced young chap have *any* notion of what he was walking into? That he was about to visit a house *oozing* with some of the most feckless, slovenly layabouts ever known to mankind? I thought not. How *on earth* had he and Angelica teamed up?

'If you don't mind me asking, how did you meet Angelica?'

'Oh, a friend of a friend. I share a little place in Hampstead with a couple of chaps and a girl called Felicity. She's a friend of Angelica.'

'Oh, *Flic*. Yes, I know of her.'

'That's right. Flic. Well, Angelica stayed one weekend.'

It all came back to me. An anxious time. To think I had spent the whole weekend worrying about the company she might be keeping. A sleepless night because she had unexpectedly stayed over in London and made one of those late-night calls telling her mother that she would find '*somewhere to kip*'. I had imagined her sleeping on King's Cross station and getting sucked into some very dubious, depraved white-girl slave trade, and us never seeing her again.

I turned into the cottage.

'*Cromwell's Retreat*? Is that a real historical association, Mr Dudgeon?'

I explained that it was reputed to be, but that local folklore lacked any substantial evidence to support it.

'Fascinating man, Cromwell,' he continued. 'Did you know that he was very active hereabouts in, let's see, November or December sixteen-forty-three, I should think. He was formidable in raising support for the Eastern Association. He and the Earl of Manchester went from village to village ... I say! What a lovely little cottage, Mr Dudgeon. Is this your weekend place?'

145

We strode into the kitchen. There was a spectacular absence of life except for the odd trace of Phil's breakfast around the toaster.

'Well, as predicted, Jacko, the welcome committee is in danger of overwhelming you.'

He grinned. 'Don't worry, Mr Dudgeon. I have a younger sister whom my father keeps threatening to send to the Natural History Museum so that she can be identified.'

I laughed. *Here* was a lad after my own heart.

'I must get Angelica up. Would you like some coffee?' I asked.

'I would, thank you very much. I had an early start. Here, let me make that while you go and make anti-hibernation noises at Angelica.'

I looked at Jacko and wondered whether to suggest that I just take him back to the station so that he could spend the weekend quietly at home, or even visit Regent's Park Zoo, which I felt sure would be light relief compared to that which he was about to endure. I opened Angelica's door and called, 'It's still Friday, Angelica, but only just . . .'

'Mumblehumumbleumble,' from under the bedclothes.

'And Jacko is here.'

'Jacko! Here! Ohmagod! Why didn't you call me? How can you do this to me?' She flicked her hair back over her head. 'What shall I do? Tell you what. Just keep him talking. Yeah, just keep him talking. I can't possibly let him see me like *this*. *Rank or what?* Shower. I need water. Lots of it. Have you done the washing, Dad? I need some clothes. Oh hell and bugger, why did I stay out so late last night?'

I left the child to do whatever she had to do and went downstairs where Jacko had found a tray and laid it for coffee, and then carried it out to the garden.

'Any luck?' he asked, raising an eyebrow.

'Not sure,' I said. 'You know what you were saying about the Natural History Museum? I think we might have another candidate.'

We sat outside in the sun, drank coffee, and Jacko chatted easily about his parents, their 'small' estate in Scotland, and his work experience at his father's office.

'He's a barrister, you see, so I've been fortunate to get a chance to work there before I go up to read law. I'm doing some research for a case. Patent Office stuff. It's absolutely fascinating. Gripping, and such a privilege. You'd never believe how complex the law is concerning patents. An eye-opener I can ... I say. Talking of eye-openers...'

Angelica drifted dreamily across the grass towards us. At least, I *think* it was Angelica. She looked groomed, was made-up, and had a beaming smile on her face ... and she was dressed! Where were the baggy shorts and the old sweatshirt with the Marmite stains that usually adorned her at breakfast everyday?

'Jacko! Darling! How *wonderful* to see you again.'

She kissed him on the cheek. I stared, and reminded myself that this really *was* my daughter.

'You're looking well, Angelica,' said Jacko. 'Would you like some coffee? Your father and I have been nattering about the Patent Office. It's been a tremendous experience. A real insight.'

Angelica stared at him in much the same passionate way that Fido looks at the Sunday joint 'Really,' she murmured. 'It sounds fascinating. Tell me more.'

I left them at that point, partly because the urge to ask Angelica what *I* had to do to qualify for breakfast-time communications of this never-before-heard-of standard was nearly overwhelming. And all before she had crammed in three statutory rounds of cream cheese and Marmite on toast, and spilt orange juice over the TV page of the newspaper.

Just as I was going in from the garden, I heard Angelica saying, 'Well Jacko, you wouldn't believe how hard I've tried to get a job up here, but it's just impossible in the country...' As the children would say under *normal* circumstances, 'Yeah, right'.

It looked as though a delightful weekend was in store. The *new* Angelica was a joy to behold. At one stage, I had to sit down to recover when, having cooked lunch, I was preparing to wash up when Angelica said, 'Daddy, you go off and do your things. Jacko and I will clear up for you.'

I was tempted to show her how the taps worked and introduce her to the plug and the washing-up liquid, but I resisted. I have to confess I felt a little insecure, a tad uneasy; the sort of feeling I might have if I had woken up, looked in the bathroom mirror and discovered that my hair was not grey but bright green. It took a little getting used to. I was mightily reassured when Greg stumbled down the stairs, rubbed his bleary unshaven face and, on being introduced to the jolly Jacko, replied, 'Oroight?' and promptly slumped across *The Times*. Up until then I had wondered if some alien force had tampered with the restored water supply and added some sort of sophistication-hormone, such was the staggering change in my eldest daughter.

Later, in the afternoon, the strain was beginning to tell. Having walked the dog, *for four miles*, most of it apparently at a steady trot, Jacko had then suggested that some exercise would do them good and the dear, dear boy offered to do some gardening.

'I fancy a bit of hedge cutting. Would you like us to tackle the front for you? I'm quite used to it. At home it's my job to maintain the topiary in the garden. Mummy's awfully keen on it being just so.'

I saw a pained expression flit momentarily across Angelica's face, but she managed a weak smile.

'You don't need to Jacko. Daddy's not expecting you to slave in the garden, *are you, Daddy*?'

'I'm not. Not at all. You really ought to relax, Jacko ... but I can see Angelica's quite anxious about the state of the hedge too, and it would be a shame to disappoint her. I'm afraid I haven't done much to it for a few weeks.'

'Well,' said Jacko, clapping his hands. 'Let's get to it then, Angelica. You can rake up, and I'll wield the trimmer. Any special instructions, Mr Dudgeon?'

Greg and Stevie, by now up, dressed and showing signs of

having had some sort of brush with the bathroom, looked on, their mouths gaping. I walked past Greg and lifted his chin.

'You'll catch flies, *Gregory*. What about a spell with the old lawnmower, huh? Or perhaps you might prefer to go out with Stevie and weed mum's vegetable patch? After that you could probably just fit in your appointment at the gym. What do you think, *old chap?*'

21

By nine-thirty that evening, Angelica was fast asleep on the settee, and Jacko was deeply engrossed in a book on the infinitely complex and fascinating legal aspects of patenting and copyright infringement. I think his efforts to enthuse her with lengthy descriptions of case law, following their mammoth undertaking on the front hedge had, in short, finished her off. Poor Angelica. She had never had a day, well, half a day, like it in her life. I've often wondered how these kids would cope with a bout on a building site. I have vivid recollections of hod-carrying on a four-storey house as a student on summer vacation. It was exhausting, and *nothing* I have done since compares with the sheer agony of carting bricks and tiles up and down ladders and scaffolding all day long. I have also, incidentally, never been more fit.

Angelica stirred just as Jacko was asking me about a suitable route for a morning run.

'How far do you want to go?' I mused.

'Well, if it's on the road, about eight or ten miles.'

A long gurgling sort of moan issued from beneath the mound of cushions on the settee.

'Ten miles? *Ten*, Jacko? Oh my God. Jacko, you *are mad*,' she said, with more than a hint of exasperation as she rubbed her aching muscles. 'And I suppose when you come back you might invite me to get up and clean all the windows with you, or cut down a few trees...' and with that, she staggered out of the living room, calling 'Night all,' over her shoulder, and went to bed.

The abandoned Jacko looked at me, and I noticed that his right eye, almost imperceptibly, twitched. I scribbled a sketch map for his morning run on a piece of paper.

'I don't think Angelica is quite used to being as ... as active as you are, Jacko. She may find it difficult to keep up.'

'I must admit, she did puff and pant a little on our walk today.'

There was a repeated banging upstairs and Angelica's voice could be heard remonstrating in no uncertain terms with Greg for the intrusive volume of his stereo. There followed a silence, as the bass sounds of *Shed* or *Garage,* or whatever 'music' he was playing, were turned off. A few seconds later Greg appeared in the living room. He yawned cavernously and stretched.

'I don't know. I haven't done anything today,' he said. 'I must get some exercise. I might pop down to the pub and get some gum.'

Jacko sat up in his chair. 'I wouldn't mind a stroll. Shall we take the dog?'

Greg stared at him with a look which I would say came as near as damn it to *total and utter* lack of comprehension. Being used to Greg, I anticipated what was bothering him.

'Stroll! Jacko, you don't *stroll* down to the pub!' exploded Greg. 'It's a bloody mile there and a mile back! *You* can walk there if you want, but I'm going in the van.'

Jacko looked thoroughly bemused. 'Right. Sorry. I just thought, well, you know, you said you wanted some *exercise,* yes? I thought you were saying that getting the gum would be...' He looked at Greg who smiled patronisingly and slowly shook his head.

'No,' was all he said.

'I was just thinking, if you were keen to exercise, you might join me in the morning for a run. Your father has given me a route which...'

Greg held up his hand and paused, before adopting the sort of posture and manner he might assume to inform us that he had had a life-changing experience; that he had perhaps *found God*. Then he spoke in a measured, profound voice.

151

'Jacko, I don't quite know how to put this to you ... I mean ... it's simple really ... it's like, I don't *do* exercise.' And with that, he left the room.

I looked at Jacko, whose right eye gave another, almost imperceptible, twitch.

Stevie came downstairs at the sound of the back door closing, slumped on the sofa and enquired after his brother.

'He's popped down to the pub. He won't be long,' I informed him.

'Miserable sod. He didn't ask me. I could have fancied a pint,' said Stevie, going horizontal with his feet on the arm.

'I...' Jacko began.

I had an inkling that Jacko was about to ask Stevie if *he* wanted a stroll down to the pub. I must have winced visibly, because the lad stopped in mid-sentence.

'He doesn't either, Jacko ... don't even ask,' I said.

'Ask what?' questioned Stevie, toying with the TV remote.

'I think Jacko wants someone to go running with him in the morning. I was just saying that you and Greg don't really, well, you know, believe in *exerting* yourselves.'

'Dad! I went sailboarding last week. I've been to the gym.'

'True. Sorry Stevie. I didn't mean to malign you, but I get the feeling that Jacko likes to stack in the *serious* exercise. You did, after all, *drive* to the gym to *watch* basketball. Jacko wants to...'

'I'm up for a run,' said Stevie nonchalantly, staring at the ceiling. 'What time?'

'Oh, er, six-thirty?'

I *swear* I saw Stevie pale.

'Okay,' he said in his most super-cool voice, 'Cool. Can you wake up on your own or do you want calling, *Jacko*?' He jabbed the remote to turn on the television. 'Mind if we take in the news?' He jabbed again, then he shook the remote.

'Oh,' I said, 'the batteries have faded. I'm sorry, I meant to have bought some new ones.'

Stevie tossed the instrument aside. 'Never mind. I can't be arsed to get up. I'll watch it tomorrow.'

I was making my early morning cup of tea at half-past seven when I heard a rasping noise. It was the sort of sound one might associate with a roll of carpet being dragged across the floorboards. Every few seconds there was a pause, and an enormous gasp, then I heard a voice.

'Take it easy, Stevie. Bend forwards a little. Deep breath now. That's it. Deep as you can. Now, relax. *Relax!*'

More rasping, before Stevie crashed through the back door heavily supported by Jacko. He lay on the stairs gasping, clutching his sides and muttering over and over, 'Ten miles. Ten *bloody* miles...'

'Morning, Mr Dudgeon,' said Jacko. 'Warm out this morning. Oh, great, a cup of tea!' He did a few bends and stretches, and looked at his watch. 'Not bad. I slowed up a bit for Roger Bannister here,' he said, nodding at the semi-prone, heaving form on the staircase. 'But he did well for...'

'*Slowed up! Slowed up!* You're a miserable bloody sadist, Jacko. You did *not* slow up!'

'We didn't do *ten miles,* Stevie. We did about three altogether. We spent most of the time leaning on farm gateposts while you got your breath back. I was so considerate it's just not true.'

'All right, you smarmy bastard. This afternoon we'll take the sailboards down to the estuary at high tide and then we'll see what you're made of.' Stevie heaved himself up off the stairs and limped painfully to the sink. 'Water, Dad. I need water.'

He drank greedily from a mug. 'Wow! That's better. Right, I'm off to bed.'

'Off to b—' Jacko began, but I nudged him before he risked further criticism of Stevie.

'I think I'll have a shower, if that's all right,' Jacko said, and sprang up the stairs as fresh as a newborn lamb.

'He,' said Stevie, venomously, 'he has a *serious* problem. He,' he continued, spitting the words out, 'is a *psycho*, a bloody *headcase.*' And with that he staggered up the stairs leaving the kitchen in peace where I sat musing over several cups of tea.

After a light lunch, Stevie persuaded me to run the two of them down to the Hard, from which they could set out into the estuary. He strapped the board and sails onto the roof of the car, came indoors, went into the hall and made a phone call.

'Hi, Leechie. Stevie. How ya doin' mate? Oroight?' I heard him say, then I lost track of the conversation as Angelica wandered into the kitchen. She paused in the doorway listening.

'Who's Stevie on the phone to?' she asked.

'*Leechie,*' I replied. 'Why?'

'I think he's borrowing his old board for Jacko to have a go on. I heard him say the one that goes like a bathtub in a pile of shit. I've got an idea it's become a bit personal between them since Jacko ran him off his feet.'

I chuckled at the prospect of Stevie streaking across the bay under the scudding sky, while Jacko brought up the rear for once.

'Jacko,' I asked him, when he came downstairs wearing Greg's wet suit. 'Have you done any sailboarding before?'

'Some. Nothing special. Just a bit of offshore boarding. My uncle taught me.'

I nodded. 'Well, do take care out in the bay. There are some nasty rip tides. Let Stevie get well out in front. Take the lead from him.'

'Rest assured, Mr Dudgeon, I will take care.'

An hour later I sat in the car on the Hard listening to the Afternoon Theatre on the wireless, and watched as the boys rigged their boards and pushed them out into the water. The tide was exceptionally high and the wind buffeted the car. Stevie was away first and travelled very quickly out into the bay, but he was holding himself so close to the wind that every now and again he nearly lost it. Jacko took a little time to find his feet but then he pushed the board hard, but not so close as Stevie continued to do, which produced a speedy but erratic performance. I knew instinctively

154

what Stevie had challenged Jacko to: a race around the headland buoy and back to the Hard. He and Greg had done it many times, and Stevie was by far the more capable. It was a demanding course, affected by the winds that seemed to spiral in the lee of the dunes. I watched with interest. Jacko was no stranger to sailboarding, that much was clear. He was about fifty yards behind Stevie but was not losing ground. Stevie was too slow at the buoy and tacked on a wide, awkward course, which allowed the other not only to catch up, but also to gain a slight lead. Then it was neck and neck. Stevie inched ahead, lost it once or twice, recovered, and all the time Jacko was there, steady as a rock on his heels.

'Steady, Stevie,' I murmured to myself in the car. 'Don't lose it now, boy.'

At the last moment, Stevie held his sail tight against the wind and streaked between the moored boats ... but he misjudged it. The momentary drop in the wind as he passed in the leeward shelter of a large yacht, broke his balance and he nearly went right over. It was just enough for Jacko to come thudding up on the heavier board, which rode out the changes, and onto the slipway. There were only three or four seconds in it. I had a shrewd idea what Stevie would be thinking.

Back at the cottage, the atmosphere was just *sub-hostile*. When the boys were out of earshot, I took the opportunity to tackle Jacko.

'Who taught you to sailboard, Jacko?' I asked nonchalantly, wondering how the hell he had learned such competence.

'My uncle. He's pretty hot. Used to be an Olympic coach.'

'I see. I had a feeling you had done more than "a bit". Stevie is good. He's reckoned to be the fastest around here. You were lucky to beat him.'

Jacko looked at me.

'Not sure "lucky" is the right word, Mr Dudgeon. He threw it away. Far too anxious. You have to keep your nerve. I kept a steady eye on beating him and it paid off. I believe in winning, Mr Dudgeon. If you are not out in front in this life, you are nothing.' He laughed.

I looked at him and realised that I could go off this boy in quite a big way. I went to ask the kids what they fancied for supper.

In the living room, Phil and Stevie were, surprisingly, in fits of laughter, but they fell silent as I went in.

'What's tickling you two?' I enquired.

'Nothing much, Dad. Phil's just discovered that our Jacko has a phobia about spiders. I just think it's bloody funny, that's all.'

The general consensus was that a chicken dish would be the order of the day. Back in the kitchen Jacko agreed.

'Chicken, yes please. Lovely. Thank you, Mr Dudgeon. I say, would you like me to cook supper? I can turn out a reasonable chicken casserole. You always seem to be doing all the domestic stuff. You could have a break.'

'That's very kind, Jacko, but there's no need. You are our guest, after all.'

'Honestly, Mr Dudgeon. Please let me. I'd like to. At home *I* have to pull my weight.'

I turned up the Aga a notch or two and left him to it. I sat with the paper while the boys sprawled in front of *Gladiators*.

'Are you sure he can cook, Dad? I mean, we don't want food poisoning or stuff, do we?' Greg said.

'I'm sure we can trust him to do it. He wouldn't have offered if he couldn't manage.'

I popped out into the kitchen once to make more tea, and found Jacko working away, rolling pieces of chicken and crushing garlic cloves. At that point, there was nothing actually cooking.

'Er, dinner at about seven-thirty? Is that all right?' I asked Jacko, as he rummaged in the cupboard and examined a tin of black treacle.

'Sure, Mr Dudgeon.' He looked at his watch. 'No problem. You go and take it easy.'

The living room was empty when I went back to join the family. I couldn't see where they had gone but, about twenty minutes later, the three boys trooped back into the house.

'Been *out*?' I asked. 'That's unlike you three.'

'Oh well, you know, Dad. We needed a bit of exercise ... work up an appetite before supper, like, you know how it is,' Stevie replied, and they all disappeared again. I should have known that something was afoot. The last time Greg, Stevie and Phil went out together for *exercise* they were in their pushchairs.

Angelica drifted downstairs and put her head round the door.

'Is it true that boy-wonder is cooking supper?'

I looked at her. 'Things not working out as you hoped, my love?'

'You could say that. He's such a try-hard, Dad. He was gloating about beating Stevie, and couldn't understand why I wasn't pleased. He's an only boy ... explains everything. Have you mended the hedge trimmer yet?'

'Mended it? What do you mean?' I asked, putting down my paper.

'Didn't he tell you? He cut the cable in half just as we were finishing off.'

'Really?'

'Yup. Thought you knew. Didn't he tell you?'

'No, he didn't. How *very* interesting.'

Supper was a little later than usual. I could see why. Whereas I would have just hurled everything in the pot and bunged it in the oven, Jacko seemed to take hours preparing the main dish. He then set to on ornate side salads, complete with those whorly tomato things and, finally, an hors d'oeuvre which was, as far as I could determine, based on liquidised melon and ginger. At about eight-thirty he indicated five minutes to 'the off'.

Everyone filed into the dining room and paused while they took in the first course, which was orangey-brown and piped onto dishes in whorls.

'Looks like doggy-turds,' Greg sniggered, while Jacko's back was turned. 'What is it?'

'I think it's melon.'

'Melon!?' said Angelica. 'Yeah, right. Whatever you say, Dad.'

We sat down and Jacko came in from the kitchen, removed my

157

very vulgar apron which the boys had bought for my birthday, and sat down.

'I hope you like this,' he said. 'It's a little dish I had in Bermuda last year. I hope I've got it right.'

'So do I,' muttered Angelica under her breath.

'Well, thank you Jacko. This is very kind of you to have done all of...'

'Paah! Phhhhp! Yaah!' Phil looked exceedingly embarrassed. 'Sorry guys,' he said, waving his hand in front of his mouth as he reached for his glass of water. 'It's a bit spicy, Jacko!'

The others tentatively dipped their spoons into the little turds of melon purée and tried the smallest amounts.

'It's the ginger. It's meant to contrast with the delicate flavour of the...'

'Contrast?' said Greg. 'I think you mean bloody annihilate. It's explosive!'

They all watched as Jacko made a brave effort to eat his first spoonful. 'You're right,' he said, colouring up. 'I may have overdone the ginger, perhaps. It is quite hot, isn't it? Not bad though. But then I like ginger.' He ate several spoonfuls. 'I thought it was okay when I tried it. The ginger seems to have ... grown. Let's have the main course.'

I'm not sure whether Jacko intended the theme of the meal to be highly spiced doggy-turds, but even the chicken looked as though Fido might have played a part in its preparation. The combination of chillies and garlic was overpowering.

'Bermuda?' queried Angelica, looking across the table at her friend.

'Mexico,' he said proudly. 'They really know how to handle chillies there.'

'It's a pity they didn't show you how to,' Stevie said. 'I don't want to be rude, mate, but it's gross. Could we wash the sauce off perhaps and just eat the chicken?'

'Hmm.' Phil licked his lips. 'What is the brown stuff?'

'Black treacle. In Mexico they...'

'Jacko,' said Angelica, pushing her chair back and standing up. 'In Strumpling Green they grill it, roast it, they barbecue it, they casserole it and even deep-fry it. What they do not do is try so hard to impress everybody that they ruin a perfectly good meal by showing off. Now, anyone else for a cheese toastie?' And with that, she stomped out.

'Don't worry about Angelica, Jacko. She's, er ... missing her mother. This is ... um, quite exceptional. Unusual, I'll give you that and, er, perhaps a little over-laced with chilli ... and garlic ... and the black treacle is, ah ... interesting. But it's good, yes and um, definitely unusual.'

Jacko sat hesitantly chewing a mouthful of his casserole.

'You're very kind, Mr Dudgeon. But Angelica's right. It is pretty dire.' He smiled, embarrassed.

'No, no,' I tried to reassure him. 'It's not *that* bad. I think the French beans and the rice are all right. The salad too. That's okay. Just a little dressing on there and ... shall I get the cheese?'

Fido rarely refuses food. The truth is, he has never been known to turn his nose up at *anything*. He will occasionally, on a walk, even sample dubious matters on the Common, but the pieces of chicken sat sulking in his bowl, quite untouched. He had various valiant attempts at them, presumably feeling that whatever appeared in his dish *should* be edible, but then he circled the dish, sniffed it, growled and gave up, scuttling away with his tail between his legs.

Poor Jacko. He was very quiet that evening after we had washed up and cleared away the sandwich maker. He took himself up to bed early and, for some reason which I could not quite fathom, this seemed to cause the boys great amusement. They nudged each other and laughed. Sensing that foul play may have been done, I ventured upstairs to find Jacko sitting staring at his bed where he had found half-a-dozen very large garden spiders beneath his quilt.

'Mr Dudgeon. I wonder if you would mind. I ... er, I am completely arachnophobic. I can't bear them. My mother has sent me to a specialist for aversion therapy, but it has not helped. Could you possibly ... get rid of them, please.' His right eye gave a flicker of a twitch.

The next morning, a bright sunny Sunday morning, Jacko made his excuses and, muttering something about having been missing from the office on Friday, he politely asked if I would run him to the station. I did so without further question and, on returning to the cottage, I found Greg and Stevie up, and sitting at the table. I surveyed the scene: spilt milk, cereal dolloped unceremoniously over the *Sunday Times* and excesses of toast and Marmite scattered anywhere but on plates. I smiled at them. The boys looked up quizzically.

'Wassup, Dad?' Greg said, his mouth full of toast.

'Nothing,' I chuckled. 'Nothing. Nothing at all.'

22

I don't want you to think that any of us at *Cromwell's Retreat* are obsessed with doggy doo-doos, particularly since relating Jacko's attempt at preparing the supper, but, in some curious way, they seem to be maintaining an unusually high profile in our lives. Whichever way we turn, we seem to find something about them. People seem either to be writing about them or, in this case, researching them and *filming them!*

I came downstairs at lunchtime to find Stevie and Phil in stitches of laughter. The newspaper was spread before them and, every so often, they would break out afresh in howls of mirth.

'Ohmagod. I don't believe it,' one of them said. 'Scoffing dog shit? How disgusting!' which as you can imagine intrigued me, not least because they were reading one of the more reputable papers. I was pleased to see that they were actually *reading,* as opposed to idly browsing the supplements, so I didn't disturb them but made a mental note to look at it later.

There it was. Page ten. Not satisfied with investigating names, animal behaviourists and psychologists had spent *another* fortune, this time researching why we find various types of poo disgusting. Can you believe it? A television company had funded a team that had come up with some staggering findings. The first was that poo is held in universal disgust. Well, blow me down, we wouldn't have expected *that*, would we? The researchers could not find a race or a community anywhere in the world that treasures their leftovers and proudly displays them on the mantelpiece for all to see, alongside photos of Auntie Ethel. The second major conclusion was that if imitation turdies made of chocolate are offered to children they feel revulsion at the idea of eating them. I think I might go along with that too. It seems fair to suggest that if you actually feel nothing negative about eating chocolate poo, there is probably something very seriously wrong with your instinct for self-preservation. Faecal ingestion is not, after all, recommended as a healthy and invigorating pastime. I have to say I am very glad that the research was not funded by the Beeb. I was also quite relieved that I was not eating my supper when the programme was screened.

I imagine that if the researchers had paid Mrs D a couple of thousand, she would have been willing to confirm from her own experiences, gained during walks with the children in the parks, that poo is not a pleasant business. Many of us have travelled that particular path and will recall the days when the Clark's Junior Sandals brought that great outdoor aroma to the living room carpet. In those days we got through more bottles of 1001 Carpet Cleaner than we did tins of baked beans because we lived next door to a park in an intensely doggy area. For better or worse, the problem has now lessened with the advent of the pooper-scooper ethic – except that nowadays the hedgerows are littered with discarded polythene bags. Personally, I prefer a well-aimed flick with my stick, sending Fido's offerings out of harm's way (or not, depending on the current state of diplomatic relations with the neighbours).

There is only one thing worse than doggie-poo and that is the dreaded fox droppings. The English language is not extensive enough, nor equipped with adequately graphic vocabulary, to describe the horrors of this particular form of effluent. If your hound has ever taken a plunge into one of these offensive little squiggles you will know very well that only speedy ejection of the animal into the garden will save you from having to sell your house and move. Quite why dogs feel the need to cover themselves in such putrid matter is a mystery. If it is just a question of acquiring a disguise, why not roll in a rose bush? Fox dung holds an almost magical, compulsive appeal to a dog, and if your hound is a 'roller', the experts say, he will always be a roller. There is *nothing* you can do to change this primeval repulsive flaw. Fido knows that if he disgraces himself in this way he will immediately be subject to certain punitive actions involving a very cold hose at full blast until he is clean again. It makes no difference whatsoever to his behaviour the next time a pile of fox dung pitches up in nostril range. I have watched him as he begins the unmistakable form of excited sniffing which is always the precursor to a balletic roll and wriggle. I have tried to deter him by shouting blue murder, but he will wait until the last moment, when I am almost in grabbing range of his collar, and then fling himself over with tears of ecstatic joy streaming down his face as he has a *wallow*.

Enough of doggie do. Not long after I had read the article, I began preparing supper, and then the phone rang.

'Mr Dudgeon?'

'Speaking.'

'This is Mandy at Costa Bomba Holidays here. I'm ringing to tell you that you have won a holiday! You may remember being stopped in the high street when we were carrying out a survey, and you very kindly answered our questions. We promised to put your response sheet into our lucky draw and guess what? You've won! Now, the wonderful holiday can be taken in a number of places: Cyprus, Crete, Corsica, Colchester, Mallorca or the Canary Isles, and will include flights to and from your chosen destination and a fortnight's free use of a self-catering apartment. You don't need to choose now, all you have to do is take down your magic holiday-in-the-sun code number, and someone will phone you very soon to confirm your prize. Isn't that wonderful? Now, if you have a pen and paper to hand, I'll give you that special little number so that you can claim your wonderful break for two in a fully furnished apartment in...'

'Wait! Please, wait. Suppose I don't want to go to any of your destinations? Suppose I would like to use my prize to take my wife to Venice or Florence? Or the Galapagos Islands?'

163

'This is Mandy at Costa Bomba holidays here. I'm ringing to . . .'

'Mandy, Mandy . . .'

'Yes, Mr Dudgeon?'

'Where's the catch? What are you selling?'

'Nothing, Mr Dudgeon. Honestly. I'm not selling anything. It's my job to phone people and tell them about their prizes. It should be lovely, but it's horrible doing it all day long because everybody is so suspicious and nasty that, quite frankly, my life is in a complete mess and I wonder why I go on sometimes. Even my boyfriend . . .'

'Mandy.'

'Yes, Mr Dudgeon?'

'The magic number, please. I'm in the middle of cooking pasta for nineteen and as much as I would like to help you sort your life out . . .'

'It's HPZ 4598215.'

'Thank you very much. That's fine. Thank you. You're a very kind girl. Have a nice life. Goodbye Mandy.'

Something wasn't right. This was what my children would probably call a *scam!* Still, you never know . . .

Sure enough the holiday firm did call and they confirmed the package which was entirely free and included travel and the apartment just as Mandy had said it would. Poor Mandy. The full details of my prize were to be forwarded in the post as soon as possible. *How amazing.*

When the children sat down to supper they were *gobsmacked* (which I think means surprised, bowled over, amazed, astounded and so on).

'Go for it, Dad. Take Mum to the sun,' said Phil, smiling at his little rhyme.

'If you don't want it, I'll go,' said Greg. Trust him to be looking for a handout.

'It's a fix,' said Stevie. 'It happened to Leechie's mum and dad, only I can't remember what they were selling . . . double glazing or something like that.'

'Time-share,' said Angelica flatly. 'They're selling time-share apartments. You wait. In the post you'll get an invitation to a presentation here in England which you have to attend in order to qualify. They've chosen you because you fall into the correct socioeconomic group. It'll be in Slough or Reading or Bedford or Newmarket ... you know, somewhere that you really want to go on a hot summer's afternoon, and you'll sit there and be bored to tears and wish you were in the garden and...'

'Angelica! *Please*! Don't spoil it for me, there's a good girl.'

Sometimes I really do wonder if she has inherited more than her fair share of Mrs D's genes. I mean it has to come from somewhere, doesn't it?

'I might have won the holiday of a lifetime for Mum and me to enjoy; a sort of celebration for getting you lot off our hands, and you sound so ... I don't know ... cynical. Has the world really made you that suspicious?'

'No, Dad. You have. You're one of the most cynical people I have ever met.'

A couple of days later the details did come. Angelica was right. The presentations were in Slough, Reading, Bedford and Newmarket. That girl, she is *so* sharp! I phoned, not to book, but to try to avoid spending a Saturday afternoon at Slough, which was the next one available on the schedule.

'Look,' I said to Trudy on the end of the line, 'I don't want to buy a time-share apartment. Let's take that as read. I've got a wife, six children, a dog, no money and an expenditure programme that would make Network Rail think they were in clover. All I want to do is to take my prize and enjoy a fortnight in the sun without going to a slideshow in Slough. What do you say?'

'No. A condition of accepting the prize is that you attend one of the meetings. You can choose from Bedford, Slough ...'

'I know *that*, but *I don't wish to go!* Nothing was said about a presentation. I was told I had won a prize. A prize is a prize. Now I would like to claim it. Send me the tickets and I won't say a word.

Don't you see that if I give up my seat, someone could go in my place? Someone with two children and loads of money ... someone who is perhaps a complete sucker ... that's what you need, Trudy, take my word for it ... loads of lovely suckers who will sign up for your apartments.'

'Mr Dudgeon.'

'Yes, Trudy?'

'Are you wasting my time?'

'Wasting *your* time! Damned cheek! Right! I'll come, but I think you'll regret it. Book me in for the 2.30 at Newmarket. I might bring Mrs Dudgeon, then you *really* will wish you had just popped those tickets into the post.'

I know exactly what will happen. Mrs D explained it all to me on the phone. Low-level brainwashing techniques, it is. She knows all about that sort of thing, having been involved in ... I'd better not say. The cults use similar techniques to hoist people in. Close seating, an airless room, just after a heavy pasta lunch, everybody speaking in hypnotic, charming voices and *no one is allowed to leave.* An hour of slides and films in a low-lit room, followed by sweet talking and a two-minute break only for the loo ... Then off they go again. More low lights and soft-soaping from an attractive blond whom nobody wants to interrupt for fear of appearing a complete geek. If you speak out of turn or question the exorbitant costs, or the colour of the cut-price kitchen units in the apartments, a big bruiser will come up to you in the break when everyone is frantic to get to the loo, and he will whisper menacingly in your ear.

'Meester Dudgeon. We think it ees time you leef, huh?' and with that you will find yourself forcibly marched away and left on the pavement outside the Odeon, Slough. Inside, someone then surreptitiously removes your chair, as if you had never existed. There is no room for dissenters if you are flogging time-shares (or a cult).

I'll show them. They will wish that they had just sent me the tickets. 'Ah, excuse me,' I will say. 'Before we begin, could we

166

open all the windows for a bit of fresh air, please? It is terribly stuffy in here. And may I respectfully suggest to the assembled company that if you have been foolish enough to bring your chequebooks or credit cards, you should put them away and resolve not to take them out until you are safely home again. Resist *any* temptation to buy. Keep your minds on one thing only: your *free* holiday prize. Remember, you owe these people *nothing*. Thank you, Mr Chairman. And perhaps while I am on my feet, could I ask you to speak up a little. Your voice is too quiet to be heard at the back. We might all go to sleep. As my elocution teacher used to say, "*enunciate* your words, please. *Enunciate* and *speak up!*" That's the key to a good presentation, my man. Thank you. Carry on.'

I'll sort them out.

23

I had been putting off telephoning Mabel and Horace, 'Granny B and Grandpa', Mrs Dudgeon's parents, although I knew only too well that I had to do so in order to confirm the proposed trip to collect Mel and Ed.

There's something about phoning old folk that is strangely off-putting. Don't misunderstand me, I love talking to them, it's just that they become completely disquieted on the telephone and, in their anxiety, actually don't *want* to talk. Having grown up in the days when the infant instrument was used only for emergencies and for *making arrangements*, they have an abhorrence of such wasteful practices as *chatting* on the phone. Goodness only knows what they would make of our three older ones who seem to have developed the skills to actually *live* on the phone for thirty-six hours at a time. *'It's good to talk'* passes Granny and Grandpa by, and each time the advert prompts the same rejoinder from Horace '. . . not at the rate you charge us it isn't'.

Horace does have a point, and, quite by chance, I have discovered one way to avoid the excessive use of phones by adolescents. I just mention it in passing as it may help you to develop appropriate telephone arrangements in your homes as your children grow up. It came to me in a flash, in a manner of speaking, during 'our little power cut' when the cordless phones all failed. I just could not work out why Angelica was behaving so oddly on the hall telephone. I cannot easily portray for you what she was doing. The first thing I noticed was that, physically, she looked *very* uncomfortable. She was leaning against the wall and repeatedly sliding down towards the floor. Then she would half-lie and half-sit across the small table, and then get up again and repeat the sliding-down-the-wall routine. All the time she was maintaining a curious and somewhat furtive, hushed conversation, punctuated with '... hang on a minute, someone's here ... okay, it's all right now.'

There are two lessons for us, the phone-bill payers, to learn from this. The first is that it pays dividends to place the phone in the most inhospitable and preferably public place in the house. Children cannot cope with *anybody* being around during a phone call. Even if they are dialling the speaking clock, they like to do so in *utter* secrecy. The second fundamental aspect of teenage phoning to understand is that they can only really talk *when recumbent*. Beds and settees are basic requisites for all adolescent calls of more than twenty seconds duration. Removing *all* potential seating from the area containing the phone thereby renders it impossible for them to sit or drape themselves over furniture. If the phone is fixed to the wall, so much the better; the floor will be the only remaining alternative to those tiring vertical positions. If you have a word with your friendly BT man next time he calls, it is possible to *shorten* the wiggly phone flex so that sinking to the floor *and* talking is tantalisingly not quite possible. I guarantee that your quarterly phone bill will immediately shrink to two healthy little figures.

During the power failure I realised that it is the new breed of cordless sets which is responsible for the maxi-bills we now incur, because they allow the phone to be taken *to* the bed, settee, soft arm chair, hearth rug, etc. The answer: do not have them in the house ... banish them to some dusty old cardboard box in a corner of the attic ... the cordless phones that is, not the children. On the other hand ...

If you don't have the bottle to tackle the cordless phone disposal in such a head-on manner, the easy way round it (which will allow you to claim total innocence) is to leave it operational in the next thunder storm. Just dial TIME and leave it on the windowsill. The ferocious electrical activity of the storm will blow the delicate electronic micro-technology to smithereens. Thereafter you have an excellent excuse for not replacing it. You won't regret it. Never again will you have to press the *Page* button and track down the lost phone as it bleeps at you upstairs from under a pile of bedclothes or a heap of mildewing socks. You will know where the phones are from that moment onwards: one will be firmly screwed to the wall in the draughty hall, and the other, if you have any sense, will be under lock and key in your desk, beside your favourite fireside chair.

I prepared what I wanted to say to Mabel and Horace, much as one might rehearse a recorded answer machine message. One only gets one short chance with Horace. You need to understand that *Horace invented the soundbite.* Mabel is slightly better.

Horace treats the phone receiver as if it was a red-hot potato to be passed on as soon as possible.

'Hello, Horace ... Horace, yes, it's Duncan ... Duncan *who?* Your son-in-law Duncan. Duncan *Dudgeon.* How are ...'

Exactly as I predicted, the panic was immediate. I heard Horace calling for Mabel in a highly agitated voice. 'Mabel! *Mabel!* Duncan on the phone. Quickly dear. Long distance! Leave the scrambled egg. Come quickly ... Just coming old chap ... *Mabel! It's long distance ...*'

'How are you Horace?'

'Fine, Duncan ... What *is* she doing? *Mabel!'*

'How have the children been? I hope ...'

'Hold on, Duncan. I think she's coming. Hurry up, dear. It's Duncan on long distance. Quickly now! Here she is old chap. Nice talking to you.'

'Hello, Duncan dear. Are you coming up tomorrow?'

'I thought I might, if that's all right with you. Are you well Mabel?'

'Yes, yes. Fine, fine.'

'And how have Ed and Mel been?'

'Oh, fine, fine.'

'I'll bet you've done lots of exciting things with them.'

'Oh, yes.'

'Right, er, well, I'll be up by lunchtime tomorrow. It will be wonderful to see you again.'

'Lovely, dear.'

'Any other news?'

'Duncan, for lunch tomorrow, I thought we'd have fishy fingers and Horace's new potatoes and fresh garden peas, followed by apple crumble and custard and we will lay the table and have glasses and knives and forks and mats and napkins and lunch will be at one o'clock sharp and we'll save you that chair which is good for your back and...'

'Mabel! Relax. Don't get yourself in a tizz. I will see you tomorrow and we will have a lovely time.'

'All right, Duncan. I won't fuss.' (*'Mabel,'* Horace hisses, *'Don't be too long. It's long distance'*.) 'Yes, yes, Horace. Goodbye Duncan.'

Brrrrrrrrr...

'Goodbye, Mabel...'

Too late.

They are such a funny and loveable couple. Their obsessions with times (notice the *'lunch at one o'clock sharp'*), planning food (good, healthy, economic food) as if they have forgotten that rationing ended about fifty years ago, and the desperate need to keep phone calls short, are astonishing. They are not poor, far from it, and they could, for example, easily afford to use a larger size of notepaper when they write, particularly as their eyesight is not what it was. Horace doesn't need to take his car out of gear and coast down long hills to save petrol any more, but, *frugality* in all things is everything. *Buying petrol* warrants the time, trouble and energy (not to mention the wasted petrol) that most people would devote to buying a house. Half a penny a litre discount, at a garage ten miles away, justifies a major expedition which must use every drop of fuel saved, if not more, and requires trans-Antarctica standard provisions, sandwiches, rugs, flasks of coffee and so on.

171

The organisation which heralds Mabel and Horace going *on holiday* is truly staggering. For weeks in advance, suitcases are dusted and laid out in the *spare room,* clothes are washed, pressed and packed into dozens of polythene bags, and the great countdown begins. The car goes in for its annual service, even though it has only amassed about two hundred and forty miles since its oil was last changed; the picnic table and chairs are given a lick of paint to ensure that they are presentable enough for Bournemouth seafront; and ponderous, lengthy negotiations are started with neighbours regarding *the house keys* and watering the geraniums.

Mrs D and I have very fond, although somewhat exasperating, memories of shared holidays with Mabel and Horace. We remember the day, for example, when one of the children dropped a cheese sandwich on the sand, and Horace insisted on taking it down to the sea to wash it before bringing it back and declaring it 'perfectly all right to eat'. It was, except that his dentures were gritty for the rest of the afternoon. On another occasion, Horace plotted all day to remove a useful piece of carpet from the hotel rubbish skip, and was apprehended by a hotel porter while taking it. Our embarrassment knew no end, and Mabel spent the remainder of the holiday with Horace on a very short lead and was repeatedly heard saying *'Horace! Don't even think about it!'* before tugging at his sports' jacket sleeve and urging him along the promenade, away from some juicy item which 'would come in useful one day'.

It is a curious in-between world they exist in, somewhere betwixt the days of post-war austerity and the wasteful throwaway times of their grandchildren. I cannot but admire some aspects of their thrift whilst at other times one has a sense that they might be a little too zealous for their own benefit. We occasionally receive letters telling us of the imminent and exciting opening of a new supermarket, usually called something like *Alfie's Bazaar* or *Grocery-Plus,* from which they will, ever after, purchase cut-price loaves of white bread (of even more dubious quality than the normal polystyrene), and tins of cheap unknown foodstuffs because the labels have mysteriously been lost. I have tried to explain to them that the haphazard lottery they operate is actually costing them more than it would if they bought conventionally packaged food. Horace believes he can tell what is in the tins according to the 'slurping' sound they make when he shakes them. He identifies them with a strip of masking tape (fifty-metre rolls from Alfie's for only twenty-nine pence) on which he writes *Tomatoes* or *Baked Beans,* which is sometimes right, and sometimes results in having nine tins of stewed prunes in the fridge as Mabel has struggled to locate the *French Beans.* We have occasionally had to suffer some curious, unconventional, associations of food: Spaghetti Hoops in a crumble with custard, because the tin turned out not to hold *Rhubarb Chunks,* or bacon, eggs and *Economy Peach Slices* because the *Whole Italian Tomatoes* proved elusive at breakfast time. One huge thing in the system's favour is that it does make mealtimes more interesting. It also accounts for our children's cosmopolitan, if not eclectic, palates.

I think that Mabel must be the original Bag Lady. She has polythene bags stored for every occasion. Countless hundreds of them are sorted, graded and labelled by Horace when he hasn't enough to do, and ones deemed to be less than clean are washed and pegged on the line to dry. When the children were small it was considered to be the greatest treat to be stood on a stool at Granny's sink, have their little sleeves rolled up and be given a bowl of *Cheapo-Suds* and a pile of bags to wash. It could amuse them for a whole afternoon while Granny and Grandpa had a snooze. Unfortunately, Granny tends to forget that Mel and Ed are now in their teens and that, not surprisingly, bag washing doesn't quite have the same appeal as it once did.

Such is the great joy of grandparents, and we will miss them sadly when they are not around to read *The Billy Goats Gruff* seventeen times in one evening, because the children enjoy Granny's frighteningly life-like impressions so much. (Not that

Greg should have spent that much time listening to bedtime stories when he was supposed to be doing his A-level chemistry revision.) I know that there will come a day when I will not be able to look at a cottage cheese plastic pot without remembering a refrigerator stacked full of them, each containing minute quantities of leftover food. I know I will miss Friday night post-shopping expedition phone calls with victorious accounts of bargain Cos Lettuce hunting and the low price of beautiful joints of pork: *'You should have seen them, Duncan'*.

I arrived at one minute to one, having been stationary in heavy traffic for an hour. The children bounced up to me, threw their arms around my neck and reported that Granny had, for the last twenty minutes, been muttering to Horace that she couldn't imagine where that Duncan had got to. 'Trust him to be late,' she had apparently said. 'I told him lunch was *at one o'clock sharp.'*

Lunch was an extravaganza of granny-dom: corned beef (eighty-seven pence in *Super-Groso* and fortunately readily identifiable), with new potatoes and peas (courtesy of Horace's labours), followed by pilchards and chocolate sauce for dessert. Granny declared, a little wearily, that fish fingers (*Alfie's* at sixty-seven pence a box) were off the menu after the children had complained that they *always* had fish fingers at her house. Horace had then told them in no uncertain terms, 'Now darlings, Granny's fishy fingers are delicious. Nothing wrong with them at all. We have three of them each for Tuesday supper and four each for Friday lunch, week in, week out . . . have done for fourteen years since I retired.'

I can't wait to be old.

24

Before we were even three miles down the road, Ed was saying that he didn't ever want to eat tuna fish again. Apparently, Horace had had an unlucky run with the fruit cocktail pieces, the baked beans *and* the spaghetti hoops. What with tuna bake, tuna mayonnaise, tuna sandwiches on a picnic, tuna-filled jacket potatoes, *and fishy fingers,* they had eaten enough fish to last them a lifetime.

'Apart from an overdose of fish, did you have a nice time with Gran and Grandpa?'

'Was okay . . .'

'Did you go out and do lots of things?'

'A bit . . .'

'What sort of trips did you do?' I asked, knowing that they had been taken to the Air Museum, a zoo, a few picnics on the beach and a country fair.

'Oh, I dunno, stuff . . .'

I gave up this remarkably fruitful conversation.

Melanie was sitting beside me in the car, picking away at her trainers after explaining that we needed to go shopping because her toe had come through her shoe. By the time we arrived home, the sole was also adrift.

'Well, darling, I'm sure you have got enough shoes to manage with until Mum comes home. She can take you into town then, and you can shop for all the things you will need for school.'

'I haven't *got* any other shoes.'

'Really,' I exclaimed. 'Some of that massive pile of shoes by the back door are yours.'

She looked at me with disdain, the like of which only thirteen year-olds can muster. 'Those! I wouldn't be seen *dead* wearing those. My friends would laugh themselves silly. They're history. They're ancient. Mum bought those for me *years* ago.'

'Actually, Melanie, it was last January, I think, just before school started. January, February, March . . .' I began counting the months. 'Eight months at the most. Not *years*.'

'Well, they don't fit me anyway,' she said, as if sending a final torpedo to sink *any* argument I might make. This particular response is guaranteed to win the 'shoes battle'. Every child knows that the responsible parent is not going to say 'Well, you can just cram your argumentative little toes into them for a few more months, and, yes, you might get bunions, ingrowing toenails and fallen arches, but never mind. The shoes aren't even worn and I'm not buying any more shoes just because black is now *out* and *Snerkers Pro-Plus with the Luminescent Soles* are in.' We just say something like, 'All right, darling, in which case I suppose we will have to then.'

'All right, darling, in which case I suppose we will have to then,' I said, and Melanie settled smugly back in her seat, blew a bubble with her gum and popped it. It is the most annoying habit, made worse by having just lost the shoe battle. Granny doesn't allow bubble gum. As a result, Melanie was suffering from gum withdrawal, which resulted in extra ferocious mastication and explosions. I don't allow gum. The only difference is that Melanie meekly accepts the rule from Granny. She completely ignores me.

We arrived and Mel and Ed quickly settled into home life. It took seventeen seconds for Melanie to take the phone to her bedroom in order to catch up with her friends (yes, all right, you've caught me out; I'm waiting for the thunderstorm to blow the bloody phone to kingdom come). Ed loaded a new computer game that he had persuaded Mabel to buy. It looked extremely unsuitable to me. I glanced over his shoulder to see the usual monsters being chased by those lurching, virtual reality flame-thrower-bearing figures whose feet never touch the ground.

'Yess!' he exclaimed, as the score came up and the game ended. *Then*, to my utter amazement, a nubile female figure appeared and, accompanied by the sound of tantalising music, she began to shed all of her clothes!

'Ed! What on earth is that game?'

'What?' he said, so absorbed by the curvaceous figure on the screen that he could not reply.

'I said, what on earth is that game?'

The figure ceased her pirouette and the screen went blank with a round of canned applause.

'Gran bought it for me,' he eventually replied, as though that made it perfectly acceptable.

'Do you think she had any idea what she was buying you? Does she know what a CD-ROM is? Did she know she was buying you a piece of . . . of pornography?'

He shrugged his shoulders. 'Dunno. Maybe.'

This probably meant that Granny thought she was buying Ed a CD of *Abba's Greatest Hits*.

While I was in the middle of preparing supper, I remembered that I hadn't phoned Mabel and Horace to let them know that we had arrived safely; a curious ritual which one has to enact after each visit. They have always said, 'Give us a call when you're safely home. No need to talk. Three rings will do; just so we can put our worries away.' What is this for? The family could sail around Cape Horn in a fifteen-foot ketch, and they would not bat an eyelid. If we leave Mabel and Horace's to travel fifty miles on the A14, we have to ring. It's *very* curious. I attempted to dial the number several times and failed to get through because Melanie was *still* on the phone. I called up the stairs.

'Mel. Off the phone, *now* please. If you don't finish that call in one minute, I'm going to open two tins of tuna for supper.'

She poked her head out of her bedroom door and dismissed my quip with a cursory glance whilst saying, 'I know. He's *so fit*. I've got a poster of him on my wall . . .'

She's obviously collecting pictures of gymnasts now. I can't believe she is only thirteen. God help us when the Olympics begin.

As I again tried the phone, it rang in my hand. I thought it might be Mabel. I scooped a pan of hot spaghetti from the cooker and stood with the phone under my chin.

'Hello. Is Mr Dudgeon there?'

'He is . . .'

'Is it possible to speak to him, please?'

'You are.'

'Oh, Mr Dudgeon. We're working in your area next week and we wondered if you might be interested to have a quotation for our double-glazing, which comes with a fifteen-year guara—'

'Is it free?'

'Oh absolutely. Our expert site survey and prompt quote is completely free of charge and without obligation.'

'Sorry. You misunderstood me. I meant, is the double-glazing free? You see, I don't buy things over the phone.'

'Free? Er no.'

'Then, no thank you and goodbye.'

I dialled Mabel. Without thinking about *three rings*, I let the phone rest under my chin while I stirred the pasta sauce.

'Hello. Middlebury two-six-four, one-three-nine.'

'Mabel. Hello. It's Duncan. Back safe. We had a backing wind, the seas were running at about twenty feet and Cape Horn was just visible through the mist . . . we're home safe and sound.'

'You don't have to make a call, dear. Three rings will do. It's so expensive these days. I won't keep you. Thanks for ringing.'

'Mabel, thank you for having the children. They obviously had a lovely time. They're *full* of it. Chattering nineteen to the dozen about all your trips out. It was very kind of you.'

'Duncan, I hope you didn't mind me buying Ed his *Abba* record . . . just a little treat for him. I can't believe how small their records are these days . . .'

Supper was a record too. An all-time record, I think. Mrs D was away, of course, but everyone else *was there*. All six children at the table at once. What a treat! A mealtime full of happy chuckles and chatter; just like the old days. There are times, not many I'll admit, when I do catch a glimpse of the brood gathered together, and I sense that very special bonding, that unique atmosphere which can only exist in a large, well-balanced family, and I give myself a metaphorical pat on the back.

'Haven't sheen you for a bit, Ed,' said Greg, tucking into his spaghetti carbonara. 'Been off shomwhere?'

'Coursh I have shtupid. I've been at Gran's for two weeksh,' said Ed, chewing.

Greg peered at him, and momentarily stopped shovelling his food in. 'Have you? Dad, why didjn't you tell me Ed hashn't been 'ere?' he said, flipping a piece of spaghetti off his chin and into his mouth. 'I'd have e-mailed or shomething if I'd known, like.'

'You can't e-mail us at Gran's can you? What are you going to e-mail us on?' asked Mel, 'Grandpa's record player?'

Greg looked at her.

'Have you bin away too?'

Melanie stared at Greg. 'No, actually, I've been in my bedroom for two weeks. Dad's been passing sandwiches under my door for the last fortnight. Of course I've been away, dickhead!'

'Uh.'

Actually, Mrs D and I have often joked that it is quite possible for the children not to see each other for weeks at a time, particularly during those in-between times when Ed, Phil and Melanie are back at school and Greg, Angelica and Stevie haven't returned to university. The young ones get up and go out at about eight o'clock in the morning, which is about the middle of Greg and Stevie's night because they come in at anywhere between one a.m. and three, and then take in a few videos, or Greg's recorded *Match of the Day*, and then go to bed at goodness knows what time. They will stagger out for 'breakfast' just as Mel, Ed and Phil are starting school (afternoon school that is), splosh a few Cornflakes around before Greg then goes back to bed with the phone. He arranges a few meetings with mates and then goes out at about four, just before the three younger ones return from school, saying 'Back in an hour'. He then returns at about seven-thirty, after we've eaten supper, when the children are homeworking upstairs, and, after a long pensive stare at the remains of the shepherd's pie, makes a Marmite sandwich. Having restocked, and borrowed a few quid from me, he then ventures out again. He returns at about one a.m., and so on. Stevie isn't quite as bad. He hasn't yet developed the full-blown nocturnal, cave-dwelling undergraduate lifestyle, which seems to require one year of university to mature. But there are promising signs that it will happen soon.

To give Stevie his due, he has tried to find himself a job. It's not easy these days. Employers want youngsters with experience, *work experience* that is, and they cannot get a job until they've had a job. They're in a no-win situation. I helped Stevie complete a number of application forms because there is always a very large and daunting space *over* the page headed *Previous employment*. We have developed a splendid line in white lies now: machine operator (washing machine); landscape gardener (he once contemplated cutting the grass); and, best of all, *Journalist's Assistant*, because he once delivered a small column to the vicar for inclusion in the parish newsletter. Mrs D had written about the village flower show, and Stevie happened to be passing Hereward's door.

To my utter amazement, he came home one day and reported that he had finally secured a job.

'Yup. Start Monday. Went to the agency in town and they signed me up.'

'That's splendid news, Stevie,' I said, clapping my hand around his and shaking it vigorously. 'What will you be doing?'

He stared at me as though my reaction was a little over the top, but that's fair enough; *he* doesn't share my perspective on the matter. *He* doesn't have to worry about having a house full of unemployed *thirty-nine year-olds* when I'm sixty eight, drawing my pension and spending months planning for our summer holiday in Bournemouth. I wondered if he knew I might react a little incredulously when he replied, quite simply 'Cleaning.'

I try to make it a golden rule never to laugh at children. One must *never ever* mock their endeavours. It has been a valued precept of mine throughout a long and demanding career in teaching. To mock is to crush their little spirits and risk damaging their fragile self-esteems. Do it once and they will remember it for all time. They will forget the hundreds of occasions when one has praised them to the heavens for their achievements, and only recall the time that they were reduced to embarrassed discomfort by our laughter.

I roared with incredulous mirth. '*Cleaning!* Stevie! You have got to be *joking!* You can't take on a *cleaning job!* You've never cleaned anything in your life, except your teeth. What are you thinking of?'

This is the boy who, when he needed a light bulb for his bedroom, came to ask me for one and I said, without thinking, 'It's in the Hoover cupboard.' He went off and returned thirty minutes later, looking bewildered and totally exhausted, and said 'Dad, where *is* the Hoover cupboard?' I have to admit, that wasn't as bad as Greg's classic. He phoned us while we were on holiday in order to ascertain where the washing machine was.

I found a chair and lowered myself into it, wiped my eyes dry and asked him where the job was.

'The Falcon Hotel. I'm going to be a . . . chambermaid.'

'Do you think you can manage?' I asked him. 'I mean, I'm sorry to laugh, Stevie, but it seems the most unlikely thing in the world. Could one of us give you some training . . . you know, making beds, dusting, that sort of thing?'

'I can do it. *You* don't think I can, *do you?*' Whereupon he went off, came back with some sheets and pillowcases, and said 'Want a demonstration?'

We went up to his room where I brushed aside the heap of dirty washing with my foot, carefully removed a pile of scruffy, juice-spattered papers, which I noticed included several red mobile

181

phone bills, and sat down to watch. He stripped his bed, which looked as if several playful polar bears had had a romp in it, stuffed all the linen in a pillow case as he must have seen Mrs D do, shook out the sheets, checked for the broad seam and put it at the head. He then made the most immaculate tucked corners I have ever seen, deftly slipped the quilt into its cover, gave it a shake, and within a minute or two the bed looked as pristine as any I have ever come across in a hospital or hotel. It was *staggering*. I was glad I had had the foresight to sit down to watch the spectacular transformation take place. I felt my knees going weak. It was one of those life experiences akin to watching a birth; a miraculous moment charged with absolute wonder. I looked at him, tears brimming in my eyes, lost for words.

'How's that, then?' he asked smugly.

'It's . . . er, brilliant, Stevie. I never thought you had it in you. I don't quite know how to put this to you, I mean, I don't want to knock you or anything, but why . . . why do you sleep in a bed that looks as though the Battle of the Somme has just been fought in it when . . . when you can do that? What's the difference between this and the Falcon Hotel?'

He looked at me for several seconds and then said, quite seriously, as though it was the most obvious thing in the world, '*Money*, Dad. *Money.*'

25

The next morning, Melanie, Ed and I set off for town in pursuit of *the trainers*. Ed came with us to spend his birthday money on some new pedals for his mountain bike, and duly trotted off to the cycle shop, on his own, agreeing to meet us at the car forty-five minutes later. Melanie flapped along beside me, her sole slapping on the ground.

I don't mind shopping expeditions, really I don't. I know some men have complete aversions to them, but *I* am not one of them. It gives me considerable pleasure to take the children shopping. It can be a time of great sharing, an excellent way to get closer to the children but, I have to say as something of a major *caveat*, if you want to purchase trainers, take my advice and *don't* go to a sports' shop. I know it sounds the ideal place to buy them, but it is not. It will present you with all the ingredients of a hideous nightmare. On entering, I was assailed first by the *sheer scale* of the choice. A wall, measuring about *seventy-five feet* in length, was covered in shelves and racks that were crammed full of sports' shoes. I cannot believe we need such a bewildering choice, but I suppose it's what happens in a free market economy. When I come across such a sight, I begin to think that there might be one or two advantages to living in the Ukraine. There, one takes one's child to *The Store*, queues at the bleak shoe counter and, if there are still any stocks left, asks 'I would like a pair of shoes, please. A size four perhaps?' A large forbidding lady in voluminous black will rummage in a few apparently empty cartons on the floor and say, 'We af da sise five. In black. Dat iss all. Take it or leaf it. You wannit?' and junior will leap up and down and say 'Oh Papa, a pair of shoes! At last. Thank you, thank you,' and plant several kisses on your cheek.

Melanie stood in front of the 'shoe wall' and stared blankly at the variety of shoes. I stood in front of the 'shoe wall' and stared blankly at the prices. *Seventy-five pounds!* Was this a bad dream? What ever happened to good old *Dunlop Green Flash* at ten and sixpence? Remember the aroma of the class as sixty-four of them were peeled off in the changing room? Ah, that takes you back, doesn't it?

My eyes ran across the price labels and alighted on a shoe that cost twenty-eight pounds. Without doubt, it was the cheapest one there. It was a nice little shoe, pleasantly coloured in a cream and olive colour scheme with matching laces and lace holes. A stylish little number. I decided. That was the one. We would be in and out in five minutes. Melanie was further down the rack and still looking. I lifted my choice of trainer down from the shelf and sidled up to her.

'This is a decent one, my darling. I love the colours, don't you? What size do you need? Five?'

To say that Melanie ignored me would, I think, be something of an understatement. Had I taken her into a restaurant and ordered *raw* tripe and onions, she could not have been more dismissive. Somehow she didn't even need to raise an eyebrow in my direction to indicate that the shoe I was holding was, as if by definition, the most nauseatingly objectionable, ridiculous suggestion for a purchase in the whole of town. She had some sort of sixth sense about it which she conveyed to me in much the same manner as an *Exocet Missile* arrives, all done without so much as a flicker in my direction. She merely slowly moved on down the racks and left me standing alone holding my olive green and cream choice. I had forgotten what it felt like to go shopping with an adolescent girl. Angelica had exhibited the same pubescent symptoms but, in some curious and subtle way, they hadn't been as polished when she was thirteen. She would at least enter into some sort of dialogue about my suggestions and say encouraging things such as: 'Dad, *pleeease* don't embarrass me,' or 'What about standing outside the shop while *I* choose, and then you can come in and pay when I call you.' With Melanie, there was nothing but a silence reverberating with disdain.

We ended up having a silent bargaining session. It was tight-lipped warfare by trainer. She walked down the rack, took down a shoe, tried it on and looked at me. I examined the price tag, gave her a look which unequivocally communicated 'No', and she would put it back with a huffy noise that sounded as though she was suffering from inflamed sinuses. She would then progress along 'shoe wall', choose another, and so on, until after about seven goes at this game she saw something less negative on my face. At this point we asked the assistant to find those for her to try on. About six shoes fell into this category. Needless to say, and I just wonder if it is a deliberate marketing ploy on the part of the sharksters who operate the place, they were not in stock. *All* of the cheaper shoes, and I use the term *cheaper* very loosely here, were in short supply, and the parents, who hovered behind their children's left shoulders like nervous consorts, were all being confronted by a team of tracksuited joggy types telling them 'Sorry. Madam. I'm afraid that at the moment that one is only available in sizes two or seventeen-and-a-half.'

We couldn't find a shoe that represented a compromise *and* was available. Melanie wanted a version which looked as though it might suddenly sprout twin exhausts and turn into a Formula One racing car. It was emblazoned with lurid advertising logos and was constructed from what appeared to be slices of old lorry tyres in fluorescent orange and black. I said 'No.' It would have cost about the same as nineteen pairs of *Green Flashes* or a week's shopping.

'Let's leave it,' I said, after fifty minutes of this rigmarole. 'I'm not paying an arm and a leg for what looks like a pair of recycled tyres.'

Melanie stared at me. 'It's *fashion*, Dad. Get with it . . . you know . . . like, *progress*.'

Progress my foot.

I indicated to our tracksuited friend that she could now box up the half a dozen pairs of shoes that Mel had scattered all over the floor.

'Dad!' she said, in that swooping way that children talk when they are thoroughly disgusted and have reached the end of their patience with the non-obliging parent. 'We can't go home without any shoes! Daaaad!'

'Oh yes we can, my sweet,' I replied, digging my heels in. 'Unless you want to go and look in Woolworth's. They have those nice black ones with elastic gussets. They were all the rage in . . .' but she was off in front of me, heading back to the car.

Ed was there waiting for us with a new fishing rod.

'I thought you were going to buy a new set of pedals?'

'I was, but I looked at them and thought a fishing rod would be more use.'

And if you can follow the logic of that, you are welcome to borrow my children, who will undoubtedly thoroughly enhance the joys of your next shopping expedition.

We pulled up outside the house where an unusual car was parked in the drive. I wasn't expecting visitors. 'I wonder who that is?' I said casually.

'*How* am *I* supposed to know?' Melanie frumped at me, just in case I had not realised that she was now *off* me in a big way and had taken the humph at my unreasonable behaviour. With that, she stomped away into the house, no doubt to ring all her friends and tell them how terrible it was living with a dad who was such a miserable old git.

From the back door, I could see that, in the kitchen, Greg and Stevie were in fits of laughter with someone who was sitting, only half-visible to me, with his back turned.

'Eric,' Greg was saying, 'we could, like, meet up for a few beers sort of, sometime?'

'I'd like that,' said the invisible man.

'Cool, cool,' Stevie concurred. 'Do you sailboard?'

I stepped through the doorway and realised that the mystery

186

guest, the figure who was drinking my coffee and who had his grubby little mitts in my biscuit barrel, was none other than Wigglesworth.

'Worgleswipe,' I said. 'You should have phoned to tel! me you were coming.'

He stood up and proffered his hand.

'I was just passing and I thought I'd drop by on the offchance. Don't worry.'

'I'm not, actually. I see you've had coffee *and* biscuits.'

'Oh yes. Your sons have looked after me. They've kept me regaled with stories of *the vicarage barbecue*. I hear Brenda Fortescue nobbled you.'

'*Nobbled* me?'

'Her wine . . . lethal. I had to inspect her. A few months ago. She had riding facilities put at the back of her saddlery.'

Stevie and Greg sniggered. 'Dad knows all about her . . .'

But one icy look from me cut Greg off in mid-spate. I spoke, perhaps a little more sharply than usual. It had been a long, and not entirely satisfactory, morning.

'Have you two by any chance got something *useful* to do? Like bringing down all the mugs and glasses that I noticed were festering gently in your bedrooms yesterday? You could take the moss rake and give your carpets a pre-winter going over, and Stevie, perhaps you could don your dapper little Falcon Hotel apron and show Greg how to convert that tip of his back into a bedroom again . . .'

'Woh!' said Greg, staring at me, eyes wide.

'*Awesome*!' breathed Stevie, and he doubled out of the door and up the stairs, muttering 'He's lost it, bro' . . . he's finally lost it.'

'Now, I've got things to get on with, *Eric,* or are you planning on wasting yet more taxpayers' money by sitting in my kitchen drinking coffee for the rest of the day?'

Outside in the garden, Worgleswipe detached his pen from his clipboard. 'I took the liberty of having a look at your wall. Not quite right yet, is it?'

'*Not quite right?* What do you mean? I'll have you know that that is now a totally authentic repair . . . river gravels and sand, horsehair, manure, lime . . . the lot. Explain *exactly* what you mean by *not quite right!*' I stared at him as he poked the stubbly ends of the straw protruding from the rendering.

'This,' he said. 'It's supposed to be smooth rendering. These need sanding off.'

'Sanding off? What's the point in doing that?'

'So that they can't be seen. They aren't supposed to be sticking out. The straw shouldn't show.'

'You mean so that no one *can tell* that the rendering is made of an authentic mixture of . . . so that it looks smooth, just as it did a week or two ago when you told me to rip it all out, or risk being deported? You mean no one will *ever* be able to tell that this repair was prepared carefully and meticulously according to a seventeenth-century recipe?'

He paused . . . for quite a time. 'Exactly so.'

I stared at him. '*Then why all the bloody fuss?!* If I've got to go over it with a pair of nail scissors and sandpaper, giving my front wall a frigging pedicure until it looks *precisely* as it did when I first had it repaired, why, please tell me, have I spent so much time being frustrated to hell and back by my insurance company? Why have I spent countless hours travelling all over the countryside collecting foul-smelling and obscure building materials . . . if . . . if no one is *ever* going to see it? I have had to suffer power-cuts, close encounters with riding school proprietors, appalling vicarage barbecues and risked devastating family traumas just to provide some sort of obscure satisfaction for the local conservation officer and some meddling biddy up the road.'

He took a step or two backwards.

'Do I need to put up a notice and provide magnifying glasses for the local pedants, just so that they will know it has been done to your satisfaction?' I asked, taking several steps towards him.

'Mr Dudgeon. I think you are being unreasonable. You have an old listed house. It is part of our heritage and you have a responsibility to maintain it properly.'

'I'm well aware of that, but has it *ever* occurred to *you* that one of the reasons that people started using bricks was because they were *better* than this stuff? When they discovered glass, they started to use it because it was better than a bit of old pig's bladder and a sack hanging in the window. . . . . It's people like you Worgleswipe, who prevent society progressing. You'd have us living in caves wouldn't you? You'd have been down at Bristol docks waving your Luddite banner and telling the great Isambard Kingdom Brunel that his cast-iron ship wasn't authentic. "Build it of wood", you'd have chanted. I can see it all. You enjoyed drinking my coffee, didn't you? Oh yes. I don't expect you asked the boys for *authentic* roast acorns and a lump of hard tack instead of my digestive biscuits, did you? No. That's right! *Why not?* I'll tell you why not. You didn't because you are a pusillanimous, malodorous, little sod of an official with nothing better to do than go round the countryside antagonising innocent people who have . . .'

Would you believe it, without so much as a word, he ran down the drive, jumped in his car, *locked it from the inside,* and hurriedly reversed out of our drive! The man had no manners whatsoever.

I walked back up the path to the back door as the phone rang. I snatched it from the wall thinking, 'All I need now is a call from "Meddling bloody Gascoigne" enquiring whether or not I'm going to replace my front gate with a piece of sixteenth-century oak...'

'*What?*' I snapped.

There was a pause.

'Hello Duncan darling . . . are you all right?'

It was Mrs D.

'Sweetest heart . . . what a surprise! How lovely to hear your voice.'

'Are you all right, Duncan? You sounded a bit . . . flustered.'

'Flustered? Good gracious, no. It's a lovely day and . . . and I've just been relaxing in the garden, done a bit of shopping with Mel and Ed . . . no, we're on absolutely fine form . . .'

189

'Duncan, I haven't been married to you for twenty-five years for nothing. What's happened?'

'Nothing really. I er . . . I just discovered the Lada is coming up for its MOT, and I had completely forgotten. It's just amazing how quickly a year flies by; gone in no time at all. Soon be Christmas before we can turn around, which reminds me darling, I—'

'Duncan! What has happened?'

'Okay. Not much. Nothing really. I took Melanie to the sports' shop to buy some trainers and she was being, well, Melanie-ish about what she was and wasn't having and, well, now I'm not flavour of the month. I refuse to be blackmailed by her concerted sulks into buying a pair of trainers that need a mortgage to finance them just because Mel feels she might be cast into permanent social disgrace if she has the wrong colour footwear.'

'Oh dear, Duncan. It's not worth all the aggro. Do what I do; offer to pay for a reasonable pair and suggest she uses some of her birthday money to top it up. It always works and, what's more, she then looks after them.'

'Right. That's easy. Twenty-eight pounds fifty she gets . . .'

'Duncan, twenty-eight pounds doesn't buy a pair of reasonable trainers! You're out of touch with things, my love. Make it thirty-five or forty, and tell her that's all she gets.'

'Forty pounds! They've got *Dunlop Green Flash* in Woolies for about a tenner!'

'Duncan. You are such an old curmudgeon. Give her the money and don't be such a dry old stick. Life's too short. Were the children all right at Mum and Dad's?'

'They were. Horace is still playing roulette with the tinned goods, so they had a few odd meals, you know, the usual, french beans and vanilla sauce, oxtail soup on apple crumble, that sort of thing. Death by tuna fish it was actually, I think. The old boy had . . .'

Mrs Dudgeon laughed at that point. 'I sometimes think you and Horace have got quite a bit in common darling, but that's probably why I love you so much.'

'And I love you too. Anyway, enough trivia from Strumpling Green. How's work?'

'Interesting.'

'Is that all?'

'All I can say. This phone has a low security rating on it, my love. I'll tell you more when I come back, but it's going well. Very productive. I'm pleased to hear that all is well with you. I must say, when I first heard you answer, I wondered if you were doing battle with the neighbours again . . .'

'No, no. That's fine. Fido has not romped through any more of Mrs Philpott's delphiniums, or whatever it was he did last time.'

'Tassel Bush. He peed on her prize Tassel Bush.'

'Well, there's not much worse than that is there? Peeing on Mrs Philpott's Tassel Bush . . . the ultimate insult really,' I laughed, and, shortly after that, we exchanged fond endearments and hung up.

I looked at the wall planner and crossed off another 'America week'. One week to go.

26

At supper, we had no fewer than *five* phone calls and not one of them on the *'landline'* as the children now refer to the real telephone. Stevie, Angelica, Greg and his chum Stonky all had their 'mobiles' in their pockets. I really must ban them from the table. One phone on the wall is quite enough. Invariably, just as we start a meal, someone calls and it will be for one of the kids. Apart from the obvious intrusion, there is a curious thing that I have noticed they all do: they shout at each other down the phone nowadays. It used not to be so. I suspect it is because they are so used to mobiles which 'crack up', or whatever they call what we used to call wireless interference. As a result, they bawl at one another and all other conversation has to cease in order to make way for theirs. It crushes the atmosphere around the meal table, turning it into something more akin to the cafeteria at Liverpool Street Station.

Travelling on trains is no longer restful for this very reason. A crowded homeward-bound commuter now has to put up with a cacophony of phones imitating the first few bars of the William Tell Overture, and loud voices talking to loved ones. What the hell did people do before they could phone home to convey fatuous messages such as *'I'm on the train. It seems to be running on time'*. No, that's too far-fetched. *'We're stuck outside Shenfield with ice in the signals'*, more like. They should have 'No Phone' carriages on *all* trains, just as they have 'No Smoking' ones. I don't want my brains boiled by a hundred and seventy-five mobiles being used around me all the way home. They say that the energy radiated by a phone is about one hundredth of that used in a microwave oven . . . so there you go. One crowded carriage and it's boil-in-the-bag time.

Mrs D and I witnessed an amusing phone incident on the train recently. It involved a young businessman called *Dave* who was repeatedly trying to put a call through to someone called *Mick*. We didn't need MI5 training to gather this much from the interrupted broken exchanges that took place, all, I may add, at high volume.

'Hello, Mick. This is Dave. No, *Dave*. Am I? Right, I'll speak up. OKAY, MICK. Oh bugger . . .'

He redialled.

'Mick? MICK? YEAH, DAVE . . . not good . . . I SAID, NOT GOOD. YOU KEEP BREAKING UP. YEAH . . . JUST QUICKLY THEN . . . Oh sod.'

He redialled.

'MICK? YEAH, DAVE AGAIN. RIGHT . . . YEAH . . . I'M ON THE TRAIN AND . . .'

At that moment the train rushed into a tunnel and phone reception was lost again. I *love* tunnels! They throw whole carriages of inconsiderate phone users into indignant outrage. At that moment the ticket inspector walked by and our man *Dave* actually had the audacity to complain. The official said, without a twitch of humour, 'Well, sir, the tunnel has been there for some time, certainly for a few years before your phone was invented. I should wait until we come out again; it will be quite all right then.'

The call which heralds suppertime at home is usually a telephone marketing one. I cannot understand the logic of attempting to abuse the private telephone at that particular time of night. By definition, the canvasser will get short shrift if they call while supper is being prepared, children are manky and the dog is cross-legged for a walk. Don't market researchers do *any* research, or do they think it will work for that very reason? Perhaps they do: 'Look, I'm really busy at the moment. I'm browning garlic with one hand and changing the baby with the other, but I'll have three of those nice conservatories, two sets of double-glazing all round, and you can *"White-o-Seal"* the exterior of my house for good measure. Yuh, yuh, okay. And a donation to *Save the Seals* as well. Just send the bill. Goodbye.'

The first phone to go off belonged to Greg's friend *Stonky*. He has some bastardised corruption of *Swan Lake* programmed into his mobile. Every time it rings, I expect him to leap up and dance the pas de deux.

'Hi Mum . . . yup . . . cool . . . yuh, yuh . . . nope . . . yuh . . . cool . . . ciao.'

At least it was brief and to the point. He looked at me and said 'Sorry. It was Mum.'

You don't say.

Stonky amazes me. Can you believe this? The boy is teaching English to *Japanese students!* It's true. He has a holiday job at a summer tutorial college. When Greg first told me, I thought he was kidding. The thought of dozens of Japanese students paying good money then to be presented with Stonky as a teacher is bizarre. I imagine one of them going back home in September and proudly meeting his parents, Mr and Mrs Nagosami, and with an inane grin, saying, 'Ah so. Yuh. Cool, chiwl out man. Wicked. See ya in ten. Ha so.'

The second call was for Angelica. She coloured up. It was . . . *Jacko*. I have never seen anyone dispose of a call quite as rapidly as Angelica flushed that one away. In the space of one second she managed to say 'Hi, Jacko. We're eating now. Can I call you back? Bye.' I don't think he got a chance to reply because it came out as 'Hijkoweetinigtowncniclubacby.' And that was it.

The third call was for Angelica as well. Strictly, it wasn't a call; it was a *text*. I gather they can tell when a text comes in because they get the *Ride of the Valkyries* instead of *William Tell*. *I* can tell when a text is arriving because the phone is plunged between the knees, under the tablecloth. The aural equivalent would be leaving the room. A text is apparently the *de rigueur* way to send messages. It's like the old-fashioned teleprinter, except that it appears on their phone screens in a series of hieroglyphics such as,

'CU2nite HopeUROK LUVU4EVA LOLGLK(-:§'. The rapidity with which they create these messages is staggering. It is done with the *thumb,* which flicks back and forth across the keypad like greased lightning. I am sure all this thumbing is going to produce a monstrous rash of repetitive strain injuries in the future. No one ever uses his or her thumbs for anything else. Mind you, looking at the little gang around the table, the same could apply to most parts of their bodies . . .

Angelica's fiddling under the table continued as her meal became cold, and Greg, Stonky and Stevie finished their food. The look on her face, as she screwed up her features and attempted to overcome her deficiencies in the dexterity department, rendered her almost unrecognisable. Finally, she slapped the phone onto the table.

'Thassit. Dumped,' she exclaimed.

'Serious? Jacko?'

'Def. Why not?'

'With a text?' queried Greg, incredulously.

'Yup. And why not?' she asked indignantly.

'Thass a bit rough, isn't it? I mean you could have, like, e-mailed him or something.'

All of which meant nothing at all to me. I just ate my supper and watched, fascinated, and quietly wondered why Angelica had developed a sudden interest in the council's refuse tip.

The fourth call was for Stevie who picked up his phone, glanced at it and then switched it off! He seemed to know who was calling him.

'Who?' said Greg.

'Rat. He's so lame.'

'Dead cert. An irrel. Sad, mate, sad.'

The fifth call was also for Stevie. He took the phone out of his pocket, looked at it and said, '*Wicked.*' Having blipped the 'on' button, he said, in a *very* loud voice, 'Alex. Mate. How yer doing? . . . Wicked, you're nearly here, then. Okay. There's a roundabout, like, coming up, yeah? Got it? Right. Take the first left; okay . . . sorry, sorry, sorry *right*; yeah right. Sorry mate . . .

Yeah, I did hear him hooting. Okay, on your left, I do mean left, yeah; there's a junction by one of those, like, bollard thingies? Take a left . . .'

The instructions continued for *ten minutes* until Stevie was saying 'Fine. Now, on your right, like, any moment now. Wicked. Drive in and park somewhere. Yeah that's cool. No, we never lock them. Come along the path and the door's in front of you . . . that's it. Turn the handle and come in.'

There was a knock at the door, and Alex walked in. It was like air traffic control talking down a troubled 747, or *Star Trek*: 'Kirk here! Beam me down Scotty'. Ah, those were the days . . . except that it has nearly all come true, of course.

The most extraordinary thing about all of this phoning is not the incredible technological wizardry that makes it possible, but the way these kids *time* calls from their friends. Supper in our house is a movable feast, so to speak; it has no fixed time, so that they cannot possibly be planning it all in advance. There's no opportunity to prearrange it: 'Make it seven fifty-three and fifty seconds, Flic.' Regardless of how many calls we have had during a meal, and I have to be fair here, we do have some meals which are accompanied only by the sound of chomping and grunting, I guarantee that as we rise to clear the trough, sorry, I meant to say *table,* a couple of the children will offer to help. 'Dad, you chill. We'll clear away,' and, *just* as they pick up the first plate, and Fido rises from his bed knowing it's scraps time, at least two phones will go off. I swear they have some sort of programmer under the table. They must bleep their friends as if to say *'Now! Do it now!'* because the synchronicity with which it happens time after time is just . . . well, *awesome.* Mrs D and I have often looked at one another as two of them disappear out of the room with their phones, saying 'Back in a tick,' and two more will rush off for an urgent appointment with *Eastenders.* The remaining ones will wander uselessly around the kitchen performing a number of domestic tasks, all of dubious value, such as putting the condiments and napkins away in the fridge.

Quite why Alexander Graham Bell and John Logie Baird are hailed as national scientific heroes, I cannot imagine. By my reckoning, they have a great deal to answer for, not least that at about seven fifty-five on most evenings I can be found alone in the kitchen, with Fido, stacking the dishwasher and scrubbing saucepans.

Pagers, those little pocket gadgets which were the precursor to the texting telephone, have of course come and gone. They are now nearly *history,* but one of the loveliest stories of the human warmth behind all this technology happened a few years ago and involved Phil, Mrs D and a lady at pager-control. Phil had set off to meet his first ever girlfriend, Cordelia, at Liverpool Street Station. Being a feckless sort of boy, he had rolled out of bed at about the same time that Cordelia's train probably rolled into Waterloo. She was to cross London and meet him under the clock at Liverpool Street. At least, that is what *he said* they had arranged. Mrs D had furnished him with the family pager, purchased for just such occasions, but, of course, Phil could not contact her. Pagers are one-way traffic. An hour after contact time at the clock, the phone rang and it was Phil to say that Cordelia was nowhere to be seen at the station. Mrs Dudgeon, trying to act as gentle broker in this touching little love affair, told Phil to remain under the clock while she tried to page Cordelia who had also been leant her parents' gadget, presumably because they, like us, had little faith in their child's ability to make a workable arrangement, and feared for her well-being in the middle of London.

Mrs D called the paging service and, on being asked for her page message by a pleasant and quietly spoken lady operator, said, 'Cordelia. Phil is looking for you under the main clock at Liverpool Street. Hope you meet up soon.'

The lady repeated the message, as they used to do before it became *digitised,* and Mrs D hung up. A little later, the phone rang and it was Cordelia to say that she was waiting under the clock, except that she was at Waterloo and not Liverpool Street as Phil thought he had arranged.

197

My wife phoned the paging number again and left a message for Cordelia explaining that she should stay where she was and that she would ask Phil to go to Waterloo to meet her. She then sent another page to Phil, saying, 'Cordelia is waiting for you under clock at Waterloo. Go to meet her. She will wait. Love, Mum.' For a while, there was no word from either of the young lovebirds and Mrs Dudgeon assumed all was well. However, the phone rang and it was Phil.

'I'm at Waterloo, Mum, but I can't see a clock. Where is it?'

Realising that the fiasco could continue forever if there happened to be *two* clocks, she sent a message to Cordelia to move to the entrance to Platform Thirteen because she knew there was only one of those. The message was accepted and paged. She then paged Phil intending to give him the same instruction: 'Ignore clock. Go to Platform Thirteen. Cordelia awaits. Love Mum.'

Quite by chance, and it was very unlikely considering the number of pager operators taking the calls, Mrs Dudgeon got the same pleasant lady who had taken her first message. 'Oh no,' the kind voice said, '*poor Cordelia.* Is she *still* waiting for Phil? I think that boy had better buck up his ideas. She won't wait for him forever, you know.'

27

Fido barked as I made tea and, glancing out of the window, I saw the postman and raised a hand in greeting. Thank goodness he doesn't come from the same depot as the Parcel Force man. I gathered the mail from the mat and sifted through it. Mostly circulars and bills. I keep receiving those annoying and, I have to say, naively optimistic letters, which are always postmarked Lima, or Amsterdam, which request that I send *twenty-nine pounds* to receive my *'Special consignment'* which will then be released from the shipping warehouse. They are usually consigned to the bin without being opened. Who, I ask, is going to send that sort of money to such an organisation? I suppose people must do otherwise they wouldn't be in business. Clearly, they are fairly desperate because as each week passes, more letters arrive telling me that it is my *'last chance* to receive the consignment' followed by my *'last ever chance'*, and more recently my *'absolutely last ever chance'*. Today, it was my *'absolutely the last ever possible imaginable chance'*. Good luck to them, I say. No doubt they are fat, rich and well and truly out of reach of the jurisdiction of British Law, and of people who might wish to have their money-back guarantee fulfilled.

I poured my tea and opened the bills. *What! Outrageous!* A bill from the Water Authority for 'removing surplus water'. I scrawled *'Not known. Floated Away'*, on the back, sealed it and put it by the back door for posting. What absolute buggers! They had eventually turned up hours after the event and done *nothing*, besides which, the problem was someone else's, not mine (not that

I could remember which organisation it should have been). As an afterthought, I added, *'Try Highways'* on the back of the envelope. All I needed was an invoice from the council for the *'Hire of Sandbags'*.

Among the mail was a reminder that any entries for the forthcoming Strumpling Green Flower Show needed to be confirmed within two days. I put *that* one to one side. *That* I could not miss. For several years it had become a major event in the lives of the males in the village as all and sundry competed in the *'Men's Bread Challenge'*. This year's entry for the weekend's show required a *Two Pound Loaf* to be submitted. Last year it had been *Five Wholemeal Rolls*. So cutthroat was the competition that even sabotage was not unknown. A friend, who had lost his entry programme, telephoned a lifelong buddy to enquire as to how many rolls were required. *'Four,'* came the emphatic answer. That caused a bit of bad blood, I can tell you. Generally speaking, in Strumpling we do not lock our doors much, but around the time of the show, security is everything. It would not be too outrageous to suggest that, last year, someone came into my kitchen and spiked my bread mixture with too much salt. I would never have put *that much* in it. Angelica's response when she tasted the bread was unprintable. A two-pound loaf, huh? I wrote a cheque for my entry. The die was cast. Men have died for lesser things.

The last letter turned out to be a cheque, not a bill. From *Serendipity*. It came with their *compliments*, whatever they may be. It was for thirty-five pounds and twenty-seven pence. Remind me to change my insurance company to another that is actually in the business of insuring houses. I'd also like to find out where Merrick Linton-Forthworthy lives. I have a sizeable amount of horse manure left.

It was a beautiful morning and I enjoyed a stroll around the cottage, spoke pleasantly to Mrs D's *Albertine*, which was looking much perkier since I had applied a good deal of liquid fertiliser to the roots in an attempt to rejuvenate it, and then I sat in the garden with a book. I felt I deserved a break. The bathroom was finished and fit for Mrs Dudgeon's return, the house was moderately tidy, at least as long as one did not open any doors, and only the lawn-mowing was outstanding. I confess I dozed a little, enjoying the early heat of a fine August day. I awoke to a cry. At first, I could not locate it at all. It came to me as a faint, rather muffled, high-pitched wail that could almost have been mistaken for a woman singing. Mrs Philpott, I wondered. Might she be pegging out her washing and, like me, be full of the joys of a beautiful summer morning? I crept close to the hedge that bordered her garden and peered through the gap, which I had blocked up since Fido did his business on her Tassel Bush. No one was around. I turned away but, as I did so, I heard the unmistakable, frail sounds of my elderly neighbour calling.

'Help me. Please help me.'

Then there was a silence.

'Somebody, *please* help me.'

Without further ado, I pushed through the hedge and into her garden. All around were the immaculate results of Mr and Mrs Philpott's labours. Stunning beds of flowering annuals, dahlias like dinner plates, and gladioli standing sentinel-like with their perfectly ordered stakes. No wonder they had taken exception to Fido's late evening visits to their propagating bed. Hastening across the lawn to the house, I was no wiser as to where the sound was coming from. I stood still, turning my head this way and that to catch the next cry. Yes! There she was! Inside a sash window, apparently standing on the sill with a large expanse of the back of her voluminous white bloomers pressed against the glass!

I hurried to the open window where the upper sash was drawn down as low as it would go.

'Mrs Philpott?' I enquired, somewhat nervously, not being sure quite how to approach an elderly lady from this particular perspective. 'Are you all right?' I asked, which was I admit, under the circumstances, not the brightest response she might have hoped for.

201

'Who is it?' she called, unable to turn round. 'Thank goodness you've come.'

'It's Duncan Dudgeon. Next door...' I was going to add '... the one with the dog,' but decided that was unnecessary.

'Please get me down, Mr Dudgeon. I seem to have hung myself up.'

It was only when I hauled myself up onto the outside sill and supported myself with an arm hooked over the sash, that I was able to thrust my head inside and see what the problem was. Mrs Philpott was not experimenting with a novel way of polishing her windows; she was actually hanging from her *bloomer elastic* which had snagged on the window clasp.

There is no doubt about it, old-fashioned bloomers are made to last. They are constructed with the same sort of built-in failsafe factors as Los Angeles freeway bridges: to withstand earthquakes and the impact of about thirteen stone of Mrs Philpott trying to bungee jump from her window catch. I was quite nervous about doing the obvious, which was to open my pocketknife and just cut the elastic that was under the most phenomenal strain. The dear old soul's feet were not on the windowsill at all; she was genuinely *suspended* from her elastic.

'Will you be able to break your fall if I cut you free?' I asked, viewing the furniture inside the room. The obvious thing was to free her from the other side, but there was certainly no space for me to squeeze through the window with her taking up the majority of the available space.

'Can I get in elsewhere?' I asked, which prompted a little gurgle of laughter.

'That's how I came to be *here,* my dear,' she said. 'I locked myself out. Just cut me down and hang on.'

Cut, and hang on? I thought, as I grasped a fistful of bloomers, which, not to put too fine a point on it, is difficult to do in a genteel manner. I hovered, knife poised.

'Ready? On the count of three, Mrs Philpott. One, two, three!' There was a silent explosion of energy as the elastic gave way and

202

the full weight of my neighbour momentarily transferred to my left hand, and I lowered her, probably too hurriedly, to the floor. She fell forwards and sank onto her knees before lying down exhausted. I slid in through the open window and within a few seconds had helped her into an armchair.

Despite the fact that Fido had once started a chilly if not quite *cold war* with our neighbours, the adventure brought Mrs Philpott and me together again, and before long we were chuckling over a cup of tea. It transpired that Mr Philpott had gone out early that morning and Mrs P had gone out to the greenhouse to water the tomatoes before the sun reached its zenith. The back door had unfortunately swung shut and locked her out. Walking around the house, she had spotted the open sash in the living room, somehow managed to climb up on the outer sill and from there she forced the sash down. Having climbed in, she was unable to lower herself to the floor and had summoned all her courage and jumped. What she had not realised was that as she had slid over the window, she had left a turn of elastic over the clasp, which is how I came to find her; suspended a few feet above the floor.

Needless to say, the story of Mrs Philpott's bloomers caused quite a stir as the children drifted down to 'lunch'. The boys became inordinately obsessed with alternative uses for Mrs P's cast-offs, which ranged from a new high-tech, infinitely variable sail for Stevie's board, to a potential launch system for the local gliding club. Quite unusually, they all roared with laughter at my imitation of the old lady's accent as I related what she had told me over a cup of tea.

'Mr Dudgeon. Oi laughed and oi croied, oi did. Oi just hung there an' oi din't know what to do. Oi went up an' down an' up an' down and oi couldn't make moi feet touch that old floor . . .'

I think she was slightly flattering herself. There was no way that she went up and down on that elastic.

Later in the afternoon, when I was walking up and down the lawn behind our old *Ransomes* mower, Angelica brought me a mug of tea. Had I given it but a moment's thought, I would have immediately concluded that something was afoot. What did she need? A lift somewhere? An extra handout, over and above her allowance? You may think me a little cynical, but over the years I have come to know this girl well. When I stopped the mower and sat on the old bench under our ancient Bramley, to drink my tea, and she came up and *sat down beside me*, I *knew* there was something up.

'Dad,' she said casually, as if in passing, 'Shona just called.'

'That's nice,' I said. 'All well?'

'Yuh. I s'pose so. She phoned from Greece. She's on an island with some friends.'

'Lucky old Shona, eh? Not the friends – being in Greece, I mean.'

I imagined it. Deep azure skies. The beckoning depths of clear, blue water. The sizzling sun. 'I bet you wish you were out there, love.' I smiled and drank my tea.

'Dad . . .'

'Yes, my darling?'

'Can I go out to Greece?'

'*Go out to Greece?* Sweetest, you have to be joking!'

'No, Dad, listen. Shona's gone out there with her friends and they've had a big bust up and now she's gone off on her own.'

Quite honestly, I wasn't at all surprised. I wouldn't have said this to Angelica, but *Shona*, privately known to Mrs D and me as *Moaner*, is the most selfish girl in the world. She is *never* satisfied. Her parents dote on her and have given her everything she could possibly want, and more. Her life is steeped in opulence, and I expect her friends had had enough of her demanding ways and given her the old heave-ho.

'She's lonely. Her father says that he will pay if I want to go out to meet up with her for the rest of the holiday. Please say yes.'

'No. You told me you were going to get a day job next week, to earn some money for medical school. If you go to Greece, you'll only spend what you have saved.'

'I won't . . . I can't. I haven't got anything saved any more . . . it's all gone.'

204

'I see. Is that Question Two? Question One is, "May I go to Greece with Shona?" and Question Two is, "May I borrow about four hundred quid to finance it?"'

'Two hundred. Shona's dad will pay for the air fare and ferry; I just need spending money and, after all, you'd still have to feed me at home . . . wouldn't you?'

I looked at her. 'I would, you are right. That would cost about twenty-five pounds . . .' I pulled my wallet from my trouser pocket.

'Oh, Daaaaad.'

'All right. *But*, when you return, you, young lady are getting a job even if it's plucking chickens down at the factory.'

'Plucking chickens . . . you are kidding. I couldn't do that! It'd be disgusting. All that mess, ugh!'

Remembering how Angelica had reacted when I cut my finger and dripped over the new bath, I said, 'Darling, what about all the *mess*, as you call it, which you are going to have to cope with at medical school? I mean, how are you going to manage that?'

'Oh, that's different,' she said brightly. 'That's clean mess. That's what doctors have to do.'

'I see.'

It would have been much more straightforward to get Angelica off to Greece if we had been able to locate her passport. As a rule I keep them all in my study, but hers was not there. Almost by definition, that meant it was *in her bedroom*. A cold shudder swept over me at the very idea. It constituted the ideal opportunity to say 'Clear up your room, and you will find it. It will be here, *somewhere*.' I took a deep breath.

'Angelica,' I said, surveying the sea of clothes and old A-level work still spread evenly over the floor, chair, cupboards and bed. 'Clear up your room and you are sure to find it. It will be here . . . somewhere.'

'Oh, Dad, don't hassle me. There's nothing wrong with my room. Anyway, I haven't got time for clearing up. I need my *passport*, not a tidy bedroom.'

An hour later I went up to see how the job was progressing only to find that, and I hesitate to say this because it seems *impossible*, there was *twice the mess*. Now, *everything* was turned out. Drawers spilled drunkenly over the floor, and the clothes and papers which had previously reached some sort of state of repose and general stability now looked as if they had been given the once-over by one of those leaf-blowers. It seemed to have all gone up and come down again. Angelica sat in the middle of the chaos, close to tears.

'Oh, I don't know *where* it is!' she said crossly, chucking a biology file onto the floor so that it burst and dozens of pieces of paper added themselves to the chaos.

'Right, Angelica. Listen to me carefully. *When did you last have it?*'

'Oh, Dad, don't start doing those silly detective games. I can't stand it.'

'They're not *silly detective games,* love. When did you last have it?'

'France.'

'Right. In what?'

'Jacket,'

'Right, get it and go through it.'

'I have.'

'Do it again.'

She searched all the pockets. 'Nope.'

'Right. What else did you take with you?'

'Nothing. We only went for a day trip.'

'No bag? Are you sure?'

'Yes. Absolutely. Nothing . . . Wait . . . I took a bag!'

'Which one?'

'I dunno.'

She sat, her head in her hands.

'*Think,* Angelica. Think. Big bag? Small bag?'

'Rucksack! That's it. The small rucksack! I had it in the pocket of the small rucksack!'

An hour later, the *search*, and the associated devastation, had spread through the hall cupboards, the cellar and every nook and cranny we could think of. No rucksack was forthcoming. We sat and trawled through every detail of their return from a post A- level celebratory trip to Calais. Then, the penny dropped.

'Flic's got it! She borrowed it to take her duty free home! I remember now! It's at Flic's!'

'And where is Flic?' I asked, pleased to be making some progress. To think, I could have been finishing the grass, or even sitting in the sun reading a book.

'Greece.'

To cut a very long story short, Angelica paid the price for 'dumping' Jacko by text, and she had to eat humble pie, as he was the only person remaining in the shared house. To give the boy his everlasting due, he selflessly hopped into his brand new Golf GTi, after work, and sped up to Suffolk for the evening having found the rucksack with the passport secreted in the side pocket. I don't think I would have done that under the circumstances, but . . . such is the course of true love. The boy is obviously *infatuated with her*. I thought: I must talk to him, and soon.

Having ascertained where it was, and gratefully accepted Jacko's offer to bring it back, she then had a mad time on the Internet buying her tickets. I kept right out of it except for the crucial moment when I had to produce my *'flexible friend'* in order to pay.

'Right,' I said to her, finally returning to my mower as the sun went down. 'I suggest you now go and clear up your room before Jacko comes. It looks as though a tornado has hit it.'

Later that evening, I found Angelica sitting on her bed in the midst of precisely the same devastation while she gazed lovingly into Jacko's eyes. They then spent no less than an hour outside saying 'goodbye' to one another before he sped off in his smart little car, promising faithfully to be in touch the moment Angelica returned from Greece.

Can somebody *please* tell me *why* we have children?

28

Not long after Jacko had taken his drawn-out and rather amorous leave, I scanned the calendar studying the remainder of the week. Thursday was earmarked for a brief overnight visit, with Melanie and Edward, to the other parents; *the Dudgeon ones*, returning in good time on Friday which was reserved for *the* loaf. Saturday was, needless to say, left clear for the Flower Show. Subject to confirmation, Mrs D was due to fly back in the middle of the following week.

I spoke to Greg, Stevie and Phil, reminding them of my intended absence with the two younger ones the following night, as I knew that the chances of them surfacing *before* we left for their grandparents were very slim. Stevie had been up for work each morning but, sadly, that phenomenon had now passed. He had come home early one day and told me, rather sheepishly, that he had been sacked. It transpired that he had been at work in one of 'his' bedrooms and, while dutifully busying himself, he had switched on the television, which predictably, but unbeknown to him, was strictly forbidden to the 'chambermaids'. One thing had led to another and Stevie had eventually been found fast asleep across the bed having dozed off while watching *The Simpsons*. The hotel owner had not been impressed, and had fired Stevie before the boy managed even to hoist himself into a sitting position.

'Make sure you feed Fido and give him some exercise, please. We'll be back by lunchtime Friday. Look after Phil. I know he can take care of himself . . . and you two come to that. Just keep an eye on him.'

'Chill, Dad,' Greg said. 'We'll be fine. Give our love to Nana and Grumps.'

I had spoken to Mel and explained Mrs D's proposal that she, Mel, add some of her own savings to the forty pounds I was planning to give her for the trainers. I wouldn't say that the suggestion was met with ecstatic jubilation and dancing in the streets, but she shrugged her shoulders and said, 'S'pose that's okay.' On the journey, she sat in the back of the car with her personal stereo headset jammed in her ears, while she played on a hand-held game machine, which absorbed the remainder of her attention. My only contact with her was the swish-swishing from her headphones, and an occasional junior expletive as she was out-manoeuvred by the box of electronic wizardry. The charming picture was punctuated by regular *Spluck* noises as she burst her bubble gum.

Ed, fortunately, was better company and we chatted and enjoyed a rather juvenile game of 'pub cricket' which would have had a very predictable outcome as we had played it so many times before on the same journey. However, just before we arrived, I took a detour to a nearby hamlet and by a circuitous route managed to pass *The Hare and Hounds*, leaving it on my side of the car by the slightly devious method of reversing down the village street. We paused outside to count the legs on the signboard.

'Eight dogs and a hare! That's thirty-six please, Ed,' I declared.

A little argument followed, because not all of the three-dozen legs were visible in the painting, but he grudgingly allowed me thirty-one and was still sulking when we arrived at my parents' house. Grumps must have wondered what had been happening when Ed walked into the kitchen and appealed for a ruling about drivers who go backwards past pubs that weren't even on the route. My mother looked totally bewildered and promptly chastised me for stopping for a drink when I knew that the meal would be on the table.

Greg telephoned just as we were about to sit down to lunch. I have to say, the boy was up earlier than usual. He wanted to know whether it was possible to start the van without a key. I suggested that he could, but that it would be easier to do so with it. 'Yuh, but, there is like, a problem there, Dad. Any idea where I might have put the keys?'

I listed all the places where they might be wilfully concealing themselves.

'Right. I'll check it out. Cheers, Dad. Any idea when you might be back tomorrow?'

I told him that it would be around midday, to which he replied, 'Cool. Yup, cool, cool, cool.'

Strange boy.

We had a pleasant time with my parents, catching up on their news, which essentially seemed to focus on a neighbour's errant flock of sheep which insisted on breaking out of their field in a bid to find greener grass... and my mother's rose bushes. After lunch, I accompanied her very patiently around the garden as she pointed out how well her *Coreopsis* had flowered during the summer, the staggering proportions of her *Deodar,* and the delightful scent of her *Boule de Neige.* When asked for my opinion as to whether the pretty blue-flowered shrub was *impressus* or *thyrsiflorus*, I peered closely at it and scratched my chin.

'*Very* difficult to say,' I agreed sympathetically. 'I'm no expert on these things,' which was a good deal more honest than she probably realised at the time.

My parents' garden has always seemed to attract the neighbouring farmer's malcontents. Although sheep were their current problem, there had been a time when it had been bullocks which would wander in, usually in the half-light of dawn. When Greg was small, a herd had strayed, making their way through early one Christmas morning leaving a myriad of hoof marks in the powdering of snow. I so exploited the chance occurrence, by taking him out to examine the 'reindeer tracks', that the memory had served as his rebuttal for those who made out periodic cases for the non-existence of Santa Claus. Until he was about seventeen, Greg, bless him, could raise the odd eyebrow by beginning Santa's defence with an exposition of the facts: that Father Christmas had once visited *Nana's garden*. Rightly or wrongly, I disabused him of the idea before he went to university, where I thought it might do more than raise the odd eyebrow among his new-found friends.

It seemed no time at all before supper was ready. Having had a substantial lunch, at home I might have opted for a sandwich or two and a cup of coffee. Such a notion was unthinkable *chez Dudgeon*. It may be a principle by which every grandmother loads her dining room table when the family arrive, but my dear mother, whom we all adore, seems to have a compulsion to test the engineering of Mr Ercol's handiwork to the point of destruction. It was not unusual for my father to be summoned to manufacture temporary props in order to support the groaning timber which was on the brink of succumbing under the onslaught of hams, sides of beef, salads, fresh bread, cold trifles, hot puddings, fruit cakes, cheese boards, fruit and so on. And all this for a 'light lunch before you travel home'. On this particular evening, the initial level of preparation indicated a modest meal for supper. I breathed a sigh of relief, not least because I had been hoping that she would not have forgotten that she only had *three* guests. An appealing fresh fruit salad was carried through to the table, and I remained heartily optimistic. It was shortly before the meal that it became apparent to me that preparations were clearly underway for a feast of some significant proportions. Up until that point it had been deceptive, as Mrs D senior has a habit of laying down substantial stocks of home-cooked food and then quite suddenly procuring major items from the freezer. She takes pleasure in seeing her guests fed well, preferably leaving the table with some great difficulty. The words '*comfortably fed*' have no place in her gastronomic vocabulary, and I doubt that there has ever been anything more guaranteed to light up her eyes than to espy a lean figure who needs '*feeding up*'. To her, these words are magic words; the promise of an opportunity to bring all of her benevolent

211

culinary talents to bear upon the needy victim. *All* children fall into this category, for they are all *growing* boys and girls, but *boys* are far better targets than girls in this respect. Their apparently hollow legs, and bottomless pits instead of stomachs, have made each of the male grandchildren vulnerable to death by *Nana's overfeeding*. The girls are not in the running. Despite having survived twenty-five years of marriage to my lovely, kitchen-competent wife, even *I* am still considered a reasonable bet. The fact that I need to watch my waistline is irrelevant. I am sure my mother still has a sneaking suspicion that I am *not properly fed.*

Realising the nature of the impending onslaught, for I had seen a whole leg of pork being lifted from the oven to be basted, I went to the garden and began vigorously to walk up and down, up and down, desperately trying to *make space.* Ed sat playing cards with Grumps. I tried to beckon him away, to persuade him to join me, but such was the strength of his hand in their game of rummy, that he declined. I knew that preprandial exercise was his *only* hope of survival. He was, from that moment on, doomed.

Had we moved from the light mackerel-based hors d'oeuvre to the dessert, all would have been well. But instead, a roast dinner intervened which would have put the court of Henry VIII to shame. Not only was there the most delicious crackling-covered leg of pork, but there were also sausages. In addition to the sausages, there was a rich accompaniment akin to stuffing (*I just thought I'd try out a new recipe*) and, in addition to that, there were roast potatoes, creamed potatoes with a hint of nutmeg, parsnips baked to that delicious shade of semi-charcoal, baby sprouts, peas, beans and apple sauce, all served with a gravy which was so thick and nourishing that it would have served as a soup. To understand the enormity of the undertaking, one needs to appreciate that my mother had, shortly before, purchased some *new* dinner plates. *They were huge.* Each was about the size of a tea tray and had been acquired, not because there was anything aesthetically wrong with her original ones, but because they were simply *not big enough.* Nana was in her element as she served lashings of pork which, frankly, would have sufficed for my fortnightly meat ration. Accompaniments and vegetables vied with each other for standing room on the plate. Ed and I looked at one another, both enchanted and appalled. This was it. *This* was The Challenge.

We both did well. Neither of us crumpled, and we approached the finishing straight with barely a sigh. We put our cutlery together and sat back. Justice had been done to the beautiful meal. Melanie wasn't even in the running with her bird-like appetite. In my mother's eyes, she wasn't worthy competition. It was *the boys* who counted at the table.

'Edward. Have a spot more, darling.'

'Er, no, really Nana, thanks. It was delicious.'

'Oh, go on. Just a little. I'm sure Dad's not feeding you properly while Mum's away. Your cheeks look hollow,' she said, as more slices were cut from the pork. 'Have a little . . . Grumps and I will be eating this for a week.'

'All right, Nana, thanks. Just a little . . . woah, thank you . . . no, only one sausage, thanks. That's fine. No, please, I don't think I can manage three roast potatoes . . . I'm really rather full. Not so many parsnips . . .'

At the end of round three we were moderately uncomfortable but nothing that a mile or two of brisk walking wouldn't have shaken down. It had been a very fine meal. I felt that a tangerine, or a nibble of Stilton, or a fresh Victoria plum would have just rounded everything off beautifully. We were, as Greg might have poetically described it, *'well stuffed'*.

'You boys sit tight. I won't be long,' said Nana, as she disappeared into the kitchen. My father adjusted his trouser belt, shook his head despairingly and settled back in his chair.

'I'm so full,' sighed Ed, struggling for breath at the same moment as his grandmother appeared round the door with a large dish.

I should explain that my mother knows that I cannot make *spotted dick*. She knows that no matter how hard I try, I cannot emulate the texture of her suet pudding, which she seems to make

213

so effortlessly. Mine are good . . . hers are exquisite perfection itself. She bore hers steaming through the dining room as though it was a trophy she had hunted down all day.

'It's lucky,' she said, without a hint of apology, 'I had this one in the freezer. I'd been wondering what I could give you, and there it was. I know you love this, Ed. It's your favourite isn't it?'

'Mum,' I tried to remonstrate, 'but you've made fruit salad as well . . .'

'Pah!'

She dismissed it as though it was lightweight food for namby-pambies, and sliced *slabs* of suet pudding onto the *old dinner plates*. I prayed for strength.

I'm not sure what it is that makes it impossible to say, 'Enough. Sorry, but I really can't manage another crumb, I'm full.' To do so would be to attack the dear woman at the heart of her motherhood *and* her grannydom; it would be tantamount to destroying her very being, that part of her which more or less justifies her existence on this earth, and worse, it would leave her doubting our undying love for her. It would be rejection at its most brutal. So we ate.

It's not often that I reach the point where I actually begin to plan where each spoonful of dessert will go when it reaches my stomach. It reminds me of an experience I once had of shovelling coal into the firebox of an express steam locomotive: one to the side near the front; one to the side near the back; one at the back, and so on. It was rather like packing the last remnants of a house move when the removal van is already fit to burst, and someone remembers that there is the garden shed to clear. Out come two mowers, a vast collection of garden tools, a collapsed Wendy house and three punctured paddling pools. The removal men blink and sweat in disbelief and, by some miracle, pack it all in. *Then* someone remembers *the garden roller*!

Ed and I finish. Melanie has somehow escaped and is eating a slice or two of apple!

'That was delicious, Mum,' I whisper, unable to breathe deeply enough to raise a normal voice. 'It was . . . fantastic . . .'

214

'Now then, Ed. How about a little more? A very small piece? It seems such a waste . . .' Nana says, looking mournfully at the other half of the pudding.

Ed is looking ill. He shakes his head.

'No . . . thank you . . . I couldn't . . . I'm so full . . .' He exhales.

'What about a spot of fruit salad?'

We look aghast. Sitting down is now impossible. I must stand. I must get to the sink, to lean gently upon the worktop and wash dishes . . . anything to support my over-burdened frame in a vertical posture.

I had the feeling that all was not well with Ed when I heard him go out to the lavatory at about midnight. He never goes in the night. I heard the door close and then there were pitiful sounds of retching. Tested beyond endurance, he was . . . *making space.*

29

The lady who was kneeling beside her front wall, gently tugging weeds from her Aubretia bed, looked up in considerable surprise as we screeched to a halt and disgorged Melanie who was promptly sick. Fortunately, Mel had the social wherewithal to avoid the woman's immaculately groomed verge and head for a farmer's field entrance where it couldn't have mattered less. I smiled awkwardly at the lady through the open window and passed a favourable comment about the weather, as various *groorping* noises emanated from behind the car.

It may have been the effects of sitting absorbed in her electronic game, or too much gum. Whichever, she eventually climbed back into the car looking very pale. I asked the question which all parents seem to need to pose on these occasions.

'Are you all right?'

Quite patently, she was not. I think that when we ask this question we actually mean, 'Is there any more coming up?' but we haven't quite got the heart to say it.

Truth be known, the countryside has, over the years, been liberally peppered with Dudgeon vomit. With six children, who have all struggled with car travel, and all passed through the 'Technicolor-yawn' stage at one time or another, we can actually supply directions based upon the locations of these kerbside traumas . . . 'You know, where Stevie honked up on that garage forecourt? Well, like, turn right there, okay? Then you get to this sort of pub place where Mum had to wash Glic down, yeah, and just after that you take a left . . .'

216

After a troubled night, Ed had been fine that morning, although I noticed that he eschewed one of Nana's full breakfasts in favour of a slice or two of toast. Reassuring Melanie that we would soon be home, we set off once more and I drove cautiously as we navigated the last few miles of road, full of endlessly twisting Suffolk bends.

I thought something was not quite right as we drove into the drive at *Cromwell's Retreat*. It may just have been the fact that Fido was lying on the lawn, in the sun, devouring a very large slab of cold, burnt pizza, or it may have been the girl who looked up from the old garden swing, where she sat with a mug in one hand and a cigarette in the other. I had *no* idea who she was and I have never seen her since. I stepped cautiously inside the house and paused. I heard Ed's sharp intake of breath.

To the right, the hall and sitting room looked as though the SAS may have recently launched a violent rescue attempt and made liberal use of stun grenades. My gaze took in the scene of total devastation. Not that the forces would have come through the windows armed with dozens of tins of lager, bottles of wine and vodka, but had they done so, I feel they may well have tidied up before taking their leave. Another lone figure, whom I did not recognise, was half-heartedly trying to scrape what appeared to be a mixture of digested olives and carrots from the carpet. I nodded to her. For one moment I wondered if we had perhaps returned to the wrong house.

'Morning,' I said, as though I was used to seeing my house trashed every morning.

'Hi,' she said nervously. 'I don't think Greg was expecting you back until lunchtime. He said . . .'

Her reference to my son reassured me. I *was* at home. I picked up a tin of half-finished beer that had disgorged itself over the coffee table, and stood it up. In the kitchen, the overall impression was the same. Quite why someone had seen fit to empty the entire contents of the fridge onto the floor and then grind it into the rush matting, I am not sure, but that is what appeared to have happened.

The sink was full of dirty plates, and every surface was covered with stale glasses and soup bowls that seemed to have doubled up as ashtrays. I suppose I should have been thankful for small mercies; at least the revellers had not ground their cigarette ends into Mrs Dudgeon's Indian dining room carpet.

Upstairs I made my way to Greg's room, stepping over various prone bodies as I did so. Opening his bedroom door was accompanied by a faint sucking noise as the oxygen rushed in. I peered across the gloomy room. There was a pungent aroma of decomposing adolescence. More bodies. I picked on one, which bore a family resemblance to my son, and shook it. It mumbled something. It *was* Greg. I put my face close to his ear and spoke firmly to him in a manner that I felt befitted the occasion.

'Can you hear me, Gregory?'

The eyes opened for a second, and then closed. I shook the slumbering form once more. I was tempted to tap on the skull to see if anyone was actually in.

'Hello, *Greg*. This is your father speaking,' I said in crisp tones, slightly louder than before.

The eyes opened wide.

'I would just like to warn you, Gregory, that you have *one minute* to shift yourself out of this bed. After that, I will not be held responsible for what I might do to you or any other prostrate creature which remains draped around my house. *Do you understand me?*'

Then I left. Stevie was awake, having been summoned by Ed. He was sitting on the edge of his bed gripping his head as if trying to hold it in place. I looked at him; one of my *professional looks*. Abruptly, he stood up, swayed, and struggled into a pair of jeans. Phil was fast asleep, propped on his side. A bowl beside his bed indicated he had suffered from threatened or actual revolt in the gastric department. I checked that he was breathing evenly and left. As I went downstairs, it occurred to me that *at least three* out of my six children had been vomiting in the last twelve hours.

By then, Greg and Stevie were both in the kitchen. They looked at me sheepishly.

'Sorry, Dad,' mumbled Stevie.

'Yuh. Really sorry. It all went, like, hopelessly wrong,' said Greg, waving his hand at the debris in a vague, despondent gesture.

'Boys . . . I am going out,' I announced. 'I am going shopping. I think that after last night, the fridge needs restocking.' I nodded in the direction of the empty cabinet. 'I will be one hour. When I come back, this house will be reasonably tidy and devoid of . . . of any of *your friends.*' I picked up my wallet and left with Melanie and Ed.

To give the lads their due, when I returned laden with shopping, they had done a pretty fair job. There was a veneer of order about the place and, despite the pub-like morning-after aroma, it looked as though we had established the basis for a spot of housework. I had a few carefully chosen words with Greg about Phil, who, I was told, was by then up and in the shower.

'I left you in charge, Greg. *You* were responsible for him. He got drunk and was sick.'

'I'm really sorry he had too much, Dad, but please believe me, I *did* look after him . . . at least, I made sure he was all right after he was ill . . . I kept checking him . . .'

Despite the folly of the whole venture, his remorse and evident concern for his brother were sincere. I told him so. Stevie came in.

'Now chaps!' I declared. 'A day of housework. I intend to make bread, but I have thoughtfully provided *you* with tins of polish, dusters, carpet shampoo, window cleaner, new Hoover bags . . . everything you could possibly want to liberate this house from the . . . the gunge of your errant ways. If you're not sure how to clean up, Greg, ask Stevie. He is a dab hand at it. Start downstairs and work steadily upwards. I will inspect it all at four this afternoon. You may stop for forty-five minutes to partake of a light lunch, which I will provide in an hour and a half. Off you go.'

30

My dough had risen beautifully, and once I had knocked it down again, I left it to rest beside the Aga for a further twenty minutes. The house was reverberating with the hum of the vacuum cleaner and the sounds of three busy lads all engaged, for once, in some useful activity. From where I was standing, I could see Phil, busy cleaning windows, and Greg on his hands and knees with a scrubbing brush and a bucket of foaming carpet cleaner. It was a rather splendid experience. Sitting in the sun with a mug of tea, amidst all the domestic endeavours, I had the feeling that I might be able to acclimatise to it. Perhaps it should become a condition of the boys staying at home . . . bed and board in return for light domestic duties. It had a certain *ring* to it.

I returned to my dough and kneaded it one more time. Quietly, I chanted over it, lest it should be in any doubt about the significance of its existence. 'You have been brought into this world to win, you will rise up and wipe the board, only red rosettes for you my little . . .'

'Dad. Are you feeling all right?'

It was Ed.

'Absolutely, old chap. On top of the world. Why do you ask?'

'You were . . . um, talking to the bread . . . how normal is that?'

'Everybody talks to his bread. It makes it rise better. Dough likes Radio Three too. This is no ordinary bread, you understand, Ed. *This is prize-winning bread* . . . it is the bread that will scoop the men's award at the village show. It's . . .'

'Dad, I don't want to interrupt you or anything, but Stevie sort of needs you. He's got the bathmat frilly-things wound round the Hoover.'

So much for my reverie about the boys competently performing light domestic duties. Having fetched a screwdriver kit and removed the bottom of the Hoover, I fitted a new belt because the old one had melted as it tried to reel in the bathmat. I returned to the loaf. A plait, that was what was needed. Something out of the ordinary. Something to bowl the judges over. Rolling it out, I cut it into three and began to plait. This was going to be the most high precision, most symmetrical loaf ever made. None of those snide little judge's comments on beige cards for this one. *'Lumpy and rather heavy in the middle'* as Hereward had had on his last year. The children had roared with laughter; they thought it was an apt description of the vicar's wife.

I set the loaf on a baking tray, brushed a little glaze over it and set it to prove once more. By the time the kitchen was tidied and everything was washed up and put away, it was time to bake the bread. Lovingly, I slid it gently into the top oven. The stage was set.

Upstairs, the stage was far from set. It looked as if Stevie was demolishing it. Having worked through the house as instructed, the boys were now beginning to sort out their rooms. An enormous pile of washing was gathering on the landing as what appeared to be two years' worth of clothes flew out of their bedroom doors. Apart from that, the startling impact of their cleaning spree was evident all over the house. I was impressed.

'How's it going, boys?' I enquired at Greg's door.

He wiped his brow and sat back on his haunches. 'Okay. How's it looking?'

'Fantastic. I think you boys missed your vocations.'

'Downstairs is nearly done,' he said. 'I washed the wood-block floor but I've still got to, like, polish it. I'll do it soon. How's the time?'

I looked at my watch. It was just after two-thirty. 'An hour and a half to go,' I said grinning. Could this really be my son? *I've washed the floor . . . I've still got to polish it!* Wonders would never cease.

The phone rang. If it had been one of their mates, I would have felt justified in asking them to call back after four, but it wasn't.

'Duncan!'

'Sweetest heart! How are you?'

'I'm fine. Actually, this is a surprise. I'm in London. Landed at midday. I'm just getting on a train at Liverpool Street. I'd finished everything over there and they twisted a few arms and fixed me a seat, so I thought I'd get back for the weekend.'

'That's brilliant, my darling. I can hardly believe it. Liverpool Street!'

'Can you meet me off the three forty-five? Must dash now or I'll miss it. See you soon!'

What an amazing surprise! Trust Mrs D to manage that! I hadn't anticipated seeing her for another four days. Just thinking about her homecoming lifted all the worries and strains of the last few weeks.

'Children!' I called up the stairs. 'Guess what?'

'What?' came a quintaphonic reply, but suddenly, without any rational explanation, I changed my mind. I wouldn't tell them. It could be a surprise for them too.

'Er, the vicar might drop by for tea. He just rang to say that he hasn't seen you guys for some time and he . . .'

'*What?* The vicar*?* Us? Hereward the Doze? Has he taken leave of his senses?' Stevie said, leaning over the banisters.

'Are you sure it's not a sabotage plot?' called Ed. 'You know what happened last year.'

'My God! The bread! Thank heavens you reminded me.'

I shot into the kitchen and opened the oven door, barely daring to peep. It was done to perfection. It was . . . a masterpiece. I set it down on the table and stared in wonder at the ripe fullness of the gleaming brown bread. The aroma was out of this world. I offered up a little prayer of thanks and removed it to a dog-proof position. Perfect!

Having got the culinary bit between my teeth, I dashed together the ingredients of a celebratory homecoming meal, threw them into a casserole and set to preparing vegetables. After a quick cup of tea, it was time to disappear to the station.

'I'm just popping out,' I called up the stairs. 'We need some petrol. If Hereward Slitherby comes by, tell him I'll be back soon.'

Ignoring the chorus of indignant protests from above, I went to the car and ten minutes later I was driving up the station approach just as the train came in. Mrs D stepped down looking wonderful. She was sun-tanned and relaxed, and chattered animatedly about Winifred's new house in Arizona. We loaded her bags into the boot and set off for home.

'How has everything been, apart from the diplomatic incident over Melanie's trainers?'

'Fine . . . absolutely fine. No, it's all gone very well . . . very straightforward . . . and the bathroom is finished.'

'Well done, darling,' Mrs D said. 'I can't wait to see it,' and she leant over to give me a kiss. 'How have the older ones been? Anyone got a job? They should have done.'

'Yes, and no. Oh . . . Angelica's in Greece by the way. She just zoomed off, all out of the blue. She does have a vague job; when she's here. Stevie had a short spell in the Falcon Hotel . . . but it hasn't worked out, but they've all been reasonable . . . you know, their usual selves.'

'*That's* what I worried about, darling. *Usual selves* means being waited on hand and foot; laid back or horizontal for most of the day. I should think you must be exhausted.'

We swung into the drive, and I was pleased that Mrs D happened to be looking the other way as we passed the still less-than-upright gatepost. The first person we met inside the house was Greg, or, to be more accurate, we met Greg's backside. The other end of him was busily engaged with waxing the parquet floor. His mother put her hand to her mouth.

'My God!' she said. 'Is that . . . Greg?'

He looked round. 'Mum!' he exclaimed, delighted, and stood up to greet her. 'I didn't know you were coming home today.'

I explained that I hadn't told them of her surprise call. 'They're expecting the vicar,' I said, but I didn't elaborate.

'Well,' said Mrs Dudgeon. 'Don't let me stop you, Greg. The floor looks . . . stunning.'

She looked at me, apparently lost for words. Greg looked at his watch.

'I'll be finished soon,' he said, giving me a knowing look.

When we peered around the dining room door, Phil was wiping down the windowsills having cleaned all the windows.

'My,' said Mrs Dudgeon. 'I can't get over this. I've . . . never seen anything like it.'

They greeted each other just as the Hoover started up again, above our heads. She looked at me quizzically.

'Don't tell me . . . Stevie?'

'Probably. He's tidying his room a little.'

Upstairs, I had to conceal *my* surprise when I looked in the door of his bedroom. At that moment, Stevie was prostrate on the floor of an *immaculate* room with the Hoover tube extended beneath the bed.

'Mum! Awesome! What a surprise! We weren't expecting you!' He extracted himself and gave his mother a warm embrace.

'I can't get over all this . . . activity. It seems, well, unreal.'

'Oh well, Mum. You know how it is. We like to keep things shipshape now. Dad's an old stickler for a bit of spit and polish.'

I put the kettle on the hob for a pot of tea, and Mrs D sank into a kitchen chair.

'Duncan . . . these children. Have they been taking something? I mean, they're not high, are they? I'm expecting to see Ed and Mel appear with the lawnmower in a minute.'

I chuckled. 'No. They're out on their bikes. They'll be back soon.'

'How have you done it, Duncan? I mean, Greg has never seen a tin of polish in his life, and yet he's in there . . .' She shrugged her shoulders. 'It feels uncomfortable. There has to be a catch. Are you paying them?'

'*Paying them?* Gracious, no. The very idea! No, I think they just, well, *enjoy* it, I suppose. All it needs is a bit of discipline . . . some gentle persuasion that there is more to life than lying in bed and propping up the bar of the *Pig and Whistle*.'

'Well,' she said, giving me a hug. 'It's lovely to be home and I take my hat off to you, Duncan. I don't think the house has ever looked lovelier. I can even smell freshly baked bread.'

I reminded her that the following day was *The Show*.

'Let's take the tea into the sitting room, shall we?' I suggested. 'I expect you want to sit down in a comfortable chair for a bit. You've effectively been up all day and all night, haven't you?'

Mrs Dudgeon kicked off her shoes and put her feet up on the sofa.

'Phew,' she said, relaxing back against the arm. 'That's better.' She pulled the cushions out and thrust them beneath her head.

'It's impossible to get comfortable on the plane. I –' She paused, and reached down beside her and, with a puzzled expression on her face, drew out an empty vodka bottle. Then, she ferreted once more and produced a half-empty packet of cigarettes and a lighter.

'Duncan, dear,' she said, smiling knowingly. 'About these children . . .'